A Poisoned Chalice

ALSO BY ALISON JOSEPH

A
POISONED
CHALICE

ALISON JOSEPH

A Sister Agnes Mystery Book 8

Joffe Books, London
www.joffebooks.com

First published in Great Britain in 2024

Cover art by Dee Dee Book Covers

ISBN: 978-1-83526-826-1

CHAPTER ONE

'But I love him.' The woman tucked a curl of shiny hair behind her ear. 'He may have got himself into a bit of trouble, but . . . I made promises, Sister. And them are promises I keep.'

A bit of trouble. The woman sitting across the desk in the hostel office was straight-backed, dark-eyed, smoothing her hair with one manicured hand. She wore gold hooped earrings, a black polo-necked jersey dress under a leather jacket.

'Your husband—' Agnes began.

'I'm not saying he did the right thing, Sister. Lord knows, it says in the Bible, thou shalt not kill. And kill he did. But . . .' She looked up. 'I love him.'

Agnes watched the red-painted nails on the black leather sleeve. 'I don't suppose it's something you can understand,' the woman went on. 'You being a nun and that. Your promises are different ones, isn't it.'

'Well—'

'I mean, they're not about a love between two people. To have and to hold, all that. Like, your promises are all about turning away from life, not taking hold of it with both hands.' She gave a brief, bright smile. She had heavy curled eyelashes, her lips a dark pink.

1

'It's a bit more complicated than that,' Agnes said.

'Well, it's true, you're not shut up in a cloister. And you dress like normal people too. Jeans and that.' The woman waved a hand towards Agnes.

Agnes wondered how much to explain. *An open Order, I could say. Being out in the world, not shut in a cloister. Ignatian, it's called, dates from the fifteenth century, all about what it is to serve God by teaching or nursing or in this case, working in a hostel for homeless young people . . .*

The woman was scrolling on her phone. Agnes spoke again.

'The fact remains that the police were here at the hostel this morning saying they were looking for a man called Jason Sorrell, and asking if we knew him. A local South London man, your husband. And now you're here, also looking for him, saying you're worried about him because of something he did in the past that may have come back to haunt him.'

'Hauntings.' The woman's voice was fierce. 'Them ghosts, they never leave his side. Never. That thing my Jay did, Sister, he's paid for it a thousand times over. A bad thing, but Lord knows he's paid the price.'

'Does he often just vanish?'

She shook her head. 'No, I'm worried. It ain't like him. Not these days. That's why I came to see you. Because my friend, Bex, she says to me, that hostel on the corner there, people come, people go. Go see them, Neave, go and ask them. They're the people in the know. And she says, they're good people there, people of God.'

Agnes smiled. 'I'm not sure the two things are necessarily connected. Though it's kind of her to say so.'

There was a silence. Agnes glanced out of the window. Outside two crows balanced on the neighbouring gutter, eyeing each other in the languid summer heat.

Neave leaned forward. 'What did the police say?'

'Not much. Routine visit, they said. A local man, reported missing, fears for his safety. Showed us a photo, asked did we know him. Everyone said no.'

'I am so worried . . .'

'Mrs Sorrell, what do you think has happened to him?'

'Call me Neave.' She flashed a glance at Agnes, perhaps weighing things up. 'He's not an easy man, Sister. If you know how to treat him, he's the best there is. But . . . but he can get the wrong side of people. And then, he finds himself in trouble.' Neave clasped her hands together in her lap. 'If he did come this way, you'd look after him, wouldn't you?'

'We're a hostel for young people. Our brief is to try to redirect homeless kids back to some kind of safety.'

'I bet you've got your work cut out.'

'There are so many kids who need help. It's overwhelming.'

'I know it,' Neave said. 'The streets, it's like a city all on its own. All with its own rules. My son, Ezra, he's fifteen. Thinks there's a world out there made for him alone. He says to me, at home, "Mum, you treat me like a child. Out there, I can be a man." I try to tell him, the world's a dangerous place for a man. Being a man won't keep him safe, but he won't listen.'

'And what does his father say?'

A blank look. 'Ah. No. Thing is, Sister, Jay ain't Ezra's father. The man that Jay killed, that was Ezra's father.'

The crows hopped to and fro, cawing loudly.

'Jay saved my life,' Neave went on. 'And he saved Ezra's too.'

Agnes watched her. *Two women*, she thought. *Same sort of age. If I'd had a child . . .*

'Of course,' Neave was saying, 'it's not as if you know about marriage.'

'I was married,' Agnes said. 'Like you, I had to get away.'

Two women, Agnes thought again. *One, with lipstick and earrings, black dress and heeled boots. The other, with her short brown hair flecked with grey, un-made-up, flat scuffed boots.*

'You ran away? To be a nun?' Her eyes were wide.

'No. I ran away to save my life. Like you.'

'Your husband . . . ?'

'He'd have killed me in the end. I had to get away. The nun bit came later.'

Neave leaned back in her chair. 'Well, well. You and me both,' she said. 'Except, in the end, it was Jay who saved my life for me.'

There was a rush of noise in the corridor outside, a slam of doors, laughter, a burst of music. Outside the sun beat down, hugging the city in its midsummer heat.

'What's he like?' Agnes asked.

'My husband?' Neave settled in her seat, allowed herself a small smile. 'He's a Londoner. He's half Irish, half Arab. Never knew his dad, but he's good-looking, Sister, I'll tell you that. Here.' She took her phone out of her pocket, scrolled through some images. She held it out to Agnes.

Agnes looked at the screen. A broad-chested man smiled back at her, his muscles straining against his denim shirtsleeves. He had a shock of black hair and dark intense eyes. 'Hmmm,' she said. 'I see what you mean.' She passed the phone back.

Neave threw her head back and laughed. 'It takes a nun,' she said. She laughed some more. 'It takes a nun to see. To see what I mean. He's a looker, right?'

Agnes smiled, nodded.

'Maybe you're not a normal kind of nun,' Neave said, laughing still.

'Maybe I'm not.'

Neave tucked her phone away.

'So, you say he never knew his father—' Agnes began.

'Oh, Lordy, the story changed all the time where Jay's father was concerned. Sometimes a refugee from Iraq who came over during the war. Sometimes a desert nomad. Lebanese, was it? Syrian, even, on occasions.' She shrugged.

'And his mum?' Agnes said.

'Oh, we knew her all right. Francie Sorrell. A good Christian woman from down the road here, born in sight of the Elephant. Oldest of five girls. Everyone round here knew Francie. Long story there. She disappeared, some years ago now.' She leaned forward. 'Give me your number, and I'll text you his photo. In case he turns up. You'll know who he is, then.'

4

'Good idea.' Agnes read out her number.

Neave typed it into her phone. 'I wouldn't send his pic to just any woman, but you being a nun . . .' She looked up. 'I guess I can trust you.'

'I may not be a normal nun. But you can trust me.'

'Yeah, I reckon that's true.' Neave got to her feet. 'Well, Sister. I've done what I can. His friends ain't seen him. His phone's switched off. All I can do is sit at home and wait for my husband to come back to me.' She fished in her handbag, pulled out a card. 'That's me,' she said. 'Any news, you call me.'

Agnes showed her out to the hallway. 'And if the police show up again?' she asked.

Neave faced her. 'Tell them what you like. I've nothing to hide from them. Nothing. And neither does my Jay, not now. He's done his time.'

* * *

Athena poured tea from a pink teapot into two pink flowered cups. The room was light with the midsummer sun.

'A leather jacket,' she said. 'I've known you all these years and I've never thought till now how good that would look on you.'

Agnes picked up a cup. 'That's what I thought too.'

'Milk?'

'Just a drop.'

'Black leather. So practical for your line of your work, surely those nuns of yours will see that. We must investigate charity shops as soon as possible.'

Agnes laughed.

Athena leaned back against her sofa cushions. Her black hair was loosely pinned up, and she wore white jeans and a pale lilac jumper. 'In fact, I'm sure I had one once. That's the problem with moving house all the time. I bet it's packed up in a box somewhere.'

'Well, now you're settled, you can unpack. At last.'

5

'Yes.' Athena sipped her tea. 'God, nomadic life really gets you down.' The room was airy, with low white cupboards, a large ornate mirror on one wall. 'I mean, not a fashionable part of London, but at least we've ended up as neighbours. South London, eh? Who'd have thought.'

'Southwark is very fashionable. You'd be surprised.

'And Nic's very happy with his new venture up east. Loft living for him, and it means I can have this flat as I want it. We could never have lived together.' She poured more tea. 'Jewellery designer, you say?' She glanced at the business card. 'Neave Sorrell.' She put the card down. 'Hooped earrings?'

Agnes nodded. 'Nice boots too, kind of chunky heel, looked expensive.'

'She sounds like our kind of girl.'

Agnes sipped her tea.

'What?' Athena said. 'What's not right?'

'It's just . . . there was a lot she wasn't saying.'

'Like what?'

'Why our hostel? That's what I couldn't work out. The police mentioned the missing man earlier, but that's kind of routine, Rob and Martha pop in when they can. But why would this woman I've never seen before think that her husband would seek out a safe house for kids that's run by nuns and is deliberately below the radar . . .' Agnes put down her cup. 'There was a kind of caginess about her, I thought.'

'Hmmm. Can't have that. Oh, heavens, let's eat these . . .' Athena pushed a plate across to her. 'Rose and pistachio macaroons. To go with my new cushions.'

Afternoon sunlight fell across the polished wood floor, shimmering against the sleek wire shelving and the marble table lamp.

'So weird, having a place of my own. It's like these cups, I've owned them for years, but this is the first time I've taken them out of their box for about, ever.' She took a bite of macaroon. 'That's what I've tried to tell Nic — if we got married, think what we'd lose.'

'And is he convinced?'

Athena frowned. 'Difficult to tell. But then, that's normal where men are concerned, isn't it, kiddo? He's happy enough in his new place too, the huge darkroom loft space, all those trendy coffee bars on every street corner. And he's all about getting rid of stuff at the moment, decluttering.' She looked up. 'You know, he's even saying we should get rid of the old Audi and just have some electric thing, to save the planet.'

'What did you say?'

'I said nothing at all. I hope he got the hint.' She smiled. 'Did you say you told this bird about your marriage?'

'It came up in conversation.'

Athena laughed. 'As you do.'

'Men being trouble, you know how it is.' Agnes smiled.

'Trouble? Hugo was more than trouble. He would have killed you. And did you explain that it was Father Julius who saved your life?'

'Didn't want to complicate things.'

'She must know Julius. Everyone knows him round here. The local Catholic priest. I mean, it was him who got you away from Hugo, all those years back, in France when he was a young curate and you were in grave danger. God knows, that husband of yours was charming enough. Even I was taken in. Our friendship forged over a complete shyster. Heavens, that was aeons ago. I guess we're older and wiser now. It would be a shame to just be older.' Athena brushed crumbs from her jeans. 'Dear old Julius. You and him, you're like an old married couple. Without the marriage bit, obvs. He's seen you through so much, fought your side with all your difficulties with the Order over the years. So absolutely reliable. God knows that's what you need in your life. Hopeless parents, ghastly husband, and a best friend who refuses to settle down.'

'Till now.'

'I thought, I'll never have the money ever again, but when that legacy appeared from Greece . . . Who'd have thought that funny old Dmitroula would have remembered

7

me in her will? Dear old thing. I mean, I was glad enough to get to the funeral last month over in Nafplion, so lovely to get on a plane after all this time, and all these relatives I hadn't seen for years, it reminded me why I left the village in the first place . . . where was I? Oh, yes, when I read that letter from the lawyers. The funny thing is, the day before, I'd found an old postcard from her when I was going through stuff. Lovely photo of Crete, decades ago. Weird coincidence, eh? Although, there's a podcast I've been listening to, this bloke, what's his name, American, lovely voice . . . anyway, he says there's no such thing as random coincidence.' Athena surveyed the wide, light space. 'A room of one's own.'

'It is lovely. It must be fun, all that shopping.'

'You should try it, kitten. I mean, there's vows of poverty in your line of business, of course, but at least those nuns have given you your own flat. Not that you ever spend any time there, holed up in that hostel of yours. I know you enjoy it but when do you ever get to put your feet up with a glass of wine and the telly on?'

'It's kind of not like that—'

'Mind you, at least you don't have to live in the convent house with all those nuns. That would drive you mad.'

It's fine, really, Agnes was about to say, *I go to the convent for Mass and vespers when I can, and the nuns are my community. I've known them for years* — but Athena was speaking again.

'Living alone. That's the thing. Last time dear Nic raised the idea of marriage, I said, "But sweetie, if we do that we'll have to live together and up till now you think I'm wonderful but more than a fortnight sharing the same house and you'd change your mind and then where would I be?" He won't admit it, but with the new Shoreditch place, he loves it, all that space for his funny old photography, and Ben and Marie and the baby can come and stay whenever they like, well, when I say baby she's two now, Daisy is, so lovely. I do think I was clever to take up with a man who already had a son, got all that out of the way and I can still buy pretty things for a cute toddler . . .' She put down her tea cup. 'No, I have to say, I'm very happy with things as they are. My own flat. And at least those nuns have worked out you need the same. Your flat is almost as nice as this one. You and me both, kitten. Best left alone.'

'Yes. Although . . .'

'Although what?'

'You can never tell when the Order will decide to move me on.'

'Nonsense, sweetie. If your God knows you half as well as I do, he'll tell them to leave you just where you are.' She laughed, then topped up their cups of tea. 'I wonder what that woman wasn't telling you.' She passed Agnes the pink milk jug. 'Knowing you, I expect you'll find out sooner or later. Drink up, then we can go on to wine. I've got a nice pink fizzy thing in the fridge.'

* * *

'You'll have had a drink, then?' Julius looked up from his desk. 'I can't imagine Athena would let you leave thirsty.'

'Oh, Julius, you're telepathic.'

'Oh no,' he said. 'Telepathy's not part of our tradition. I just know your friends very well.'

'Or me, perhaps.'

'Perhaps.' There was a flicker of amusement in his blue eyes. He stood up. His office had a high, sloped ceiling, a wide, ancient desk and an arched doorway which led through to his church.

'I was going to pour you a whiskey,' he said. 'Irish, of course.'

'Just a small one, then.'

She heard the clink of glass. The sun was lower now, filtering through the leaded window, warming the heavy oak panels and worn red carpet. He carried two crystal glasses across, lowered himself into his desk chair with an out-breath. He looked up at her. 'What is it?'

She smiled. 'I was just thinking that we must have aged, in all the time we've known each other.'

He leaned back in his chair. 'I blame Athena. You always say things like that after you've seen her.'

They chinked glasses.

'You think she's bad for me?'

He smiled. 'Oh, no. Every nun needs a best friend like Athena.'

'That's not what they tell you in convent school.'

'Shows how wrong they are, then.' He looked up. 'And how are you?'

Agnes leaned back in her chair, reflecting on her conversation with Neave. 'A woman came to the hostel today, looking for her husband who she said had gone missing. It was weird, because the police had mentioned him earlier.'

'That kind of gone missing?'

'He doesn't sound like a straightforward kind of guy,' Agnes said.

'Ah.'

'But what I don't get is why come to us? How did she even know the address? I can't work out why she'd think he came to us. Nothing she said rang true. It's an ordinary Victorian terrace, just like the houses either side. It's hardly got a neon sign saying, "Troubles Solved While You Wait".'

Julius laughed.

'And it's not like he's some kid on the street looking for a safe place to stay.'

'Strange indeed,' he said.

'Look.' Agnes drew out her phone, leaned across to him. 'This is him.'

Julius looked at the image. After a moment he said, 'I suppose people go missing all the time.'

They sat in silence. Beyond the wooden door there was bustle, a glimpse of two women carrying armfuls of flowers.

'Are you all right?' Agnes said.

'I think so.'

'You seem . . . a bit . . .'

'A bit what?'

Tired, she wanted to say. But it wasn't quite that. He looked as he always looked, with his white hair, his blue eyes behind their half-rimmed glasses, his purple vestments. But there was something about him . . .

'It's probably just this funeral on Thursday,' he said. 'Ivy Wharton, lovely lady, a stalwart of the parish. Did you know her? She was only seventy-nine. That's what all these preparations are for.' He nodded his head towards the door.

Agnes watched him, as he put down his glass, fiddled with a pen.

'What's that?' she pointed at an object on his desk.

'What?'

'That.'

'Ah. That.'

'Well?'

'It's an hourglass. A sand timer. Seventeenth century. Dutch, they think.'

'Why . . . why has it appeared on your desk?'

That hesitancy, again. 'Ah. Well, just one of those things.'

'Julius?' She waited.

His desk chair squeaked as he settled back on it. 'You know the church, across the way there, the derelict one?'

'St Bruno's?'

'That's the one. The one with old crypt, people used to sleep in it. The diocese has finally decommissioned it. And in clearing it, they opened the safe. And—' he gestured at the glass timer, 'a few things came to me.'

She picked it up, watched the sand trickle through the glass waist. 'It must have a huge value.'

'All rather a worry,' he said.

'What else did you get?'

'Oh, you know. That tin. Funny old antique tobacco thing there. A book or two. One in particular, very old, leather thing. Other bits and pieces. I've tucked them away in my safe for now.'

11

She picked up the tobacco tin. It was golden yellow, with an ornate picture of a Manhattan skyscraper on it and a Greek name.

Outside, the rumble of traffic from the main road, the flicker of sunlight.

Dear old Julius. So absolutely reliable . . .

'Jason Sorrell, he's called,' she said. 'Known as Jay. His mother was local, Catholic. Francie Sorrell, disappeared a few years ago, there was some kind of estrangement in the family.'

He seemed to breathe again. 'Sorrell? Doesn't ring a bell.' He shook his head. 'No,' he said. 'Can't say I know him.'

She turned the sand timer over. They sat in silence, as the slow trickle of sand counted out the passing time.

CHAPTER TWO

'But sweetie—' Athena's voice on the phone was concerned. 'Julius never lies. He just doesn't. Are you sure you're not just—'

'Making it up?' Agnes raised her voice above the traffic noise on her mobile, walking along the warm dusky street.

'I don't mean that. I mean, just because of your own concerns, allowing that anxiety to take hold . . .'

'I know the man.'

'Well, that's unarguable. You know him better than anyone, I reckon.'

'He recognised the photo on my phone. And he said he didn't. It's so strange . . .' Agnes reached the hostel steps, rummaged for her key with one hand, opened the door.

'Are you still there, sweetie?'

'Just arriving back at the hostel.'

'What the hell's that noise?'

'That — oh, that.'

'A baby crying?'

'Akeela.'

'You're taking them young these days.'

'Her mother. We're trying to put a roof over their heads. I'd better go.'

'Well, sweetie, keep me posted about Julius's change of personality. All very odd, I must say.'

* * *

'So,' Agnes said, walking into the kitchen, 'I'm trying a Catholic charity home. I've asked for a place for you both, Dina. If they talk about sin, just take no notice.'

The baby had a sweet face and tufts of black hair. The crying briefly stopped as the baby looked up. She was wrapped in a delicate white woollen shawl, held tightly in her mother's arms.

'Listen, Sister, Akeela is the best thing to have ever happened to me. No one's going to tell me different.'

A young woman in black stood at the stove, stirring a large pot. 'Bean stew. And there's cheese on the table for the non-vegans.' She turned, ruffled the baby's hair. 'Aww . . .' she said. 'I love this baby. If the Catholics won't have you, I'll get my mum to adopt her.'

'I'd like that, Aysha,' Dina said.

'You'd have to do Friday prayers,' Aysha said.

'Cool.'

Aysha smiled. 'My mum — we always used to grumble when we lived at home, me and my brothers. To have someone who thinks it's cool, she'd adopt you too. Here, have a bowl.'

Dina laughed and settled to eat. Agnes took Akeela who smiled up at her.

Eddie put his head round the door. 'Agnes,' he said. 'Someone's at the door, asking for you.'

Agnes handed back the baby and went out to the hall. It was warm and dark outside, and beginning to rain. A man stood there, hunched and thin-faced with wiry red hair. 'I'm looking for Jay,' he said. 'Jay Sorrell.'

'I think we all are,' Agnes said.

The smallest blink. He faced her, straightened up. 'He's not here? I was told—'

'Who?' Agnes said. 'Who told you?'

He went silent, suddenly guarded, standing there on the doorstep, and now another figure appeared behind him, small and slight and female. 'Is she here? Neave Bennett?'

'He ain't here,' the man said to her.

'But Neave . . .'

They both looked at Agnes.

'I met a Neave, this morning,' Agnes said.

'Was she, like, wearing pink lipstick, high heeled boots?'

'Yes. She called herself Neave Sorrell.'

'She what? She never took the bastard's name. Neave Sorrell? She's got a damned cheek. And where's he, then, where's Jay?'

'She was looking for him,' Agnes said.

'Her too? Oh God.'

The rain had come on more heavily, dripping from the guttering on to the steps. The night was heavy with thunder. Agnes looked at them, the woman in an orange peaked cap over short dark hair, the man eyeing her, waiting.

'You'd better come in.' She stepped aside, closed the front door behind them. They stood, damp and silent, in the hallway. Agnes studied them. 'So,' she said at last, 'this Jay Sorrell. What is your connection to him? And, more to the point, why does everyone think he'd come here? We've never even heard of him.'

The two looked at each other, him rangy, staring down, her gazing up. Then they turned to Agnes. 'He always said . . .' he began. 'He'd point at this door, whenever we passed. "Safe house," he'd say. "One day I'll need it."'

'But we're a hostel for teenagers, we couldn't even give him a bed if he needed one — if he knew about us, he'd know that. And how did he know we were here?'

The man shrugged. 'He said someone had told him. Someone from the church. If he ever needed a bed for the night—'

'Absolution,' the woman interrupted. 'That's what he needs. He don't need a bed for the night. He needs remission from his sins for the rest of his fucking days.'

Agnes faced her. From the kitchen they could hear the clatter of saucepans. 'What do you mean?' Agnes spoke again.

'He killed a man. Bet the cow didn't tell you that. Six fucking years ago. Remission for his fucking sins in this life maybe, but he can rot in Hell in the next.'

Agnes looked at her, her face tight with rage, her eyes bright in the dim hall light. 'The man he killed . . .' she began.

'The man he killed was my brother Reece,' the woman said. 'I'm Daniella. And this is my partner, Aidan.'

'Would you — would you like to sit down?'

Agnes led them into the empty lounge. Along the corridor there was noise, loud chatter, the clatter of supper.

They sat on the faded armchairs. Agnes drew the heavy curtains, golden yellow in the lamplight.

'Reece Bennett,' Daniella said. 'He was my brother. And he and Neave were together. They had a kid even. And then Jay came along and he broke it all up, broke everything up, smashed it all to bits . . .' Her voice cracked. She slumped against the cushions.

'Ezra,' Agnes began.

'Yeah.' Daniella leaned forward. 'My nephew. A good kid, but he ain't been the same. Well, you wouldn't, would you, if a guy killed your dad and then took your mother away, and you're supposed to act like he's your dad now. I can't bear it, can I, love?' She turned to Aidan, who was sitting on the edge of his seat, his elbows resting on his knees.

He shook his head. 'She can't be around it,' he said.

'I miss him so much,' she said. 'We were close, him and me.'

'How . . .' Aidan began. 'How did she seem?'

'Upset,' Agnes said.

'It's an act.' Daniella's voice was steely.

'Babe — she might be upset. I mean, if he's really gone missing . . .'

'Uh-uh.' Daniella shook her head. 'I know that cow. Did she go on to you about Reece being violent and Jay rescuing her?'

'Well,' Agnes began.

'See?' Her eyes blazed. 'Told you.' She flung herself back against the chair, her arms folded across her quilted jacket.

Agnes turned to Aidan. 'So,' she said. 'Was he?'

'It wasn't,' he began. 'It's not the whole story, that's what Danny means. They were dealing. Both of them. Just small-time, you know, nothing mega. He was the man, Jay was, Reece was the runner. He did the missions for them, that's all.'

'And they fell out?'

'Jason wanted Neave.' Daniella brushed her fingertips along her sleeves. 'And what Jason wants, he gets. He was the big guy, he was making money, he'd go on at her, "Look what I can give you, girl, why are you with that no-hoper?" He didn't give up. And one day Reece had had enough. He challenged him. And they were armed, innit. Both of them, drawing out their blades, and Reece, he got chinged. Aid was there, weren't you, babe?'

'Jay was yelling at him, "Don't go, please don't go." Someone called an ambulance. But . . .' He shook his head. 'They were there for a while, trying to save him, all that kit and that out on the road. Didn't do no good, did it?'

'And Neave . . .' Agnes prompted.

'Next thing we know, she's moved in with him. And according to her, he's stopped the dealing, stopped the traffic, he's working as a DJ instead, laying down tracks, you know.'

'And now he's gone.' Aidan glanced around the room at the old cast-iron fireplace, the thin jumble of books on the shelves.

'And is that characteristic?' Agnes faced them both.

'That I could tell you, if he had just one character,' Daniella said.

There were footsteps on the stairs, a faint cry from the baby, as the house settled into the evening. Agnes wondered at this strange invasion, this tale of lost love and small-time criminality and vengeful, fatal rage. Once again she wondered, *Why us? Why here?*

17

'Have you always been local?' she said.

Daniella nodded. 'Grew up in the flats across the way there, you know the ones by the park? Half of them sold off now, all the gardens where we used to play have been fenced off. And that church, that one where the windows are all broken? There was a youth group there. We'd all go there. Brave the witch and everything.'

'The witch?' Agnes asked.

Daniella smiled. 'There was an old woman who lived next door. We told ourselves all sorts about her. Poor old thing. Though, she wasn't a nice person. But the church was like a second home. We'd play table tennis and then smoke weed out the back. Probably shouldn't be saying this to you.' She smiled again. 'Not him.' She jerked a hand towards Aidan. 'He's from Somers Town. Wasteman. Can't think how I ended up with him.'

'So . . .' Agnes turned to her. 'Why now? Why are you so keen to see Jay, all of a sudden?'

'It's because he's gone,' Aidan began.

'I'm not having it.' Daniella's voice was firm. 'I'm not having him get away with it again.' She looked up. 'Or her, for that matter,' she added. 'Neave fucking Bennett. Like my brother never existed, she's written him out of the whole fucking story.'

Agnes settled in her chair. 'What was he like, then, your brother?'

Daniella softened. 'I'm not saying he were an angel, because he weren't. But . . . more than anything in his whole life, he wanted to look after me. There was only him and me, and our mum. And our mum's not well. Well, you wouldn't be, would you? Her lungs. Grief, they say.' She took a long breath. 'He promised me, promised us both, he'd always look after us. And you tell me—' She sat upright, her eyes fierce. 'You tell me how a boy like that is going to make a living round here? And it all kind of worked. Until Jay fucking Sorrell came into our lives.'

There was the slam of a door. Laughter. A burst of music. 'We should go, hon.' Aidan got to his feet.

'If she comes back—' Agnes held out her phone.

'Yeah. Good idea.' Daniella punched her number in. 'Tell her we were here,' she said. 'Eh, babe?'

He gave a nod.

Daniella stood up, slung her bag over her shoulder. In the corridor she offered her hand. 'Thanks for seeing us, Sister. Keep in touch.'

Outside there was rain, the swish of rush hour traffic in the dark wet streets.

'Perhaps he's at that church,' Aidan said. 'The one with the witch. Maybe he went back.'

'I thought of that,' Daniella said. 'It's all locked up.'

They stared out into the rain.

'And the witch is long gone,' Daniella said. 'She died years ago.'

'Or that other one.' Aidan pointed at the city skyline.

'St Simeon's,' Agnes said. 'I don't think Jay has been there. My friend is the priest there. He'd have mentioned it.'

'He wouldn't go where there was a real live priest,' Daniella said.

They shook hands once more with a murmured goodbye. Agnes watched them go out into the wet, humid evening.

* * *

That night Agnes settled with her prayers.

'. . . when you, O God, went out before your people, when you marched through the wilderness, the earth shook, the heavens poured down rain . . .'

Her room in the hostel was neat and newly painted, with a single bed tucked against the wall. She sat at the desk, lit a candle, looked up at the icon of St Francis, the single patch of colour on the wall. Outside, car headlights beamed white against the rain.

'Extol him who rides on the clouds, rejoice before him, his name is the Lord. A father to the fatherless, a defender of widows . . .'

She closed the prayer book.

It was a long time ago, that Julius rescued me. That he took me away from my violent marriage.

Athena's right. He saved my life.

So — why is he hiding from me now?

Or — am I imagining it?

* * *

'Then the earth reeled and rocked, the foundations also of the mountains trembled, and quaked . . .'

The words cut through her sleep.

'As smoke is driven away, so drive my enemies away; as wax melteth before the fire, so let the wicked perish at the presence of God . . .'

The voices echoed in her dreams, with the noise of sirens and the flashes of blue light. Suddenly she was awake, her eyes wide open, her senses full of burning.

She pulled the curtains open.

St Bruno's church was on fire.

* * *

The small crowd stood in the street. The rain had eased, and the sky was blue-grey with the early dawn.

They stood in the choke of smoke, faces shadowed in the darkness, vehicle headlights cutting across the warp and weft of smoke, the swish of hoses. Shouts from the firefighters, 'Is anyone inside?'

'No one. It was derelict—'

'Homeless?'

'All clear, sir, we checked—'

And then Julius was there, his voice raised against the noise of the engines and pounding water.

'The crypt,' he was saying. 'People used to sleep there—'

'We're just clearing—'

A hush fell.

A stretcher. A man, lifeless, blackened, shrouded in rags, his clay-grey arm swinging at his side; his trainers strangely bright and white against the smoke.

A single cry, a scream, cutting through the night. Neave ran towards the scene, caught by a fireman as she struggled against his grip. 'Sorry, madam, you can't—'

'My love,' she was shouting. 'My Jay . . .'

Agnes looked across at Julius. Again, that tightening in his face, that flash of recognition as he looked at Neave, still fighting, still shouting, 'I knew they'd do it.'

The fireman steered her firmly away from the scene. The stretcher was loaded into an ambulance. Neave's voice rose in a loud, high wail. 'They killed him.'

Agnes looked back. The church was black, skeletal against the soft grey dawn.

Smoke spiralled upwards.

'Can we go back to bed now?' someone said, a hostel resident. Then Eddie from the hostel was there, shepherding them all away.

Agnes and Julius stood, side by side. Damp grey smoke rose up to meet the early day.

In the ashes, at her feet, an ornate cigarette tin, gold letters against a crimson background bearing the inscription *M. Melachrino*, and a Manhattan skyscraper. She bent to retrieve it, turned with a bleak smile to Julius.

Another coincidence, she wanted to say, but he'd already moved away. She could see him through the lingering crowd, standing across the road with one of the fire crew. She pushed her way towards him, away from the site of the fire, but by the time she'd got there, he had gone.

CHAPTER THREE

'See?' Athena tapped the tobacco tin. 'Just what I was saying. No such thing as coincidence. Just like that podcast says.'

Agnes stood in Athena's kitchen, unwrapping smoked salmon sandwiches.

'Eau de nil,' Athena said, waving towards the kitchen units, the pale, tasteful green. 'That's what the decorators said it was called, this colour.'

'It's lovely,' Agnes agreed.

'And the blinds, that was their idea. Allow the light in.'

The midday sun warmed the pale granite counter tops.

'Greek tobacco money,' Athena said. 'That's where Dmitroula's family wealth came from. They all settled in Manhattan, last century, found a gap in the market . . .' She carried plates and knives to the dining table. 'The fact is, real life is full of coincidences. But you know, like, when you're reading a book and the whole plot hinges on a coincidence and you think it's just a cheat? You think well, that wouldn't happen in real life. It makes you think the story is unbelievable. It's as if we have higher standards for when something is made up than when it's in real life.' She studied the tobacco tin. 'Melanchrino. It definitely rings a bell, not actually Dmitroula's family, but I'm sure they were connected.'

She finished arranging the sandwiches on a plate. 'And the church is a smoking ruin?'

Agnes yawned. 'All roped off. Signs saying *Danger* everywhere. And police tape.'

She'd passed it that morning, after a few hours' sleep. The air was still heavy with smoke, in spite of the drizzle. People were still stopping to take it in. They stood in ones and twos, murmuring. There was an old man leaning heavily on the railings, trails of grey hair against a ragged collar. He seemed to be speaking, perhaps to himself, perhaps into a phone though none was apparent. As Agnes passed she had heard a few words, a lament, perhaps a psalm: 'How long, O Lord, are we to be forsaken . . .'

A scent mixed with the smoke, the hint of kerosene.

'And Julius was given one like this?' Athena pulled up a chair, and they sat at the table.

'Along with some other stuff. Much more valuable stuff. He said it all came from the safe of the church.'

'Which then burned down. Perhaps that's why he's avoiding you, some scam that involves selling priceless ecclesiastical antiques on the open market.'

'Julius? Involved in a scam like that?' Agnes laughed. 'It's just not him.'

Athena nodded. 'No. You're right. So weird, all this coincidence. This podcast I'm listening to — *Random Divination* it's called, had I told you that? — Doctor Mitch says that we're all wired into the universe in ways we don't understand, and that there's no such thing as coincidence, it's just us noticing the connections . . . He has such a lovely soothing voice, very West Coast, really makes you pay attention. He says it's about discernment, like, if a lot of the same kind of things start happening you have to see what the universe is trying to tell you, and that way you can harness those forces to make changes in your life.' She looked up, sandwich in hand. 'No need to look like that, Agnes.'

'I wasn't—'

'It's different for you lot. You can call it God's will, but what about the rest of us trying to make sense of it all? And you can just obey the rules, doing as you're told, being happy with the needy young people of South London—'

'Hmmm.'

'What is it?'

'That feeling I had, about how the Order are about to move me on . . .'

'What? They're not thinking of moving you. That would be a terrible mistake. Like I said, any sensible God would tell them that. Do you remember when they decided you should go and teach French at that ghastly school of theirs up north? That didn't last long. No, they've got the right idea. You've got your work at the hostel; you've got your own flat up the road. Though seems to me you're always in your room at the hostel and never at home, they should give you more time off.'

'There's a nun, Sister Winifred. She's visiting the Order's house in Hackney; she's come from Calais. She's part of a project in a camp there, supporting mothers and children, and she was talking to me the other day, saying how they need more workers, and I speak French, don't I . . .'

'They're mad. You? With mothers? And children? It's not going to work, however many languages you speak.'

'I will try to tell them.'

'And they won't listen, I bet. For a community based around Christian charity they are the most steely bunch of women I've ever encountered.'

Agnes laughed.

'What's she like, this Sister Wilfred?'

Agnes sighed. 'Winifred. She seems to eat nothing, need nothing, is quite happy living in a tent . . . She practically glowed with fulfilment when she talked about taking a baby in her arms and keeping it warm against the sleet . . .'

'Oh dear.'

'She has this way of looking at you, a kind of frown, like she's judging you.'

Athena placed her cup on its saucer with a clatter. 'It's out of the question. You can't possibly hang about with people like that. What are they thinking of? Just say no. Emphatically.'

'We're supposed to practise obedience,' Agnes said.

'Yes, but even your God must understand there are limits. You can't possibly live in a tent with a bird who lives on thin air and is happy feeding newborns or whatever she does . . . and anyway—' She squeezed lemon on to smoked salmon. 'And anyway, Julius needs you. It seems to me that that's the takeaway from this, as Doc Mitch's podcast says. He says discernment is about asking what does the universe want from me, and it's quite clear to me that whatever the universe is, it has no interest in sending you to live in a tent with a load of do-gooders. Not when Julius is behaving so strangely.'

Agnes took a sip of tea. 'It's so weird. He's never like this with me. The last time was when he was ill, do you remember, that cancer treatment he had to have and he didn't want to worry me . . .'

'Go and see him.' Athena got up, went to her fridge. 'Talk to him. He's your best friend. Apart from me, obviously.' She took out a bottle, peered at the label. 'Elderflower. It'll have to do. Much too early for wine.'

* * *

On the way to the hostel that afternoon, Agnes passed the church again. The column of smoke was thinner now, the air clearer as the sun broke through the clouds. There was the beginning of scaffolding, men in hard hats, to-ing and fro-ing, the scrape of long metal poles. Blue and white police tape trailed along the ground.

Furniture had been stacked on the drive, heavy wooden pews, a lectern.

A woman was watching the activity. She wore a fake fur coat in zebra print and tall shiny boots. 'Can't see that lasting long.' She sniffed. 'Perhaps they want everyone to make off

25

with it, 'cos that's what'll happen, round here, that's what it's like. And as for that . . .'

They both watched as a statue was brought out of the door on a pallet, feet first. It was of a woman, cast in bronze, her long skirts in dark frozen swirls, her calm metallic gaze framed by her turbaned head.

'Do you know who it is?' Agnes asked, aware she'd never seen it before.

'Francie Sorrell,' the woman said. 'I knew her. She got on with everyone round here, but you know how it is, she fell out with her family. Lots of bad feeling. There was some trouble with her son. Then she vanished. They said she retired, to Scotland, maybe. Or was it Grenada . . . ? No one heard from her. So then they did that memorial thing and put up the statue, maybe two, three years ago now. Befitting, really. I liked her. Did a lot for the community round here.' She glanced at Agnes, then back at the statue. 'They'd better not leave it there. It'll be melted down and sold on before you can blink.'

They watched as a white van appeared. Four men in overalls got out of it, lifted the statue and, with some effort, loaded it into the van.

'Council,' the woman said. 'Or thieves. Take your pick.' She threw Agnes a pinched smile and went on her way.

Agnes watched the van pull away. In the front passenger seat was a woman. Agnes could make out wisps of white-blonde hair and a dark blue beret. The van turned the corner and went out of sight.

* * *

'They could have checked the fucking chapel. That bro might still be alive . . .'

'All them wastemen use the graveyard and shit—'

'You think one of them threw a match through the window?'

'Takes more than that to burn down a church.'

26

Agnes stirred a large pot of spaghetti on the hostel stove, listening to the swirl of rumours. People gathered at the table among the mugs, old teabags, scattered biscuits. Dina jiggled Akeela on her knee.

'On purpose, isn't it.'

'Why set fire to the old church on purpose?'

'Maybe the witch never went away . . .'

Agnes put the pot of spaghetti on the table, as the doorbell rang. 'Help yourselves,' she said and went to open the door.

* * *

Neave was standing on the doorstep. Next to her stood a teenage boy, nearly the same height. He was staring at the ground, in hooded sweatshirt and baggy jeans. He wore a football scarf draped around his neck, in blue and white.

Neave pushed past Agnes, shoved at the door of the lounge and threw herself into a chair.

'I told you,' she said. 'I told everyone who'd fucking listen and he still ended up dead.'

The boy had followed and was now standing in the middle of the room. 'Ez, sit down, for fuck's sake.'

He went to an armchair, curled into the cushions, still staring downwards.

'I went to the feds,' she said. 'They wouldn't see me to start with. I knew it was him, Sister. I knew it.' Her voice faltered. She dabbed at her long-lashed eyes with a fingertip. 'So I says to them, "Look. Here's his passport." Like, I was at the front desk up the road there, waving his photo at them. So then they called someone, a woman, and they let me in and we sat in a room, and I told them. "It's Jay. My Jay," I said to them. "I have a right to know. You call it a fucking crime scene — you can tell me what the crime is."' She straightened her black leather skirt, crossed her legs in their black clumpy boots.

'So then the woman, pretending to care, asks me about Jay. Was he in any trouble that I knew of? So then I says,

27

"You tell me. He didn't die from fucking smoke, did he? He was dead long before that fire started," I was saying, "I know he was." And the woman is saying she can't tell me nothing, and I'm saying, "I'm his fucking wife and the mother of his son."' Her eyes flashed rage. 'So then this bitch writes down my details on a form and says they'll keep in touch. And then she says, like she's not sure she should be telling me, that they're "looking at unlawful killing". That's all what they had to say to me, before they chucked me out, because all they see is just another girl from the estates with a drug dealer boyfriend. Not someone who's lost the fucking love of her life . . .' Her words stopped short, choked by tears.

Agnes realised that she'd been hoping for a quiet end to this story — a man already unconscious, drink or drugs or something, breathing in smoke as the life gently left him. An accident, just one of those things. She felt her hopes fade.

'He was killed,' Neave said. 'Like I was trying to tell anyone who'd hear and no one did—' The sharp trill of her phone sounded from her bag. She snatched it up. 'Yeah? Not good, no . . .' She got to her feet, went to the door, 'Sorry, got to take this, my cousin . . .'

Agnes heard her out in the corridor, narrating the story so far.

The boy hadn't moved, still curled into the smallest space he could find.

'You're Ezra?'

A small nod.

'This must be tough,' she said.

A shrug.

'What was he like?'

A glance upwards. 'Who?'

'Jay Sorrell.'

Another shrug.

Ezra had bright white trainers, sculpted hair.

'I like your shoes,' Agnes said, and he almost smiled, but then Neave came back into the room. 'Tash,' she said, 'wants to know how we're doing, I said not good, babe, not good.' She flung herself back into her chair, pulled her skirt down over her thighs. 'Tash said they should have burned the church down years ago with that old priest in it and I said what about the witch and she said, nah, all the witch did was spells, you could live with that.' She almost laughed, and her face softened briefly.

Agnes could smell the smoke, again, the trace of paraffin. 'Which priest?'

Neave closed her handbag with a snap of gold buckle. 'Father — what was his name? Something foreign. Years ago. He had a reputation. You know, like they did. The boys would joke about not being alone in a room with him.' Again the almost-laugh, tightened by grief.

Agnes wondered about this priest. 'He was someone you knew?'

'Only by sight. We were Kingdom of God, me and my brothers. It were the Catholics who went to St Bruno's, the Irish boys, you know. We'd just hang out in the crypt with them after hours.'

There was a burst of music from the kitchen as supper came to an end, voices, banter, laughter.

Ezra looked up towards the door, then back at his feet.

'I thought this place was full of refugees,' Neave said. 'Not . . .' she jerked a thumb towards the door.

'Homelessness,' Agnes said. 'Affects all kinds of people.'

'Us,' Ezra said. 'We nearly came here that time.'

Neave's expression hardened.

'After Dad was killed,' he said, and now his gaze was direct, and he sat tall and still.

'The only dad you ever had was alive until yesterday.' Neave spoke roughly. She got to her feet, slung the gold chain of her handbag over her shoulder. 'Come on, we're going.'

Ezra stood up slowly. He followed his mother out of the lounge, one heavy step at a time. On the doorstep she took another call, stumbling unevenly down the front steps in the dusk, raging into her phone. Ezra hesitated at the door. He held out his hand to Agnes. His brown eyes held hers. 'Thank you,' he said.

They reached the end of the street, Neave still on her phone, Ezra walking tall at her side.

* * *

It was late when Agnes left the hostel, hurrying to reach the Order in time for Compline. A humid dusk had settled, the air still warm. She waited at the bus stop.

Outside the church, a lone woman stood, motionless, her hands clutched against her face, her hair smooth-white under her blue beret. She had low-heeled shoes, a dark mid-length coat. Agnes thought of approaching her, but then the bus was pulling up, its red bulk drawing nearer.

Agnes looked back as the bus drew away. The woman was pacing the churchyard, one hand trailing along the old stone wall.

CHAPTER FOUR

'You can still smell the smoke,' Agnes said.

Julius nodded. 'All the roof timbers went. It's taped off now, unsafe structure.'

She went to the window, touching a fingertip on the dusty frame, and looked out at the morning sky. Even at this time of day, the heat was already stifling.

'This weather doesn't help,' she said. 'Nothing to clear the air.' She turned back to him. 'And was it arson, they say?'

Julius was stacking the books on his desk into a neat pile. 'Nice policeman came to see me this morning. That was the impression, yes. He said the safe had been wrenched open. Empty, of course.'

The sand timer was on the mantelpiece, above the old fireplace. 'Did you tell them you had half the stuff from it?'

Julius shook his head. 'Best not mentioned.'

'Why?' She was still standing, and now she faced him as he sat in his old desk chair. Something about him looked old, but perhaps it was just the thin June sunlight on his face.

'Why what?' he said.

'Why not mention it?'

'Oh, you know . . .' He tried a smile but it just made him look more weary. 'A crime scene. All that police tape. A poor man died . . .'

31

'That's what I mean. A man that half my neighbourhood near the hostel was looking for.'

'Best left to the police, don't you think?'

'Julius . . .' She sat down opposite him.

Their eyes met.

She was silenced.

He sipped on a cup of cold coffee. 'What really worries me about all this . . .' he began.

'Yes?' She looked up.

'What's missing, from the bequest,' he said.

'Missing?'

'All this, I have. That sand timer. The old religious text I was given. A couple of bibles. But there was another thing, part of the family's treasures, very valuable. The family was connected to that church, a long time ago. And this treasure, it's the Judas chalice. It's a silver cup, probably about fourteenth century. It went missing years ago, never found. There were always rumours it was somewhere in that church. And then, with the safe broken open . . .'

'Why Judas?'

'It has an engraving on it. Of our Lord, with the thirteenth apostle. It makes it unique, people think.'

'And you thought it was in the safe?'

He shrugged. 'I hadn't really thought about it.' He traced a circle on his desk with a fingertip. 'Thirty pieces of silver,' he said. 'That's what Judas was paid by the Romans in order to betray Jesus, to tell the soldiers which man was Jesus so that they could arrest him. So to put that on a chalice, is a very strange choice indeed.' He seemed to be talking to himself, but now looked up at her. 'Anyway, all lost, it seems. I just ended up with that, the sand timer, and the old theology book . . .'

'So — so why?' she said. 'Why have you got it now?'

Once again, that hesitancy, that shutting down. 'I knew — I was friends with — I mean, in the old days, when it was still a church . . .'

She waited.

He took a deep breath. 'The family, you know, they went back a long way here. And I was the priest for them, so when they were clearing the safe, I suppose they thought I should have the things, only for safekeeping, you understand, not to own . . .'

'Who gave them to you?'

'What do you mean?'

'What I said. Who brought them here? Things don't just turn up,' she said, trying not to shout. 'First they weren't here, and now they are, and then the church burns down with a poor man inside, and now I've met his son, or stepson, can't quite work it out, really lovely young man, and you're behaving as if—'

'As if what?' He smiled, and for a moment everything was as it used to be.

She stood up, went to the mantelpiece. She turned over the sand timer, and they both watched the swirl of the grains.

'It was Orla St Fleur,' he said. 'She brought them to me, the sand timer, the books. Her family, the St Fleurs, are an old Catholic family. They've been connected with the priory since medieval times. Lots of land in Suffolk, originally, though how they ended up in London is anyone's guess. Most of the wealth has gone now, I understand.'

The minutes passed. The sand settled.

'Does she wear a blue beret?' Agnes turned to him. 'Nice coat. Chic white hair . . .'

Julius's expression tightened.

She sat down again, faced him, waiting.

'Agnes,' he said. 'I know the workings of your mind. Here you are, piecing things together. But what if they don't go together? I know you. You've met this poor boy—'

'Ezra.'

'Ezra,' he said. 'And you can sense his need, and you can sense that he knows more than he's telling you, and you feel responsible, for him, for the woman who came to you to talk about this dead man, whoever he was—'

'Jay,' she said. 'Jay Sorrell.'

'Ah,' he said. 'Yes. And,' he went on, 'and the safe was emptied a few days before the fire, and I happen to know a woman who you've subsequently seen, and . . .' He stopped to catch his breath. 'And . . . here you are, as ever, trying to make order out of chaos. It's what you're like. Studying the evidence. Making a story. Giving it a structure. But what if these are just random events? What if there is no story, and all we have to do is sit with the chaos and wait for the police to do their work?'

He leaned back in his chair, breathing heavily.

Julius, she wanted to say. What is the matter?

From outside there was a passing blast of rap music.

He got to his feet. 'I expect you need to get back to the hostel.'

She followed him to the door.

'Agnes—' He glanced down at her. 'You and I — the life we have chosen has few rewards. But one of them is that we can turn away from our passions. We can live quietly. I could cling to these artefacts, lock them away . . . but I have no need.' He gave a brief, thin smile. 'The Judas chalice,' he said. 'It was said to absolve you from sin, if you drank from it. But only on Maundy Thursday.' He opened the door for her. 'Judas, of course, betrayed our Lord. So it's a double-edged thing — absolution in some way, but with the shadow of betrayal.'

She felt the light touch of his hand on her back.

'See you soon,' he said. 'Have a good day.'

* * *

The morning at the hostel passed quietly. Agnes sat in the office, typing names into search engines. *The Judas chalice* brought up no results. *Bermondsey Priory* told her a bit about the old ruin in between a series of articles about the recent blaze, and there was something about a wooden drinking cup, a mazer, now in the Victoria and Albert Museum. There was nothing about the St Fleur family. *Francie Sorrell* brought up a local newspaper article about the statue of her, commemorating 'a much-loved local woman who had done so much for the community'. She'd trained as a nurse, but then got involved in campaigns for local housing, and she'd also run a food bank. Something about a birthday celebration for her sixty-fifth. Then nothing. There was a more recent article about a dispute concerning the final resting place of the statue, 'feelings running high', 'statue stored in the church for safekeeping until a decision is made . . .'

She thought of the bronze form being loaded into a van. She thought of the passenger sitting in the front seat, smoothing wisps of white hair. She thought about making order out of chaos.

Her phone trilled with a text. From Athena: *How is Julius? Still lying?*

Still lying, she typed back.

There was a ping of a reply from Athena, with words of support. *He must have been replaced by an alien, it's the only possibility. J lying to you it's like we've slipped into a parallel universe . . .*

Something about this made her want to cry.

There was a loud ringing of the doorbell. Agnes blinked back tears, gathered herself.

Aysha put her head round the door. 'Someone on the doorstep for you. Again. Call this a safe house — everyone knows where we are.'

Agnes got to her feet.

'You all right?' Aysha eyed her.

'Well—'

'Knowing you, you'll say you're all right even if you aren't, so there's no point bloody asking really, is there?' She brushed an affectionate hand against Agnes's shoulder as they went out into the hall.

* * *

Standing on the doorstep was a middle-aged white woman with tight grey curls. She was small, hunched and angry.

'You the nun?' she said.

'I am *a* nun, yes.' Agnes felt weary, and much too tall.

'Don't look like one. In my day they were draped in black. You know, like angels of death.'

'Would you like to come in?' Agnes stepped aside.

The woman didn't move. 'Jeans?' She raked Agnes with her narrow gaze. 'Them shoes? Adidas, are they?'

'Are you coming in or not?'

The woman cocked her head to one side and blinked, bird-like. 'No need to be like that.' She strode past Agnes into the lounge.

'I weren't going to come, but then I thought about that boy dead in the church, and I know who they'll accuse, just because the stupid lad keeps saying he's glad he's dead, and I couldn't let them lock him up when he ain't done nothing wrong, and someone said there was a nun here so I thought, let bygones be bygones, and I came.' She stood, breathing hard. She wore a beige raincoat, tightly belted.

'Would you like to sit down?'

She eyed the chairs warily, then chose one, perching on the edge, still in her coat. She had neat lace-up shoes, a pleated skirt.

'You knew Jay Sorrell?' Agnes said, sitting down opposite her.

'Oh, I knew them all, those lads. I worked as a childminder. Raised them like my own. Better maybe, not having my own. So when the Preedy boy was standing in my kitchen cursing the dead boy's memory, I thought, I can't have this. Them cops will be scooping him into their van as soon as look at him and I'll never seem him again.'

'Aidan?' Agnes guessed.

'Yeah. Obviously. Swore vengeance over the Bennett boy's killing, all them years ago. Reece, you know, his girlfriend's brother. Much good it's done him ever since. I don't even think the Sorrell boy was responsible for that killing neither, but then everyone else thinks he was, so what do I know? Whoever it was, they got away with it. Jay Sorrell did time for it, and then was released. The police just melted away. I thought it strange at the time. All I know is, that Jay's mum Francie knew. She knew it would all go wrong, that's why she went when she did. She warned anyone who'd listen. Her fears for that kid, the grandson . . . She'd say, we women, we have to be watchful how life shapes boys into men.' She smoothed her skirt over her knees. 'It defeated her, in the end.'

The Sorrell boy, Agnes thought. And the killing of the Bennett boy.

'Jay Sorrell killed Reece Bennett,' she said.

'That was the story at the time. Six years ago, no— six and a half. It was winter. Something about a drug deal gone wrong. Money mattered to both of them, that was the problem. Mattered too much in my view.' She sighed. 'Jay was there when Reece died, a stabbing. He insisted on his innocence, but what were the police going to do? But then, after a few months inside, something happened. Lawyers got involved — his mum was behind it all — and he was released.'

She relaxed a little now, sitting slightly further back on her chair. 'It's what you do, isn't it? Fight for your child. Any mum would do the same. Not that your kind know about that sort of thing — although,' she added, kinder now, 'you seem better than most.'

'Thank you,' Agnes said.

She glanced around the room, at the worn green rug, the lampstand with its odd, fringed shade, then back at Agnes. 'Francie was right, about how boys become men. But thing is, I'd say to her, they're good lads, deep down, all of them. I've seen them grow from tiny dimpled things into clumsy great teenagers, I know what they're like.'

'And Aidan still visits?'

'It's like a second home to those lads. I lived nearest to their school. They'd always stop off at mine on the way home. So, yeah. They still do.'

Agnes studied the keen bright eyes and pinched face. 'And — what is your name?'

'My name? I'm Bridget.' She smiled politely and put out a small hand. 'Bridget O'Leary. You must have heard of us. You ask anyone round here, they know the O'Learys. I married into them, for my sins.'

'What were you before you were an O'Leary?'

She looked up. 'What kind of question is that?'

'Nothing at all. I just wondered.'

'Well, you can keep your wondering to yourself. You may not look like the others, but you're all the bleeding same.' She was brittle with sudden rage, her fingers entwined tightly in her lap.

'I asked because I care.' Agnes's voice was loud in the quiet room. 'Because something has made you overcome your fears and knock on this door.' There was a silence. Agnes spoke again. 'That church seems to be at the centre of something. And that poor young man died because of it. I agree with you that Aidan isn't guilty, even though he might seem to be. So if I ask about your maiden name, it's just curiosity—'

'St Fleur,' she said.

The name was a shock.

'But I never carried the name. I was illegitimate. A shame on the family. Brushed out of view, like so much about that lot. Parcelled out to be raised by my mother as best she could. Then, when I married, the O'Learys smelled money. More fool them.' She smiled her muted smile.

'Do you know Orla?' Agnes said. 'Orla St Fleur?'

'I certainly do.'

'White hair. Blue beret,' Agnes said.

'What — she's never back, is she? You seen her?'

'I've seen her, yes.'

'My half-sister, though she'll never say so. I thought she was in Ireland, in a castle somewhere. What the hell's she doing, lurking about here?'

'I don't know.'

'She used to live up west when we were younger, big house in Harrow or somewhere. She'd always ignore me.

Never married. Someone said she was in love with a priest, an Irish Jesuit. They said he was a kind man who took pity on her once. But he was always going to be a priest and so it fizzled out. They said she never got over him.'

Agnes tried to breathe normally. 'Do you — do you happen to know the name of this priest?'

'What? No . . .' She shook her head. 'I think he stayed in London, though. I don't have much to do with the Church. The Good Lord he may be, but to be honest he ain't done much for me over the years, so I'm keeping my distance.' She fiddled her raincoat belt. 'There was another priest,' she said, suddenly. 'Only just thought of him. Not a nice priest, not like the one Orla was in love with. He was round here years ago, then he disappeared. Funny name . . . Greek sounding. No one liked him. Creepy, you know. Like he was after something. He tried to befriend my mum when he knew she was struggling, but she wouldn't have any of it, bless her.'

'Do you know about the Judas chalice?'

Her face was blank. She shook her head.

'Do you know why Orla St Fleur would steal a statue of Francie Sorrell?'

Bridget stared. She leaned back on her chair, her hands working in her lap. 'Orla . . . ? Francie . . . ?'

Agnes nodded.

'Are you sure?'

Another nod.

'You mean — that statue — it ain't in the churchyard anymore? That's very strange.' She shook her head. 'But — Orla and Francie . . . Are you sure it was her?'

'I saw her,' Agnes began, as her phone trilled on the desk beside her. *DS Rob*, she saw on the screen. She snatched it up.

'Perhaps you made a mistake,' Bridget was saying, as Agnes answered the call.

Agnes listened, said, 'I'll be right there.' Then clicked the phone off.

The older woman got to her feet. 'Something wrong?' She gestured to the phone. 'Sounded like it to me.'

'Yes. Police.' Agnes gathered up her bag, her keys. 'I've got to go — my friend's church — there's been an attack on it, some kind of break-in . . .'

'I'm not surprised,' Bridget said. 'People round here, they see God for what he is these days. Well, thank you for listening,' she said, as they went out into the hallway. 'I've done what I promised. I won't be back.'

'And if I see Orla St Fleur?' Agnes was putting on her coat, unhooking her scarf from the rack.

'I can't imagine she'll be hanging around. And anyway, I don't have no hard feelings towards her. She's still my half-sister. It's the rest of the family who behaved like criminals where my mother was concerned.'

She glanced up at the icon of the Virgin that hung by the front door. As she went down the steps, she briefly crossed herself.

The evening was threatening rain. Agnes wrapped her scarf over her hair as she set out for St Simeon's.

CHAPTER FIVE

'He should have CCTV, your mate.' DS Rob Coombes was standing outside Julius's church, broken glass crunching underfoot. 'Look.'

One of the leaded windows was smashed, hanging from its hinges.

'That's how they got in. Safe bashed up too. A determined attempt, but I reckon they were surprised. Didn't expect Father there to be in the church.'

'He was there?' Agnes felt a sudden chill.

The dusk was settling over the church's spire, a softening twilight muting the city's hum.

'Did he see them?'

Rob shook his head. 'He said he was in the church and heard a noise from his office, so he went to see, but they'd gone by the time he got to the safe. Must have legged it sharpish through the window here.' He fingered the blue police tape that edged the site. 'Not happy about it, me. An old man like that, all alone. Not happy at all, especially given they torched the one across the way there.'

Agnes was glad to have Rob by her side. She'd known him for years, seen him from DC to DS, always supportive of her and the hostel. He was tall and rangy, with a thin mousiness that disguised a fleet and powerful strength.

'But it's not connected, surely?' Agnes looked towards the church door.

Rob shrugged. 'They tried the empty safe in the old church, didn't they? And now this.' He sighed. 'People will stop at nothing for the next fix. I'm just glad your friend didn't encounter them. The funny thing is, they wrecked the garden too. Like in revenge for—' His attention was caught by the crime scene team. 'I'd better go. Yeah, mate, on my way.' He jogged over to the team and joined their choreographed search.

Agnes walked to the gate and gazed at the devastation in surprise. The garden was trampled, pots overturned, branches lopped, hydrangea heads severed. Revenge for what? she wondered.

'Marjorie won't be happy.' Julius was standing at her side. 'Look at the roses. The Ancient Mariner, it only started flowering this year. After all her hard work.'

Crushed petals littered the damp flagstones.

'She was going to cut some for Ivy Wharton's funeral tomorrow,' he said. 'I told you about that, didn't I?'

'Julius.' Agnes turned to face him. 'You shouldn't stay here. All alone.'

He smiled. 'Where else am I going to go?'

'But—'

'An opportunistic break-in, that's all it was. They won't come back, not now they know how impossible these windows are. And that the safe's empty.'

'Empty? You have those things . . .'

'Ah, well, that's where you're wrong. I took them all across to the house. There's nothing here of value now.'

'But these people — they don't know that.'

'Which people might they be, Agnes?' He was smiling still.

'Julius.' She held his gaze. 'You were given those things. They appear from nowhere, just before that young man is

42

found dead in the old church. And then the statue is taken away — and it's all about Orla St Fleur.'

He flicked her a glance.

She went on, 'Orla took the statue out of the old churchyard, the statue of Francie Sorrell. And it's Francie's son who they found dead in the old church. And now they've gone after this church too. You're not safe, that's what I'm trying to say.'

'Och, Agnes.' He shook his head.

'I saw him. I saw the body. We both did,' she said. 'Don't tell me I'm inventing things.'

'Wouldn't dream of it. Only . . .' He looked up. 'It's come on to rain and I'm getting damp here. I've got a lot to do before tomorrow's funeral, and the glazier is on his way. I'd really better get on, if you don't mind.' He touched her arm. 'You take care of yourself. I'll see you soon.'

Another smile, another pat of her arm, and he'd gone.

Agnes looked at the withered pink petals in the fading light.

The police team was already loading the van. Rob got into his car, gave a brief wave as the engines revved and they pulled out on to the main road.

Behind her, the lights went on in the church.

* * *

Agnes walked aimlessly, found herself outside St. Bruno's. She sat down on the garden wall.

A tall figure emerged from the dusk with a saunter of white trainers.

'Ma'am.' He smiled. 'Sister.'

'Hello, Ezra, what are you doing here?'

He sat down next to her. After a moment he said, 'Your friend. Break-in, then.'

'Yes,' she said.

'I heard,' he said. 'And my nan's statue gone.'

'Your nan?'

43

He flashed her a smile. 'They tell me, this one's your dad. And then, no, it's this one. But Francie, she was there for me. I may have been the kid with two dads, but she was always my nan.' He glanced at the empty space where the statue had been.

'People took it away,' Agnes said.

'Yeah.'

'I saw them.'

He turned to face her. 'Saw them?'

She nodded. 'A van came. And a lady. I think she was Orla St Fleur.'

A slight flinch. A nod. After a moment he said, 'That's that, then.'

'That's what?' She took him in, his elbows on his knees, his head in his hands.

He lifted his head. 'Someone to watch over me,' he said. 'That was my nan. I always thought, that statue . . . ever since she left, I was only a kid, and I'd think, well, she's there. In the statue. When I pass it, I do a lucky thing, like, go and just touch her hand. Her right hand. And now I can't.' He ran his fingers through his hair. 'Don't tell no one that, I sound stupid. I'm only telling you because she's gone. And now my dad's gone and my stepdad too, one because of the other and I'm on my own. It's like one of them plays, Sister, know what I'm saying?'

'Shakespeare—' she began.

'Aeschylus. That's the man. Brother against brother. Child against father. A mighty hero who will torch a whole land over a woman — the Greeks got that.'

'Aeschylus,' she said.

'Them classics. My nan used to read them to me. Big book, pictures and that. Soldiers, gods, monsters . . . Still got the book.'

'So — torching the whole land?'

He smiled at her. 'Well, all right, Sister. Just the ends where my dad was concerned. But, y'know, it's still bad.'

'And a mighty hero?'

'Uh-uh.' He shook his head. 'I wish.' He sighed. 'He tried. God knows he tried. But my nan, she would always say, "Whatever happens, little Esau," she called me that, don't know why, "whatever happens, I shall be here to watch over you."'

'Esau was Jacob's brother. In the Bible.'

'Yeah. I know.'

There was a silence. 'They're gonna charge Aidan and it weren't him, Sister. I know for a fact it weren't him. He ain't clever. He's so fucking stupid, if he tried to ching a man he'd end up slicing his own thumb. Both of them. It ain't him.' He bent to his shoes, fiddled a lace on his trainers.

'How do you know?'

Ezra faced her. 'My mum, she ain't so friendly with the truth. I know that Jay was really my dad. It was my nan who looked out for me, before she vanished. But my dad was a restless soul and it was Reece what raised me, at least when I was a kid, and when Jay came a-claiming me, that was when the trouble started.'

'What trouble?'

He pulled on his sleeves. 'My nan was scared of Jay, even though he were her son. He had a rage about him. She said he carried it in his bones. And she'd say to me, "One day, Esau, you're going to be a man. And when you feel that rage, when you feel that heat burning in your heart, you must put down your sword and walk away."'

A whispering of leaves from above, as birds settled in the branches. Agnes waited.

'But my dad, Jay, he weren't like that. He'd walk towards the fire. And then they said he killed a man, the man that raised me, that I called Dad. And it broke her heart. And she went, then. Won't talk to anyone now. I get a birthday card, like, in the post, once a year. No address. Nothing.' He brushed his eye with the back of his hand. 'What I don't get is what Jay were doing in that church. The stuff he knew about that church, he wouldn't have set foot in it. For him to be in that crypt, then, he would have needed a damn good reason. I think there was some big man what reeled him in, making promises. That's what I think.'

'Promises of what?'

A shrug. 'Girls. Weed. Money.' He looked up. 'A simple man, my dad.'

'And a good one?'

Ezra stared at the ground. 'Sister, if a man has killed, can he ever be a good man?'

'What does Aeschylus say?'

He looked up. 'With them Greeks, you can always blame the gods. Man might ching another man, but it's, like, out of his hands. Them gods go placing bets on it.' He smiled at her. 'I guess your God, he don't go around placing bets on man's stupidity.'

She smiled back. 'No.'

'Though he'd be a rich man if he did,' he added. 'Win-win, if you ask me.'

The drizzle had abated. There was a rustle in the brambles at their feet, a flick of a sleek grey tail.

'Ezra,' she began, 'you said Jay wouldn't have gone into the church, that he knew something bad about it. What was it? Everyone round here seems scared of it.'

He stretched out his legs in front of him. 'Sister, I don't know the answer to that. They used to play there, when he were a kid. And his mum, she ran a community group there, looking after the mothers and the babies. There was a food bank too, and a sports club for the older kids and then it all went wrong. There was a priest, he didn't like my nan. She wouldn't give up, but she got tired, and ill, and he knew he was winning. And then there was the big row, and she went. And after that, he was in charge.' He sighed. 'Maybe his God had bets on him winning. Because I reckon his God was the gambling kind. Not your God, not the God of love.' He faced her, and his eyes were wet. 'She always said she'd watch over me. And while that statue was there, I believed it. I knew she was here for me. But now . . .' He shook his head. 'I don't know who will look after me now.'

She wanted to hold him, to take him in her arms. *Another one*, she thought. She gathered words to speak, about love, and inner strength, and caring for oneself—

'Do you believe a statue can come to life?' His words were sharp in the chill air.

'Well . . .'

'She promised me. She said, "Esau, when you really need me, I shall be here." I've always thought that, sitting by her here in the churchyard, I've always thought, when I really need my nan, the statue will come to life.'

'In my faith, miracles happen.' It was a feeble answer, she felt.

'Maybe.' He began to get to his feet, brushing the dust from his knees. 'But then, your God, maybe he's placing bets after all?' He reached out an arm, and helped her to her feet.

She smiled. 'In my faith, the gamble is for us humans. We take a risk to believe in God.'

He nodded, met her eyes. 'Yeah. Well,' he held out a hand to shake. 'Good night, Sister. Thanks for the chat.'

'You know where I am,' she said. 'Any time you need someone to watch over you, I'm here.'

He tilted his head. 'It ain't the same, Sister. It ain't the same.'

She watched him walk away, his easy stride cutting a path along the narrow darkness of the streets. A fox emerged and faced her warily from the brambles, staring hard until she too left the churchyard.

* * *

The night passed fitfully. Agnes heard baby Akeela crying in the darkness.

Awake in the hours before the dawn, Agnes wondered how it was that Jay Sorrell killed Reece and only got a few months in prison, yet everyone knew.

She wondered about the power that Francie Sorrell seemed to wield, even now, when she'd long since gone away.

Ezra had mentioned that the priest there hadn't liked her. Perhaps he was the reason they all feared the Church. Ezra had recognised the name of Orla St Fleur, but why? She must have left long before he was even born.

Akeela's crying ceased. Agnes imagined her being held, soothed, loved, made safe.

And yet some of us, after a while, learn not to ask.

CHAPTER SIX

'You can't possibly come over all maternal now.' Athena crossed her long legs in their light blue linen trousers.

'Maternal?'

'You know.' Athena poured coffee into two large bright cups. 'Catching sight of a pretty baby, thinking, how come I let that pass, I'd have been great at motherhood. It's all cuddles and warmth until the baby lets out a godawful squawk and then you remember that no, actually, things are fine as they are.' She handed Agnes a cup. 'And what are you wearing — that awful jumper?'

'This?' Agnes touched the mustard yellow cable knit. 'From the hostel. We've been having clear-out, Eddie organised it. There's loads of stuff that's been left behind over the last few months. I got this jumper and a pink dotty umbrella. Though I'm not sure it works.'

'It's horrible. Not a good colour on you. Never wear it again, okay?'

'Oh. Okay.' Agnes took off the jumper. 'It's too hot in any case.' She sipped her coffee. 'I didn't mean I wanted the baby,' Agnes said. 'I meant, what would it feel like to be mothered like that.'

'Ah.' Athena leaned back against her cream and pink cushions. 'I see what you mean. Though, perhaps, when you were a baby, perhaps your mother did care for you then.'

Agnes shook her head. 'I have no memory of having my needs met at all. Ever.'

'Didn't you have a nanny?'

'There was Jeanne, that's true. But she was dismissed when I was seven. "Old enough for governesses now," my mother said. I cried for weeks.'

'Well—' Athena put down her cup. It was a bright morning, with a twitter of urban birdsong in the trees outside. 'We're too old to be bogged down with all that now, don't you think? We've survived pretty well so far.' She raised her cup. 'I'll drink to that.'

Agnes raised her coffee cup too, laughing. 'Me too.'

'And poor Julius is pretending everything's okay?'

'It's not like him to hide.'

'Perhaps he's on anti-depressants,' Athena said. 'Half my acquaintance is on them. Maybe it's the answer. Maybe the brain really is just a load of chemicals that have to be tweaked from time to time. Even Nic, he's been going on about taking daily passion flower for anxiety, when in the old days he'd have been much happier spending thousands on years of therapy. Nic says that life is so challenging, everyone needs a strategy. He's got a plan for compiling a list of "things that work for coping with life". The problem is, it's an ever-growing list.'

Agnes laughed.

'But then,' Athena went on, 'how would you make sense of the world if it's all just chemicals in your brain?'

'What does Doctor Mitch say?'

'Ah, there you have it. He says we have to see what the universe is telling us and shape our own future. It's not brain chemistry at all. But between his worldview and Nic's, I really don't know what to believe. And I would try and work it all out, but there are far more important things to talk about, like, these trousers, I bought them to go with that cashmere

50

cardigan I never wear, you know the one, but now I think they might be the wrong shade of blue . . .' She poured more coffee into their cups.

'I was just thinking how well those trousers would work with that cardigan, actually.'

'You were? Ah, good. I knew I could count on you.' Athena stirred milk into her cup.

'All these strange events.' Agnes took a sip of coffee. 'Julius thinks I should just ignore them all.'

'Ah. Of course. That's why.'

'That's why what?'

'Why you're suddenly envying little babies being held by their mothers. Because Julius is making you feel uncared for. Cast adrift. Don't blame you at all, sweetie. I mean, I know I'm always celebrating how Nic and I keep a distance, but the other day . . .' She picked up her coffee cup, then put it down again. 'The other day, Nic said how he wanted me to know that he couldn't manage without me. He just said it. I was holding a shelf for him in the new loft workspace while he fixed it on the brackets, and he just turned round and said it.'

'What did you say?'

'I said, "If I wasn't here this whole shelf would fall down." Then he got cross because I wasn't taking him seriously.'

'Oh. Then what happened?'

She leaned back on her sofa. 'Well, then there was lots of loud hammering of the bracket and stuff. And we put up the shelf. And then we weren't really talking, but a bit later, he was huffing and puffing over the drill that wasn't charging properly, and I went over to him and said, "I couldn't manage without you either." And he said, "That's not going to get this drill to start, is it?" And then we both started laughing. Couldn't stop.'

She circled her cup on the table. The cups were straight-sided, maroon with a yellow stripe. 'I found these with the rose ones when I was unpacking. Those rose ones are for tea, I thought. These are better for coffee.'

'Yes,' Agnes agreed. 'Definitely.'

'When will you next see Julius?'

'There's this funeral this afternoon. I said I'd help. An old lady from his parish.'

'Ah.'

Agnes shifted on her cushions. 'It's the children who give up asking,' she said. 'That's what worries me. Not the small children having a tantrum, being demanding. Because those are the ones who expect their needs to be met. But the dead-eyed ones. The ones who've given up expressing any need at all, because they know they'll be ignored. But it doesn't go away, that pain. It festers. You see it all the time in the hostel,' she said. 'All that untreated pain, it's dangerous.'

'Yeah.' Athena sighed. 'But look at you. You're okay.'

'Me?'

'Yes. I mean, you might have been unmothered, and your father didn't really have any idea how to be a parent either, but here you are. Being good at life.'

'Me?'

Athena laughed. 'Yes. You.'

'Oh.'

'Perhaps it's your God. Perhaps Nic could add Him to his list of things that work for coping with life. Do you think God would mind?'

'Knowing what I do of God, I think he'd be very pleased.'

* * *

I'm okay. Agnes wondered at the words, as she crossed the main road, the flashing of the green man beating time to her steps. She felt wrongly dressed for a funeral: scuffed black boots, a pair of black cotton trousers that were itchy with age, yellow sweater tucked away into a carrier bag. 'At least that jacket is timeless,' Athena had said. 'Black linen. Can't go wrong with that.'

Not for the first time, she wondered what it would be like to wear a habit, to make a statement as soon as you walked out of your door, to say: Look. Look at me. I am a nun.

Whatever that means, she thought.

We can turn away from our passions, Julius had said.

That doesn't mean they're not still there.

I'd rather keep them in plain sight.

* * *

The churchyard was across the road from Julius's church. It was tumbledown and overgrown, a mass of stone and moss and bramble. 'Reopening a grave,' Julius had said. 'It happens sometimes, if the family still own it. It's nice to be able to do what priests before me always were able to do.'

The trees swayed slowly in the warm air, casting golden light against the lichen stones.

A group of people had gathered, a mix of height, age, colour. Agnes merged with them, quietly. She noticed Bridget O'Leary standing at the back.

A graveside service, Julius had said. No fuss.

He began to speak the words of the funeral service.

'. . . I am the Way, the Truth and the Life . . .'

A hesitation. Agnes saw his eyes flicker upwards. Then he gathered himself, took a breath, continued the prayers. '. . . whoever believe in me, though they die, yet shall they live . . .'

The air seemed to still, the traffic rumble silenced. A small, thin woman dabbed at her eyes with a large white handkerchief.

Agnes shifted and scanned the small crowd. Someone had appeared, late, and now stood at the back of the group. He was grey-haired and tall, draped in a loose jacket and a black silk scarf.

'. . . Rest eternal grant to her, O Lord, and let light perpetual shine upon her . . .' Julius's voice floated above the bowed heads.

Agnes watched as the newcomer joined the prayer, his lips moving with the words. He raised his head, flicked a glance towards her, as if aware she was staring, then away.

Then the blessing, and the pallbearers stepped forward to lower the coffin into the freshly dug grave.

A symbolic sprinkling of earth. A pause. And then, slowly, life started again, the birds sang overhead, a lorry thundered past, people turned to each other, smiled in greeting, began to group in conversations and introductions.

'Haven't seen you for months.'

'Dear Ivy, we will miss her.'

'A peaceful passing, at least.'

'Isn't that her brother Len over there? I wouldn't have known him. He's lost weight, hasn't he, ten years younger . . .'

Julius was nowhere to be seen.

'I didn't really know the deceased.' The voice was deep, and Agnes turned to face him. The scarf shone with luxury, and the jacket collar was turned up.

'I'm afraid I'm rather an imposter,' he went on.

'Funerals are public events,' she said. His hair was thick, she noticed, his face lined with age. His eyes were grey and heavy-lidded.

'I wanted to see the graveyard,' he said. 'I haven't been in this area for a long time. And with the sad fate of the old church . . .' He waved a hand towards the main road.

'Yes,' she said.

People were drifting away. There was talk of a nearby pub, conversation, laughter. 'I'm sure they'll do you a cup of tea if you ask nicely . . .'

'The vicar here,' he said. 'Still Julius?'

'Father Julius,' she said. 'Priest, not vicar.'

'Roman, of course.' He held out his hand. 'Andras Swift,' he said.

She allowed his hand to grip hers. 'Sister Agnes,' she said.

A flicker of interest. 'Sister?'

'I'm a nun,' she said.

'Ah.' He studied her. 'Ignatian, then.' She was about to answer, but he went on, 'Father Julius — I knew him once, a long time ago,' he said. 'I'd like to see him again.' He looked around, as if hoping to see Julius appear. 'And isn't that — Bridget?' His eyes raked the crowd. Agnes was just in time to see her slip away, a flick of beige raincoat against the wrought-iron gate.

'You know everyone,' she said.

'I used to be . . .' He hesitated. 'I used to be part of this community. But my work drew me away.'

He turned his gaze towards the gate, the main road beyond. 'I gather . . . I heard that someone died, in the fire.'

'Yes,' she said. 'A young man. Jay Sorrell.'

His expression gave nothing away. 'I'm sad to hear that,' he said. 'People used to sleep in the crypt,' he said. He was still scanning the crowd, but now turned back to her. 'A burglary gone wrong, I assume?'

'Perhaps,' she said.

'I mean . . .' he shifted from foot to foot. 'They can't have expected to find anything. Not in that old church, the safe would have been emptied long ago, surely?'

It seemed to be a question.

'Well,' Agnes began. 'Who knows? I mean,' she added, 'there was a break-in at St Simeon's yesterday. You can never tell.'

'Here?' His voice was sharp. 'This church? Where Julius is the priest? What did they get?'

'Nothing,' she said. 'The safe was empty, of course.' She smiled. 'He keeps it empty because of the risk of break-ins.'

Andras didn't smile. He was studying the church, the main door, the side door, looking up towards the guttering. He turned back to her. 'They got nothing, you say?'

'Nothing.' She watched him.

He seemed to breathe again. 'All these centuries have passed,' he said. 'And they still walk upon this land as if it's theirs.' He allowed himself a small smile.

'Who do?'

He looked at her again. 'The Protestants won, but the old families will never accept it. Their Norman roots go too deep.' He touched a gravestone, stroked its worn antiquity. 'Their bones are still under our feet. Staking a claim.'

Agnes wondered if he'd sought her out just to lecture her on Catholic landownership.

There was a silence, then he said, 'There were objects,' he said, and suddenly he seemed breathless, his tone urgent. 'From the old church. Things from the vestry— Ah, here's Father Julius.' He broke out a smile.

'Marjorie is struggling with the hot water urns.' Julius addressed himself to Agnes. 'I wondered whether you could—'

'Yes, of course.'

The visitor held out his hand. 'Dr Andras Swift,' he said, still smiling. 'Perhaps you remember me.'

'I remember you,' Julius said. His eyes narrowed as he held the man's gaze, then he turned back to Agnes. 'If you wouldn't mind,' he said. 'And there's Father Gregory from up the road, I must have a word with him . . .' Julius turned and left.

The silence was awkward. 'I might give you my details, perhaps,' Dr Swift said. He pressed a card into her hand. 'In case . . . in case anything turns up. From, you know, across the way there . . .' He gestured towards the old church. 'I write about church art, religious artefacts.'

'It's still a crime scene,' Agnes said. 'It's been cleared for evidence. Someone died, don't forget.'

He turned towards the path. 'There was a sand timer,' he said. 'The St Fleur family acquired it. What did they know of its value?' He turned back to her, his voice oddly fierce, his manner clipped. 'Centuries of acquisition, driven only by value, not beauty. Traders, that's all they were. No expertise, no connoisseurship. Just value,' he repeated. He seemed to collect himself, turned back to her, held out his hand with a warm smile. 'Delighted to meet you, Sister,' he said. He grasped her hand. 'That sand timer, you see. Grains of sand,' he said. 'Counting out the minutes, chasing the years. A challenge one can only lose.' His hand dropped to his side. 'But that's typical of that family. They think you can just turn the whole thing over and start again.' He tucked the end of his scarf into his collar. 'I'll come back,' he said. 'I'm glad your friend Father Julius remembered me. I hope to see him again.' A touch of his hand, and he'd gone.

Agnes stared after him, gathering her thoughts. Then she went to help Marjorie with the tea urn.

* * *

Later, she found Julius in the scullery, washing up the mugs.

'I thought that went all right,' he said, not looking up.

'A blameless life,' Agnes said.

'Indeed.'

'Bridget O'Leary came. I thought she didn't approve of us.'

He nodded. 'But she was fond of Ivy.'

Agnes picked up a tea towel. 'Do you know Bridget was also a St Fleur?'

Julius placed a mug on the drying rack. 'So they say.'

'So — who was her father?'

'There are all sorts of tales about Ralph St Fleur.' His voice was tight.

'It just seems very odd,' Agnes began. 'I'd never heard of this family till now. And then that poor man is killed and there's all this safe-breaking and now all the connections with that family are appearing from nowhere.' She opened a cupboard, began to stack clean mugs noisily inside.

'Careful.'

'I am being careful.' She shoved the last mug into the cupboard. 'And as for Dr Andras Swift — what a strange man. Didn't shut up. Went on about old Catholic families. How come you knew him?'

'I only know him slightly.' Julius closed the cupboard. 'And I wish I didn't.'

He led the way back into his office, sat down at his desk. The sunlight was fractured by the temporary glazing placed hastily across the broken window. He looked up at her, and his face seemed lined and weary. 'Ever since that fire across there,' he said, 'it's as if the scorching of those timbers has awakened sleeping ghosts.'

'Dr Swift said the St Fleur family think they own the land under our feet,' she said.

He gave a thin smile. 'Catholics. Protestants. It's an ancient war, and never won.'

'He was talking about the sand timer too.'

'He was?' Julius smoothed his white hair. 'Perhaps he was our burglar.' He gestured to the safe in the corner, the heavy door wrenched half off its hinges. 'They came equipped, the police said. That was the noise I heard, but by the time I came in here, they'd gone. Empty-handed,' he added.

'I didn't let on,' she said. 'I pretended not to know you had it.'

'Good,' he said. 'Good. I don't hold with lying, but there are times when, well . . .'

'Orla St Fleur,' she said. 'Those things — the timer, the books . . . they came to you because of her.'

'And?'

'I hope she's not a danger to you,' she said.

'A danger? Why—'

'So far, she's given you stuff that people will stop at nothing to steal back. She's made off with a full-size statue in a van . . . And now I'm told that her family still walk these streets as if they own the land they're built on.'

He sighed. 'Dr Swift has a point. They're an old Norman family, and the medieval priory was part of their estate.'

'So — why do you wish you didn't know Dr Swift?'

He leaned back against the old worn leather of his chair. 'What's he up to these days?'

'He says he writes about art history. Church art . . .'

'Ah.' There was a silence. 'He used to be a priest, over in Southwark. He was known as Father Anselm. He knew people round here.'

'What happened?'

Julius shifted on his chair. 'He had a crisis of faith. It happens. He reverted to his secular name, moved away. I was surprised to see him again.'

'And you don't like him?'

'No. No I don't.' Julius picked up the tobacco tin that still lay on his desk. 'One of his friends died. They were a little group, old friends. Devoted. Two were priests, one of them was an artist. And then, the artist died and suddenly they'd fallen out, lots of bad feeling, people frozen out. I was on the edges of it all, tried to help but couldn't. Anselm left the priesthood and became Andras again.'

'So — why don't you like him?'

'Many reasons. He's a selfish man. Ambitious. Stops at nothing. And all this pretence at expertise in art history . . .' He tapped a finger against the tin.

'And the other priest?'

He hesitated. 'Oh, him. He went away. Went to Greece, apparently, joined a monastery, I heard.'

'And after that the church closed.'

'Yes,' Julius said. Their eyes met, briefly. 'What did you say about a statue?' he asked, after a moment. 'Orla has taken away a statue?'

'The one of Francie Sorrell,' Agnes said.

'The — the commemorative one? The one they argued about where it should go?'

'Yes.'

'Are you sure? It must weigh tonnes?'

'That's what I saw. She was in a van, with four burly chaps. Straight after the fire, on Tuesday. They carried it out of the churchyard, put it in the van, and drove away. And she was in the passenger seat.'

'Ah.' He seemed nervous, tracing the lettering on the tobacco tin with one finger.

She took a breath. 'Bridget said that Orla used to be in love with a priest round here.'

Suddenly, Julius was on his feet. 'Agnes — I am not interested. Don't you understand?' His eyes blazed, his face was flushed. 'Why do you always do this? Poking around, making up stories, seeing connections where there aren't any?' He strode to the door, flung it open. 'And now if you don't mind, I've got work to do.'

Agnes stared at him. Slowly, she got to her feet. She walked past him, out of the door, out into the street.

It was a warm, pink sunset. She felt the paving stones hard against her soles. She felt tears pricking her eyes. Julius's rage, so entirely out of character, so utterly strange. As if the still-disputed land beneath these streets had cracked in the summer's heat, and ancient enmities erupted into the here and now, circling wealth and value, chalices and sand timers.

The old families, she thought, counting out the centuries in grains of sand. As if you could just turn the whole thing over and start again.

She thought about the scorching of the church awaking sleeping ghosts, stirring the bones beneath.

She thought, There is work to do.

CHAPTER SEVEN

Agnes sat in the hostel office with a cup of tea by her elbow and the landline tucked under her chin. Bright morning sunlight dazzled against the computer screen.

'Yes, I know it's early,' she was saying. 'But there are things I need to know.'

Neave's voice was faint at the other end of the line, something about disturbing people from their sleep when they'd only just got to bed and what fucking time is it anyway . . .

'How did Jay get away with it?' Agnes said.

'Oh God, Sister, this now?'

'He was found guilty of Reece's death. Everyone said he was there when Reece was stabbed. And then he's released. No one else was charged.'

Agnes heard a weary sigh. She went on, 'Francie was somehow involved in getting him released.'

'Yeah. One helluva woman, Francie. Wherever she is now.'

'Ezra's grandmother.'

'So?'

'You left Jay. Why did you leave him?'

'What? You ask me that? At this time in the morning?'

'It just seems strange, considering you claim he's the love of your life.'

'Sister, that is one whole other story and not one I'm going to start talking about now.'

'You raised Ezra with Reece. And then Jay came back, fighting for you. Fighting for his son.'

'Any real man would do the same.'

'To the death?'

'If that's what it takes, then, yeah.'

'So, Reece is dead. Jay is released from prison, and somehow, everyone keeps their silence about it, Francie goes away, you and Jay and Ezra are family again and then some years later, someone kills Jay?'

'Yeah. That's about it, Sister. Can I go back to sleep now?'

'Not yet. Neave, what was Jay doing in that church? You all avoided it. Since you were kids. Since the youth group . . .'

'Oh my Lord. The youth group. What was his name?'

'Father Anselm,' Agnes tried.

'Oh my days, I ain't heard that name since I was kid. Him. And the other one. They'd talk about him, the lads. Like, laughing and that. But I never thought it was funny, things they were saying.'

'Who would know? Who would be able to tell me about him?'

There was a silence. 'Jay,' she said. 'And Reece.'

'What about Daniella? Aidan?'

Neave was quiet. Then she said, 'It's up to you. Me, my life is over. There's just me and Ez, and I'm trying to keep it all together for him. And I don't know how I'm going to do it.' Her phone clicked off.

Agnes sipped her cold tea. She picked up the phone again, dialled Daniella, who didn't answer, and left a message asking her to call. Then she went to help Aysha serve breakfast.

Later that morning, DS Rob Coombes came by. They sat in the deserted kitchen, which was weirdly tidy. 'Eddie was on washing-up duty, that's why. He says it's his OCD . . .'

She placed a mug of coffee in front of Rob, and watched him stir two large spoonfuls of sugar into it.

'Forensics report,' he said. 'Thought you'd like to know. Early days, but Jay Sorrell was already near death when the fire was started, maybe already dead. Severe head injury, signs of a struggle, bruising, asphyxiation, not from smoke inhalation.'

'Whoa.' Agnes looked at him. 'Big news,' she said. 'Though it'll be no surprise to anyone round here.'

'No,' he agreed. 'And Aidan's gone missing. The Preedy boy.'

'He has?'

'We've got CCTV of him now. There's a security camera on the flats across the road, shows him walking away from the church on the night of Mr. Sorrell's death, about five, ten minutes after the time of death, we reckon. Walking fast, you know. Looking about him. Nervous. And then the safe break-in at your friend's church, he's in the frame for that too once we've gone through all the CCTV.'

'I tried phoning his girlfriend earlier.'

'Any answer?'

Agnes shook her head.

'They're lying low.' He sipped his coffee. 'The problem is, no one is going to tell us a damned thing. And why should they? Coppers, we're the last people they trust. Goes back years. Old DI Wharton worked this area all his career. He's retired now. He called into the office the other day, just passing through. He'd been at a family funeral. He said it was the same in his day. Old tribal families, always at war, always silent when you tried to find out what had gone on.' He gave a tight smile. 'It's all right for you. People will talk to you.'

'Not always.' In her mind's eye she saw Julius, on his feet, flushed with rage, pulling the door open for her to leave.

'Are you okay?' Rob was watching her.

'Yeah. Sure. I'm fine.'

'DI Wharton said you need just one person. Mrs Sorrell was that person here, apparently. The mother of the dead

63

man. She was at the heart of things in this neighbourhood. Someone who is trusted by both sides. But we don't have that these days.'

'He knew Francie Sorrell?'

Rob nodded. 'Everyone knew her.' He brushed at some sugar grains on the table with a fingertip. 'He reckons we let her down. Something happened in the community, and she asked for our help, but she didn't get it. And after that she got ill, and then she moved away.'

'Jay, her son — he did time for murder.'

'The Bennett boy. Charged with manslaughter. Provocation. No intent.'

'Ah.' She sipped her coffee. 'But — remanded and then released?'

He frowned. 'Insufficient evidence. There was nothing to actually put him at the scene of the crime. No DNA, nothing. So the case was dropped and he was freed.'

'Was Francie involved?'

'She was on his side, yeah. Fought for his release. Thing is, she knew what he was like. I mean, Jay might have been released without charge, but she knew. He'd already done time. He had previous, minor offences, nicking stuff, going equipped. He was a troubled young man, like a lot of them round here.' He drained his cup. 'So, even once he was out, she still struggled. D I Wharton reckoned her difficulties were about something else. There was something going on in the community that she tried to bring to light and failed because we didn't support her.' He looked up. 'Every copper has a story like that. Something we should have followed up but didn't. The one regret.'

Agnes smiled. 'You're lucky if it's just one.'

He gathered up his coat. 'Well, this one ain't going to be mine,' he said. 'Her son was left lying there for dead in the old church and it went up around him — he may have been a no-good boyo, but he's still owed the truth.'

* * *

Agnes went back into the office after she'd let Rob out and sat at the desk. From her bag she took out the business card. *Dr Andras Swift*, it read, with a landline number. She put it back in her bag, just as her mobile rang.

'The thing is, sweetie, it's so weird,' Athena said as a hello, 'I was just listening to Doctor Mitch again, and it was *Nothing Happens Without a Reason*. I was unpacking one of the boxes and I came upon a photo of your house in Provence, the old family home, isn't that weird, and you'd been on my mind anyway, so I thought I'd ring — are you okay?'

Agnes was aware she was fighting tears. 'No,' she said.

'What's happened?'

'Julius got really angry with me and threw me out of his office.'

'What? When?'

'Last night. There was the funeral, and I'd been helping. We were chatting. I'd met this odd bloke there who wanted to know about the stuff from Julius's safe, and I asked him about it — and then he just stood up and told me to leave.'

'Bloody hell.'

'He's never spoken to me like that. Ever.'

'A complete personality change?'

'Well, yes.'

'He's been taken over by aliens. An implant in his brain. It's the only explanation. Right,' Athena said, 'this calls for emergency action. This evening. Gin, at least. If not vodka cocktails. That bar on the corner, by the Tube? The sparkly turquoise one we've had our eye on for a while?'

Agnes smiled. Sparkly cocktails seemed suddenly appealing.

Athena was still speaking. 'What time do they let you escape from the ravages of South London poverty? Let's say eight. Fab. See you then.'

Agnes looked at the phone, which still bore Athena's name on the screen, and then at Dr Swift's card. In the silence, in the bright mid-morning light, she thought about the house in Provence, her childhood home. She thought about Julius, his brittle rage.

She wondered why it was so quiet.

But then the landline rang with a council referral, and Eddie appeared asking when Room Five would be free for that new lad, the runaway from Sunderland who'd been promised a room from tonight, and Dina walked into the office with Akeela, who was shrieking and wailing, 'I've had enough, Agnes, what's wrong with her now . . . ?'

Agnes found herself walking a now quietening baby up and down the corridor while Eddie sat in the office on the phone and Dina bashed saucepans loudly in the kitchen in an attempt to help with lunch.

So it was only later that she saw her phone had a missed call from Daniella. She clicked on the number.

'Ah, there you are. I'm at my mum's,' Daniella said. 'Aidan's keeping safe. You can find me here. Connie Bennett. I'll text you the address. See you as soon as you get here.'

* * *

'I couldn't get away earlier.' Agnes stood on the doorstep, breathless and apologetic.

'It's all right. We've got all the time in the fucking world now.' Daniella was in pale grey jogging pants and sweatshirt, un-made-up, her hair awry. She yawned, then stood aside to let Agnes through the narrow doorway with its peeling green paint.

'Mum,' she called upstairs, 'that nun is here.'

She led Agnes into the kitchen, slumped down at the table.

Agnes took off her coat, put it over a chair, sat down opposite her. The room was a semi-basement, with a high barred window. On the windowsill stood some empty milk bottles and a collection of drooping plants.

'I've had enough, you know?' Daniella curled a lock of hair around her finger. 'I want it all to stop. My Aidan had nothing to do with it and now he's the one having to hide from the feds. And meanwhile that two-faced cow is swaggering about as if she's the victim.'

'Your brother,' Agnes began.

'I think about him every day. And my mum, she's never got over it. Well, you wouldn't, would you? Me and Trig, my other brother, we do what we can, but Trig is up north, working the rigs, we hardly see him.'

'I spoke to Ezra,' Agnes said.

Her face softened. 'How's he doing?'

'Not well.'

Daniella sighed. She leaned her head on one elbow. 'My brother did his best, the Lord knows. He tried to raise him as his own, it's what that bitch said she wanted until she changed her fucking mind.'

From somewhere in the house, a cuckoo clock struck the half hour. Outside, the sun had clouded over. There was a pile of washing-up by the sink. On the windowsill the weary cacti fingered the stained cream tiles.

'And Francie?' Agnes said.

Daniella raised her head. 'Francie Sorrell?' Her expression tightened. 'The saintly Francie. There's a long story there, Sister. A devil's pact, if you ask me.'

To do with what? Agnes was about to ask, but there was a clatter from upstairs, followed by a burst of swearing.

'Ah,' Daniella said. 'Here's Mum.'

Connie Bennett stumbled into the room. She wore loose jeans and a baggy green cardigan, and her dark frizzy hair had an inch of grey at the roots. She glanced at Agnes, managed a thin smile, and went over to the kettle. 'You didn't even offer her a drink,' she said to her daughter.

Daniella didn't look up.

'He's gone into hiding,' Connie said to Agnes. 'Aidan. Did she tell you that?'

'Yes.' Agnes held out a hand. 'I'm Sister Agnes,' she said. 'You're Mrs Bennett.'

Connie ignored the hand. 'I am,' she said, above the noise of the kettle. 'Connie to my friends.'

'Of which I'm one, I hope,' Agnes said, and it sounded clumsy.

'That remains to be seen.' Connie took three mugs from the shelf, opened a tin and thrust a teabag into each mug.

'We were just talking about Francie Sorrell,' Agnes said.

Connie placed a mug of tea and a bottle of milk in front of her.

'You were, were you?'

'I ain't said nothing, Mum.' Daniella flashed a glance at her mother, as she took the mug of tea from her.

Connie sat down at the old Formica-topped table. 'Not a bad word to say about her. You ask anyone round here. But those of us who know . . .' She clicked sweetener into her tea. 'A pact with the devil,' she said.

'That's what Daniella just said. You see,' Agnes went on, 'I don't see how Jay got away with it. When Reece died . . .' She looked at Connie.

Connie squeezed out her teabag and placed it, wrung out and shrivelled, on the table surface. Daniella dropped hers next to it.

'People think London is a great big city,' Connie said, staring at the teabag on the stained table top. 'What they don't realise is that it's lots of villages stuck together. And people in villages, they behave like they always have. Always will. You get the wrong side of the village and you're stuck there.' She looked up. 'And like in all villages, all through time, it depends on two things: who owns the place, and whose God you believe in.'

In the silence, Agnes added her own teabag to the two on the table surface.

'There was a priest.' Connie looked up. 'Francie Sorrell and that man . . . they was like *that*.' She touched a thumb and forefinger together. 'Close as anything. I don't mean in a sexual way. For them it was power. Them two, and the family that owned the land under the church. It was like a triangle. Like three steel pegs on which the whole thing rested.'

Daniella was silent, staring at her tea as it grew cold before her.

'Was this priest . . . was he called Father Anselm?'

Connie sat upright. 'Now there's a name I haven't heard for a long while.' She shook her head. 'No, it weren't him. Although, he knew them all.'

'Was — was it — the Greek one?'

Connie almost laughed. 'Greek? Who told you that?' Her lips twitched with a smile. 'He was about as Greek as I am, and I'm ninety-eight per cent Irish. I did one of them tests, didn't I, Ella?'

Daniella smiled, nodded.

'Not that it told me anything I didn't already know, I could have kept the money,' Connie said. 'Father Darius, he was called. No one liked him. But him, and Francie Sorrell, and that family. They ran things. Money from the family to the Church. Money from the Church to Mrs Sorrell's community centre. Everyone praising Francie for her good works. So, when Francie's boy loses it with my boy, and it all goes wrong . . . things get hushed up. Police get involved, questions asked, Jay Sorrell has his day in court, manslaughter, provocation—'

'It was victim blaming, plain and simple,' Daniella interrupted.

'Yeah. Victim blaming.'

'In what way?' Agnes asked.

Connie spoke. 'Like, my boy was asking for it? Like, just because our kid gets a bit clever out there, like all the other lads, does that make him a gangster? And does that give another gangster the right to stab him to death? You tell me if nine months in jail is justice. Jay comes out swaggering, just the same, only better connected.'

Daniella picked up her phone. 'Ez was only nine. Poor kid.'

Agnes watched her scroll, briefly, then put her phone down on the table.

'This priest,' Agnes said. 'Father Darius.'

Both women looked at each other, then back at Agnes. 'Yes?' Connie said.

'You said he and Francie were close, but — I'd heard he didn't like Francie.'

There was another glance between the two. Connie took a deep, decision-making breath. 'It all went wrong, you see. The old family, there was a brother, Gerard, he took his own life. He made accusations — against his family, against the Church, and then he hanged himself. And suddenly, the priests went, the church got closed. Francie was never herself after that. That's what made her ill. She moved away then. Talk of her going back to Grenada. Though some said Scotland, was it?' She looked at Daniella, then went on. 'And then there was that statue, like she was a saint, or something.'

'Bridget O'Leary said—'

'Oh. Her. What's she got to say now?'

'She said that she doesn't think Jay killed Reece.'

'She means well, that woman. It's a nice thought. But . . .' Connie shook her head. 'Witnesses. Everyone knew. And in any case—' She looked at Agnes. 'It's like I said. Like in history, isn't it? In the end, it's us mothers, standing by our children's graves. Nothing changes.' Her voice cracked. 'Nothing changes,' she said, again.

A chirrup from the cuckoo clock floated on the silence.

'Francie Sorrell,' Connie said. 'I think about her now. Wherever she is, she never got to see her boy dead in her arms. She's been spared that, at least.' She looked up. 'Do you think she knows? Someone must have told her. Bet the old family knows where she is. If anything brings her back, it'll be that. But even then . . .' She pulled her cardigan around her.

'Do you know why she moved away?' Agnes asked. 'If she was ill, wouldn't she want to be close to her family?'

Connie shrugged. 'There was a big row, that's what everyone said. She went on about bad influences, she was frightened for her boy, with good reason it turned out. But this was Church stuff. And then there was a big falling-out with the old priests. That's the thing with Church people, they go on about God, but in the end it's always about money.' She fished in a baggy pocket, pulled out a packet of cigarettes, placed it on the table. She went on, 'All rumours. All hearsay. Superstitions, all of it. Like holy water keeping ghosts away.' She turned to Daniella. 'Do you remember talk of that magic cup? Like, a church thing, you know. Old, it was. Said it could save you from your sins, like, you'd be saved from the hellfire.'

'The Judas chalice,' Agnes said.

'Yeah.' Another almost-smile. 'That was it. Funny you know about it. It came from like, the old days, when all the church land was a monastery or priory or something. Before them Protestants pulled it all down. They're like that, aren't they. They never change. Bastards.'

'Mum!'

'She don't mind,' Connie said. 'She's one of us, aren't you?'

Agnes smiled. 'Go on,' she said. 'About this chalice.'

Connie leaned back in her chair, pushed a teabag around the table. 'It disappeared. And they was fighting over it, them churchmen. And Francie was accused of stealing it, and she was furious, hopping mad, and that's when she left. It's like it was the last straw, after that man's death, and getting her boy out of jail, and then all the church turning against her. She looked ill, in those days. Then there was this fight about that special cup, and then people said she'd gone.'

'Do you know where it went? This chalice?'

Connie shook her head. 'I never saw it. But you just reminded me. That priest you mentioned, not the Darius one, the other one. Father Anselm. He'd go on about it, looking for it. He'd unlock old cupboards in the church. He climbed into the loft, once, got his foot stuck between the rotten boards, they had to call someone to get him out . . .' She shook her head. 'People said it was in the church some-where, but then the church closed, and no one ever found it.'

There was a sudden loud animal wailing outside. 'Them cats!' Daniella jumped up. 'And ours always comes off worse.' She ran out to the hall. Agnes could hear shooing noises from the street.

Connie reached for the packet of cigarettes, tapped one out of it.

'I knew a kid,' she said. 'Well, Reece knew him. Through the church choir. I mean, we were never church, like that, you know, but they were kind of friends . . .' She struck a match, lit her cigarette. 'But this kid, I can't remember his name now, Albert I want to say, but it ain't that, something like that . . .' She drew in a deep breath of smoke. 'He sang beautiful he did, this boy. Lovely voice. Quite a bit older than the others, but he was kind, like a big brother to them. Troubled, though. Lived in the children's home across the main road there, closed down now. No one really to look after him. And then one day he disappeared. He were older then, about seventeen, maybe eighteen. I asked around, but no one knew where he'd gone. He often absconded, people said, had problems with drugs. People said he'd moved away, but there was something about him . . .' She took another drag of her cigarette. 'And the thing is, it wasn't long after that that the St Fleur brother died. Gerard. Found hanging in the churchyard.' She fiddled with a button on her cardigan. 'I've always avoided the church after that. We all do. I'll walk round it. There's a short cut I can take through the churchyard from the bus stop, but I never do. Too many ghosts. Restless spirits, that's what I think. So when they said the Sorrell boy was found there, I thought, what was he doing there? None of us would set foot in that place. Not that I care. He can go to Hell as far as I'm concerned.' She placed her cigarette on the edge of the ash tray. She looked up. 'I didn't like that priest. Father Darius. Didn't like him.'

The front door slammed, and Daniella appeared holding a large, struggling tabby cat. 'I got her,' she said. The cat leaped from her arms and hid under the table.

Connie got to her feet. 'And now someone said the statue got stolen.' She went to the sink, rinsed out the empty milk bottle, placed it on the windowsill with the others.

Agnes gathered up her coat. 'Yes,' she said. 'Orla St Fleur took it away.'

Connie froze on the spot. Behind her, the cacti seemed to wince. 'She did, did she?' She turned and gave a weary smile. 'Like I said. The old connections. Too strong to fail.' She looked at Daniella. 'You can show our Sister out, can't you?'

The warm clouds threatened rain. On the doorstep, Daniella reached out a hand. 'Thank you for coming.' The gesture was strangely formal. 'Don't mind Mum. She's mostly tolerant, my mum, but don't get her started on the Protestants.'

'It's okay,' Agnes said.

'She liked you. I can tell.' Daniella's eyes filled with tears. 'The problem is it don't change nothing. My brother was killed by that shite, and now someone has finally brought justice upon him. But unless something changes, the man I love is going to do time for it.'

'Is he safe, Aidan?'

She gave a nod. 'I hope so. For now.'

Agnes touched her arm. 'I won't give up.'

Daniella raised her tearful face to her. 'Thank you,' she said.

CHAPTER EIGHT

'So you said, "I won't give up"?' Athena took a sip from a cocktail glass. 'That is so fucking typical of you. And I bet you had no idea what you meant.'

Around them was the buzz of noise, the chink of glasses raised. The London Friday evening crowd jostled and bantered. Beyond the lighted windows, the dusk was cut through with headlight streaks.

'Poor girl. I just wanted her to feel someone was on her side.'

'That's typical too.'

'Thanks.'

'It's a compliment, sweetie.' Athena was wearing a plain cream dress draped with a scarf, layers of silk in blue and yellow.

'I know.'

Their drinks were bright pink, chunky with ice, adorned with fruit. 'Pomegranate juice. Terribly healthy. And extra vitamins too. And vodka, obviously.' She popped a blueberry between her painted lips. 'So — what are you going to do?'

'Well . . .' Agnes leaned back against the soft turquoise cushions. 'There are all these threads, you see. Something happened, with a priest who worked in the old church.

Daniella started telling me about a kid, a choirboy, who disappeared, and this priest with a Greek name who no one liked.'

'Oh God. One of those stories. Not the Greek bit, but just, in general.'

Agnes stirred a striped straw around in her large glass. 'And Francie, Jay's mum, she knew something about it. She was very involved with the church, and then suddenly she wasn't. No one will speak ill of her, but something happened to drive her away. And even with her son's death, no one has seen her since. But whatever it was, it left people vulnerable, and angry. As you would expect. And I think this odd church art man knows a lot about it. He used to be a priest but left the church, which is why I think the next thing I've got to do is contact him.'

'What, this creepy art dealer? You can't really mean to tell me you were thinking of seeing him again? It's the opposite of what you should do, surely?'

'But . . .' Agnes put down her glass. 'The real problem is, Julius isn't telling the truth.'

'Hmmm. That is serious, I agree.'

'It all seems to stem from this Orla St Fleur. Connie, Daniella's mum, she said that Orla had a brother who killed himself. And then Bridget O'Leary, the half-sister, she said that Orla was in love with a priest. A kind man, a Jesuit—'

Athena shook her head. 'No. I won't have it. Not Julius. I know there was that woman in Ireland centuries ago, but she was the love of his life. He's not the sort of chap to have two.'

'Exactly. And when I mentioned her name, he didn't behave like someone who'd heard the name of the love of his life. He behaved as if he'd seen a ghost. And as if it was all my fault.' Agnes speared a piece of mango and laid it on a saucer. 'None of it makes sense. I mean, a woman from his past is one thing, but this is a real murder, a real dead body in the church.'

Athena put down her glass. 'Maybe he's got a point, Julius. If going about digging all this up is going to be so upsetting, and from what you're saying, there's something dark about a youth group and priests behaving badly. God knows there's enough of that around, don't get me started on the old priest back home. The old ladies would send all the children out to play whenever he visited. We knew it was odd, it was the only time we were allowed to roam the out-of-bound caves. We'd only come back at tea time when we were sure he'd have gone . . . Where was I? Oh, yes. Maybe Julius is right.'

Agnes looked at her. 'What do you mean?'

'It's like this.' Athena twirled a paper parasol between her fingers. 'Julius is the most honest person I know, for one good reason: because he doesn't lie to himself. I mean, you and me, we make an effort to be straight with people, but sometimes — what I mean is, there are times I am not straight with someone else because I'm lying to myself.'

'You? When?'

'Ummm . . . Oh, I don't know. Telling Nic that of course we'll get rid of my lovely red Audi and replace it with some kind of electric thing which only does twenty on a good day.'

'That's just lying, not self-deception.'

'Or promising I'll spend some of my inheritance on solar panels for the studio.' Athena stared at the pink paper in her fingers. 'But Julius — he never lies. There's something in his past that he doesn't want to awaken. And knowing Julius, there'll be a very good reason for it. So, you should trust him, you owe him that. What I'm thinking is, whatever this woman has brought back into his life, it's not about love, or regret, or anything soft and sentimental. It's hard as nails and a hundred times more dangerous. There, I've said it. And now I need a wee.'

She got up, smoothed her dress and tottered towards the ladies' on her high black heels.

Agnes drained her glass. *Turning our back on our passions*, she thought.

I'm on my own.

The hubbub around her had become very loud, the pulse of laughter and chatter now broken by the tapping of Athena's heels as she returned.

She looked at Agnes's face and reached across to grasp her hand. 'Oh, don't listen to me, sweetie. I'm not myself. I always thought that all I wanted was a distant Greek relative to leave me a fortune and now it's happened it's causing nothing but trouble. Nic's right, we should invest it in property, and the loft space is wonderful . . . And he's got other plans. He wants to move out of London. He's looking at thatched cottages somewhere in Kent or Essex. Not far, commuting distance, that's what he said, and he can still have his studio . . . Can you imagine how he'll manage without decent coffee within two minutes' walk?'

She settled back down on the bench. 'But it doesn't change anything, does it? You know, back in Greece, I was sat there, at the funeral, all that lovely music, and flowers, and the beautiful sculptures in the old church, all that . . . and I stared at the coffin. And I was listening to dear old Yiannis sobbing, the love of his life lying there dead. And I thought, he's done all the right things. He's followed the traditions, we did holy water and oil and stuff, flowers everywhere, all the chanting, followed all Dmitroula's wishes . . . He's done all that, but the only thing he really, really wants to happen is for his wife to come back, and that's the one thing that can't happen. And I started thinking about what happens when it's Nic. When I'm sitting there, looking at his coffin, listening to lovely music . . . and I thought, really we've got it all wrong. I mean, sweetie, you know me, I'm just an ordinary bird who doesn't believe in God, but in that moment I thought those dour-faced Lutherans in plain Nordic churches have got the right idea. Nothing to celebrate, nothing to hope for, just sitting in their awful chilly buildings being depressed. Accepting the reality of it all. No pretence that anything can be fun and pink and sparkly and joyful. And no disappointment either.'

Agnes looked at her. 'Perhaps this personality change thing is catching.'

Athena twiddled her glass between her fingertips. She shook her head. 'No, not me. In the end, I concluded I'm just too shallow. I can't be dour. There's too much to love about life, like these drinks, aren't they fun, and do you know, I saw this beautiful winter coat the other day, leaf green, tailored, it would go so well with those expensive white boots I bought last year that I never wore . . .' She looked up. 'Why are you laughing?' She laughed too. 'And the great thing is, all the thinking I had in Dmitroula's funeral, it's made me *so* much nicer to Nic.' She drained her glass. 'I just hope he notices, you can never tell, can you?' She leaned across and gathered up her coat. 'We should go. Make sure you visit the ladies' on the way out, there's a beautiful mirror in there and they've got rose-scented soap and proper hand towels.'

They had stumbled, arm in arm, along the street. At the corner, Athena gave Agnes a hug. 'Please don't feel I'm deserting you, sweetie. Knowing you, you'll do whatever you want, regardless of what I say. Speak soon.'

* * *

Now, Agnes was sitting by the window in her flat, looking out at the London night. After so many nights on call at the hostel, she was glad to be back home. One-bedroomed, first floor, low-rise, 1950s, near the hostel in South London, acquired by the Order rather by mistake, used for visiting bishops and dignitaries, and only reluctantly given to Agnes in the absence of such visits and because it was convenient to the hostel and, as Sister Christiane had said, 'all that commuting from the convent house in Hackney is a dreadful waste of time and anyway I'm sure we'll continue to see enough of you . . .'

The room was warm, the curtains half drawn, the lamp a bright pool of light across her desk. A mug of mint tea sat at her elbow.

Gerard was on her mind. What was it Connie had said? This brother had made accusations, against his family, against the Church, and then he took his own life.

She picked up her phone and tapped on a number.

It rang for a long time, and then was answered. A woman's voice. 'Hello?'

'Oh. Um . . . I wondered . . . Is Andras Swift there?'

'Andras?' The voice was abrupt, an accent slightly foreign. 'No.'

'This is his phone?'

'This is his phone, yes. But he is not here.'

'Can I — might I leave a message?'

'Good night.' The phone clicked off.

Agnes looked at her phone. She put it down on her desk.

I should listen to my friends, she thought.

CHAPTER NINE

'Sister, you do look tired.' Sister Dominique nudged her, joking. 'Or maybe it's a hangover?'

They were in the corridor of the Order's main house, waiting to go into chapel for Saturday morning prayers.

Yes, Agnes wanted to say. *A hangover. You know what it's like. You have a few too many margaritas, and then you phone some guy you've only just met and his girlfriend answers, you know the kind of thing . . .*

Instead she nodded and smiled, as the door opened and they filed into chapel.

'. . . Why are you so full of heaviness, O my soul . . .' The words of the psalm sounded softly around her.

She knelt in her pew, head bowed.

'. . . and why are you so disquieted within me . . .'

She thought of Julius. His rage, his distance. The disquiet within him.

* * *

Afterwards the sisters caught up over coffee. Sister Judith had to go and nurse her father who's ninety-three and fell off a ladder pruning his apple tree. Sister Winifred would be back tomorrow with news from the Calais project. Mother Abbess from the Burgundy Benedictines was insisting on coming to stay again next month. 'Two whole weeks she wants, you remember how bored she was last time, tapping her fingers during vespers and always complaining about the food . . .'

'Agnes,' Sister Christiane asked her, quietly, as they sat in a corner of the parlour. 'Are you all right?'

Agnes faced her, as she sat, serious, attentive.

'You can lie if you want,' Sister Christiane said.

Agnes smiled, shook her head.

Sister Christiane had been Provincial Director of their Order for some time and was currently based at the Hackney house. She was ageless, at least sixty, and now considered Agnes, her head on one side, neat and grey and bird-like. A large wooden cross hung against the crisp black of her dress. Christiane laid her hand on Agnes's arm. 'I know you. You are once again embarking on one of your journeys. No doubt, you are going a long way away. But make sure you come back. We need you. And,' she added, suddenly business-like, 'we need to talk about you going to Calais.' She squeezed her arm, got to her feet and went to join the conversation about Mother Marie-Therese and whether an art gallery would be a good idea. 'Remember her theatrical yawning all the way through the Raphaels at the National Gallery . . .'

A long way away. Making up stories. Seeing connections where there aren't any, isn't that what Julius had said?

Agnes watched Sister Christiane, who had now joined their new novice Sister Birgitta in gathering up coffee mugs, sharing a kindly word or two.

Make sure you come back.

Agnes stood up and left the convent house.

* * *

It was a bright, sunny morning. Agnes took a detour through the park on her way to the bus stop. She looked over at the slide where a mother in a red coat was laughing with her child.

Tomorrow she would meet Sister Winifred again. *Perhaps that is the next step. Perhaps I should lay this investigation to rest and concentrate on being obedient to Sister Christiane and her plans for me.*

Her phone chirruped in her pocket.

Andras Swift, she read, as she clicked to answer.

'Hello,' she said.

'I'm sorry about Ginny.' The voice was warm, deeper than she remembered. 'Sharing phones, you know . . . crazy idea. I wondered if you were busy today. I know you nuns must have duties . . .'

'It's my day off,' she said.

'It is? They give you a day off? Times have certainly changed since my brief sojourn in the priesthood. Well, what do you know? We could go for a walk as it's a nice day, what do you think?'

Agnes found herself making arrangements. 'Two o'clock,' she echoed, 'yes, fine, very happy to come to you, the riverside, very good idea . . .'

She walked through the park, aware of a heaviness within her. Sunlight sparkled on the lake. She wondered why she had said yes to a man disliked by Julius who crashes about in lofts in search of lost artefacts.

She thought of Athena's Lutherans in their cold grey churches and wondered if that's what obedience would feel like.

* * *

By the time Agnes had got back to her flat the sun had given way to cloud. She wondered whether to call Julius. She wondered whether to call Andras back and say she couldn't meet him. She looked at the gathering rain. She picked up the pink polka-dot umbrella and put it in her bag.

It was only when she was on the way to Southwark Bridge that she remembered the umbrella was broken.

* * *

They strolled west along towards South Bank, dodging the walkway's crowds. Across the river the towers of glass refracted the hazy sunlight, the scudding clouds. There was the gentle splash of the pleasure boats on the river, the megaphone narratives of London's past.

'It's kind of you to see me,' he said. 'I thought perhaps you wouldn't want to.' He looked somehow younger, in a pale cream jacket, a shirt tightly buttoned at his neck.

They walked in silence. Then he said, 'It was nice to see Father Julius again. A reminder of old times.'

'Mmm.' Agnes watched a boat pass under the bridge, noisy with revellers.

'He seemed unchanged,' Andras said.

'He is always unchanged,' Agnes said.

'Does he still see Orla?'

'Orla St Fleur?' Agnes glanced at him.

He gave a brief nod.

'She has reappeared,' Agnes said. 'Before that, not to my knowledge.' She took a deep breath. She paused, mid-step, realising what she needed to ask. 'Dr Swift — why are you so interested in this sand timer?'

He stopped, and looked down at her. The tension in his face seemed to soften. 'That's a very good question.' He began to walk again, and she fell into step with him. 'The short answer is, because I fear that I am one of the few people who know its true value.'

'And the long answer?'

He slowed, shook his head, then picked up his pace again.

'Julius seemed reluctant to see you.'

'As well he might,' he said, with an odd emphasis. 'They were difficult times. Very difficult. He won't want to be reminded of me.'

'So why come back?'

He turned to her. 'That young man who died — in the church—'

'Jason Sorrell,' she said. 'Known as Jay.'

83

'Yes.'

'His mother — Frances,' he said.

'Yes?'

'There was a priest, a colleague.'

'You were Father Anselm?' she said.

He took a breath. 'Yes,' he said.

'And there was Father Darius, the Greek priest.'

A small nod.

'Although people say he was more Irish than Greek,' she added.

He laughed. 'People always say what they want to say.' He hesitated. 'There was a lot of bad feeling. Between him and Mrs Sorrell.'

'What happened?'

'Friendships were broken. There was terrible anger. I moved away.'

He seemed reluctant to say any more.

'I've heard,' Agnes began, 'from a few people now, that you were looking for the Judas chalice. Did you find it?' She was unprepared for his response.

He stopped dead, and seemed to sway as if he was about to fall. His hand reached out to a nearby lamp post and he leaned against it, breathing heavily, a sweat breaking out on his forehead.

'Are you all right?' she asked.

He took out a linen handkerchief and mopped his brow.

A group of young people passed close by, in big puffa jackets, slouching along to the beat of music from their phones.

He faced her. 'I wasn't expecting . . .' He took a breath. 'Doesn't he know?' His voice was low. 'Julius — he must know where it is.'

She shook her head. 'No one knows where it is.'

'They didn't get it, then?'

'Dr. Swift — who are "they"?'

'Julius's safe . . .' he began. 'The break-in . . .'

She looked at him. 'Julius's safe was empty,' she said.

He seemed not to hear her. 'The other church,' he said. 'The one they set on fire . . .' He seemed to be talking to himself. 'They said that safe was empty too. . .'

He began to walk, his pace uneven. She walked next to him. It was more crowded now, with people, swirls of noise, eruptions of music.

'If you don't mind—' He gestured to a low wall. She sat down next to him. His breath was still in short bursts, and again he dabbed at his face.

When his breath seemed more even, Agnes tried again. 'So, what is it with this chalice?'

He shook his head.

'It's medieval,' she said. 'That's what I've been told. Silver. Very valuable.'

He gave a brief nod. 'Beyond value,' he murmured.

'Why?' she said.

He turned to her. 'Why?' he repeated. 'There is only one in the world, as far as anyone knows. Judas the Betrayer. No one would put him on a communion chalice, and yet, someone, some medieval silversmith, had reason to.' His voice had settled now. 'When it was known, when it was used, all these stories gathered around it, apparently, that it would cure ills, but only on particular days in the church calendar.'

'And why do you want it?'

'Because — because I am expert. Because I will do it justice, make sure people know about it. I will be true to its past.'

He seemed to choose his words carefully. She wondered what he had been about to say.

She spoke again. 'When did you decide not to be a priest?'

He straightened up next to her. 'A crisis of faith, Sister. You must know of such things.'

She gave a brief nod, a smile.

'I was born of Dutch stock,' he said. 'My great-grandfather. Traders in jewellery in Amsterdam. Then they settled in London. It was that, you see.' He turned to her. 'I mistook

85

the beauty of the Church for faith. I would look up at a paint-ing, a carving, and see the love of God for the world. But after some years I realised I was making a mistake. I began to study history of art and ended up doing a PhD. I specialised in church artefacts from the thirteen and fourteenth centuries. The Church in those centuries supported a wealth of talent, engravers, painters, ceramicists, not just in Europe, across the East too. Without those abbeys, those monasteries, it would have been a cultural desert. And I began to feel drawn to that way of thinking about things, celebrating creation with art and beauty.'

His face softened as he told her about miniaturists and the groundbreaking advances in fifteenth-century oil paint-ing. Agnes found herself wondering why Julius didn't like him.

'And then I met Ginny,' he was saying. 'She worked at an auction house I used to visit. And now,' he spread his arms, 'here I am.'

'Julius said things went wrong,' Agnes began. 'There was a group of you. There was a youth group. And someone died.'

'Gerard,' he said. 'Gerard St Fleur.'

'Ah.'

'He died by suicide. Julius will have told you, no doubt.'

She nodded, feeling a tightness in her chest.

'He was a great friend, Gerard.'

They watched the river, the passing boats.

'You see—' Agnes braced her feet against the paving stones. 'One man is dead. Another is liable to be charged with his killing and it all seems to be tied up with Orla St Fleur, and Francie, and safe-breaking . . . and this chalice,' she finished.

His voice was soft. 'The clue is in the name. Judas, the betrayer. Do you have any idea what that means?'

She shook her head.

'These chalices, they were believed to be redemptive. The idea was that drinking the wine during the Eucharist from this chalice would aid the process of the remission of sins. It was a popular belief when it was made, in the fourteenth century. But this one shows the Judas kiss, the moment when Judas betrays Christ, the moment that leads to the fulfilment of the prophecies, the crucifixion, the resurrection. It is unique, this very unusual portrait of the thirteenth apostle engraved within it. So much church silver got melted down in the Reformation, but somehow, this chalice disappeared into the vaults of the St Fleur family, and then ended up in the old priory. And then the priory was rebuilt, and the church became derelict, and it disappeared. The family have always maintained a silence about it.'

'So — so why do you want it so much?'

He closed his eyes, briefly. 'No one else knows. No one else can be trusted with it. All these years, I tried to tell them, only me . . .'

'To own it?'

'Certainly, to own it. If I was to begin to talk about its provenance, to tell you all I know about it, we'd be here all day. But the history is fascinating. Its roots in the Netherlands, the probable silversmith, the Arab merchants trading these things, the families who bought them, but this one — this particular, extraordinary one — why did the engraver choose that image? There is still so much unknown. It would be a lifetime's work to find out. But they wouldn't listen. They just wouldn't listen to me.' He dabbed again at his forehead. 'Gerard might have understood, but he died before . . . before anything could be sorted out.' He took a deep breath, exhaled.

'There were other things,' Agnes said.

'Oh, the books, yes, and that sand timer. Another beautiful thing, whose value has been ignored by those philistines. There's a psalm about sand, isn't there, "How deep I find your thoughts O Lord. Were I to count them they would be more in number than the sand . . ." Isn't that it?'

'Yes,' she said. 'Yes, it is.'

'The words remain, even if the faith has melted away.' He smiled. 'The idea of ownership, of inheritance — in the wrong hands, that's how art works get ruined, that's how beautiful creations get spoiled, or lost . . .'

'Like the chalice.'

'Exactly.'

'But—' she began. 'It's lost.'

'No.' His voice was emphatic. 'Not lost at all. They're lying. I've seen it.'

'You've seen it?'

'Once,' he said. 'Once. She was there, Frances, laughing at me. And Orla was holding it. They'd collected it from the St Fleurs' bank on the Strand or somewhere. She said it was going back where it belonged. "It's time it went home," Orla said, and the Sorrell woman took it from Orla and they both laughed, their sticky fingerprints on it, looking at me, laughing, as if it was a joke, when only I . . .' he stopped to get his breath again, 'only I knew. And Orla knew I knew. She knew that what she was doing was wrong and she did it anyway. I almost seized it then. I moved towards them, and that woman held it above her head, laughing still . . . I remonstrated. It became unpleasant. I had to leave.'

'Unpleasant?'

He waved her question away.

Something they'd said. How he'd stop at nothing. She watched him now, dabbing at his temples with his crumpled handkerchief, stuffing it back into a pocket, his face marbled with stress.

'Shall we walk?' she suggested.

The late afternoon air was heavy, squeezing drops of moisture from the thickening clouds. Two musicians nearby played a folk song with violin and a guitar.

'Dr Swift, why did you come back?'

Again came the thin smile. 'Sister Agnes,' he said. 'I never went away.'

'Biding your time?' she asked.

He held her gaze, then gave a nod. 'You could put it like that.'

'How well did you know the St Fleur family?'

He was walking more easily now, as if on safer ground. 'They were my friends. The St Fleurs: Orla and Iris, her sister. And Gerard, of course. But you know all about that.'

'I know very little.'

He flicked her a questioning glance. 'Well,' he said, 'Gerard and I were very good friends. He promised me the chalice. He said I would look after it. He was right. I would have found a safe home for it, but after Gerard's untimely death, feelings ran high, as you can imagine. Those friendships were fractured. Orla and that woman were on one side. Darius, he coped less well than the rest of us. No one was coping very well, to be honest, but he . . . he lacked resilience. He was angry, he said things . . . It broke everything up. And then Orla moved away. That woman did her disappearing act, and Iris went back to the family home. Their mother was still alive in those days and needed to be cared for . . . and so we lost touch.'

'And is the loss of the chalice connected to that time?'

He nodded. 'I blame myself,' he said. 'They were good friends. I was disloyal.'

'In what way?'

He stopped and faced her. 'Even if I tried to explain, I'm not sure you'd understand.'

'Try me.' She stood still, facing him. He seemed reduced now, stooped, his hair dishevelled. Again, he gave his narrow smile, but said nothing.

'Is it about the youth group in the church? Someone said there was a boy, some years ago, he went missing . . .'

He was silent, and so she went on, 'The church that recently burned down. Arson, they're saying. And the one person found dead, carried out of the ashes, is Francie's son, Jay.'

He gave a deep sigh. 'Oh, Sister, I wish I knew. I wish I could help. Like you, I feel that these recent events are connected to the past. Like you, I have a sense of the history at play, of being in a continuum. Perhaps that's what your faith gives you.' He smiled. 'The chalice was said to give absolution.

That's why the depiction of the great betrayal is so unusual. Of course, for you Catholics, the wine becomes the actual blood of Christ. The holy grail . . .' He turned to her. 'That was where I drew the line,' he said. 'Transubstantiation. That's when I realised that in my bones I was a Protestant. The Dutch side won in the end.' He laughed.

The heavy clouds had gathered, and now it began to rain.

He looked at his watch. It was high-tech, new and expensive-looking. 'Well,' he said. 'I'd better get back. Ginny will wonder where I've been all this time.' Another smile. 'You'll get wet,' he said. He rummaged in a large pocket, produced a neat, black folded umbrella. 'Here,' he said. 'You can borrow this one.'

She shook her head, falling into step beside him. 'I have one.' She pulled the pink polka-dot umbrella from her bag. 'Thanks all the same.'

They parted at the Tube station. 'Well—' he offered her his hand, 'this is my stop. Thank you for the conversation. If there's any further news, you will let me know, won't you? And if there's anything more I can help with, do not hesitate to ask.'

She shook his hand and walked away, feeling the rain against her face, shaking out the broken spokes of the pink umbrella.

I am no further on, she thought.

Who were these men? What was the darkness in their friendship, the story of betrayal that circles this chalice, that led to suicide, that collided so harshly with Francie Sorrell.

And with Julius.

She went along Southwark Bridge Road, back towards the old church. Her hair trickled rain against her neck.

She found herself in the old churchyard. The blackened door was padlocked now, a brand-new steel chain thrown across the threshold.

Pointlessly, she tugged at the lock.

'Ah,' a female voice said. 'There you are. I gather you've been asking about me.'

CHAPTER TEN

Coincidence, Agnes would say, later, to Athena. Orla St Fleur, standing there in the graveyard, in the rain. Or perhaps no coincidence at all, she wondered now, as she looked at the china blue eyes, the pale hair still neat and dry under a plastic hood. *Perhaps Orla St Fleur has followed me and chosen her moment,* clipped and precise as the well-cut coat, as the elegant black shoes that now tapped on the gravestone at her feet.

Orla looked at Agnes. 'You're very wet,' she said. 'Don't you have an umbrella?'

Agnes produced the tangle of pink polka dots. 'It's broken.'

'Ah.' Orla turned towards the South Door. 'We could sit in the porch?'

The porch had walls of thick sandstone, mottled by the years.

'Let's just hope it's safe after the fire,' Orla said with a smile. 'This is the oldest part of the old church, you know.'

She took off her coat and spread it across the damp stone shelf, and gestured for Agnes to sit down next to her. 'Part of this wall has been here for centuries.' She touched the stone with a pale finger, then looked up. 'I decided to seek you out because Julius thinks so highly of you.'

'Thank you.' Agnes kept her voice level. 'The odd thing is, he's never spoken of you.'

A flicker of a smile. 'There's a reason for that. But not one I can tell you. Of course, I don't see him often. Hardly at all, really.'

The rain was easing with the dusk. Beyond the railings, streetlights flickered into life.

'I expect Julius expressly warned you not to speak to me,' Orla said.

'He did,' Agnes admitted. 'I don't suppose you'll explain why?'

Orla shook her head. 'Not now. Not without his blessing.'

Agnes stretched her legs out, aware of her muddy flat boots next to Orla's polished heels. 'Given that that is the case,' Agnes said, 'let's talk of something else, then. For example, why did you take the statue away?'

Orla's gaze went towards the empty stone base at the centre of the churchyard. 'Because I promised her,' she said. 'And I keep my promises.'

'You mean Francie? And where is the statue now?'

'Safe.' Her tone had a hard edge.

Agnes waited, but Orla didn't elaborate.

'Ezra believes that statues can come back to life,' Agnes said.

Something softened, briefly. 'Ah,' Orla said. 'Ezra.' She shook her head. 'If only they could.'

'What is she like, Francie Sorrell?'

'She was my friend.' The voice was suddenly fierce. 'And I don't say such things lightly, coming from my background . . .' She looked up at Agnes. 'You're not like me. From what Julius says, you're strong, and self-contained, and of course what you have, what you both have, is faith. It must help.'

It occurred to Agnes that what this woman was expressing was envy. It was unexpected. Orla's air of privilege, of Englishness, reminded her of her father's sisters, her elderly aunts, who managed somehow to exude a disapproval of her

92

mother's family, the foreign-ness, the being 'continental', the unaccustomed food . . .

'We owned this, once upon a time.' Orla flicked her thin fingers to indicate the space around them. 'The St Fleurs. We never converted, when those Tudors made it so dangerous for us. We refused.' She spoke as if it was a few years ago, not centuries. 'We lost so much. We retreated, back to East Anglia, and this became a ruin. And then a church was built on top, and now, that's a ruin too.'

They both gazed out of the old stone doorway at the scaffolding, the hasty signage warning of danger, the remaining walls streaked black.

'You can still smell the smoke,' Orla said, in the silence.

'Who would want him dead?' Agnes asked.

'Jay Sorrell?' She shook her head. 'What you must know is, Francie was like the spider at the heart of the web. And I mean that as someone who loved her very much. She held it all in balance, she paid attention, she mended broken threads, she kept it all safe. And when she went . . .' Her hands clutched together in her lap. 'The threads broke. The centre collapsed. Jason went bad. She was frightened he would. And more to the point — she couldn't keep him safe from those that meant him harm.'

'Reece's family, the Bennetts? Jay was accused of stabbing Reece to death, a few years ago. He did time in prison for it.'

'Reece?' The question seemed to surprise her. 'Oh. Yes. Them too.'

'Who else?'

Orla touched one of the stones at her side with a gentle finger. 'All this . . .' she looked at Agnes. 'Do you fear death?'

'Me?'

'I imagine you don't,' she went on. 'You have your Heaven. Although Julius is strangely silent on the subject whenever I have raised it in the past.'

Agnes smiled. 'It's not a huge part of his theology.'

Orla met her eyes. 'That's what he says too.' She leaned back, exhaled. 'I gave up on Heaven. I was raised with it, of course, but the more I thought about it, a hereafter where sins are forgiven, the less it made sense. And the idea that God loves us, where is he, then? Where is he when there are wars, or famine, or when these young men can kill each other out on our streets here?' Her voice was harsher now. 'It all seemed to be wishful thinking, an excuse not to take responsibility. So I stopped making excuses.' She touched the stone again. 'Francie had faith, you know. In the face of all of it. "Orla," she'd say, "you may not believe in God. But he believes in you."' She laughed. 'I found it strangely comforting.' Her smile faded. 'For all I know she still does.' She gave a sigh. 'I miss her terribly.'

'When you say the statue is safe—'

'The statue is safe,' Orla said. 'And wherever Francie is, I suppose she's safe too.'

'Does she know her son has died?'

A moment's hesitation. 'I hope so,' Orla said. 'But to be honest, I've no idea. No word from her. Nothing. She might as well be dead.' There was another silence. They watched the shadows of the graveyard, listened as the birdsong drifted into the quiet of the night.

'I met Andras Swift,' Agnes said.

A brief turn of her head. 'Poor you.'

'He's very interested in the Judas chalice.'

'Oh,' she sighed, irritated. 'Still?'

'Apparently.'

'I didn't come here to talk about that man.' Again, the tightness in her voice.

'Why did you come?'

Orla gave a small smile. 'I often come here.'

'And did you know I'd be here?'

Orla shook her head. 'But I knew I wanted to talk to you.'

Agnes waited.

Orla spoke again. 'You spoke to Bridget. Bridget O'Leary.'

'Yes.'

'What did she tell you?'

94

'She said that you're related,' Agnes said.

'And what else did she say?'

'Just that.'

'Half-sister, was it?'

'Yes.'

Orla gave a brief nod. 'We used to play together, as children. My mother made allowances for her. In fact—' she shifted on the hard stone, 'I think my mother preferred her. She could give her back at the end of the day. Unlike us.'

'Who was Bridget's mother?'

'A local woman, here. It was an affair, my father had a tendency for them. He didn't expect them to produce children, though. It was my mother who acknowledged Bridget, at least when we were little. Then I was sent away to school, and after that . . .' She gave a small shrug. 'It destroys things.'

'Yes.' Agnes glanced at her. 'I was sent away too.'

'You were?'

'Your mother sounds rather like mine.' Agnes smiled.

Orla studied her. 'If one has never known love — one either seeks it out in a way that leads to danger, or one backs away from it. Or in your case, one chooses an imaginary God, perhaps.'

'It's not quite like that,' Agnes began.

Again, the impermeable look.

'Perhaps not,' Orla said.

'And your brother?' Agnes said. 'Connie said he died.'

'Who is Connie?'

'Connie Bennett. Reece's mother.'

'Ah. Them. I'd forgotten her name. I've been away, you know. Rather out of touch.'

'What brought you back?'

There was a hesitation, a silence.

'You see,' Agnes went on, 'everyone seems to have gathered, around the time of Jay's death and the fire here in this church. 'Jay himself. And Andras Swift, obsessed with the contents of the safe. And Bridget braved a conversation with a nun to tell me her views. And you. And now my friend

Julius seems to be entangled with the past, and refuses to talk to me about it. And, worse than that . . . there is some dark heart to all of it, about the youth group here and Father Anselm as he then was, and another priest, and a choirboy who disappeared and your brother having died—'

'That's enough.' The voice was loud. Orla held her hand up. 'You are treading on shifting ground, and you don't know what you're doing.'

Agnes faced the brittle gaze. 'That's definitely true,' she said.

Orla's hand went to her lap. 'I hadn't seen Julius for years,' she said. 'Not until I gave him those things for safe-keeping. You see, he helped me once. A long time ago. He's a very good man. People said we were in love, but that wasn't true. The people who said that kind of thing didn't know him, that's all.' She looked up. 'My brother, Gerard, he killed him-self. There's a tree, in that corner there by the wall, an old oak . . .' She closed her eyes, briefly. 'That's why I come back, from time to time. There was a police investigation at the time, it was very difficult. Francie was my friend, she helped lay it all to rest. And Julius . . .' She settled on the cold hard stone. 'He helped me to see beyond my rage.' She looked up. 'He's a good man,' she said, again. She smoothed her coat at her side. 'The St Fleurs had always had a say about the priest of this church. In the old days. Then it was ruined, and that was that.'

'Why did Julius end up with the things from the safe?'

Orla studied her hands in her lap. 'I gave them to him to look after. I needed a safe place, someone I could trust. They are priceless.'

'Someone tried to steal them from him,' Agnes said.

'Yes. I heard. He had the good sense to move them.' She smiled. 'That sand timer. I love that old thing. I like the expression, "running out of time". It always makes me think of that. It used to be on the mantelpiece in our home, until someone pointed out to Father that it had rather more value than the old pipes and dusty paperweight that sat next to it.' She gave a small laugh.

'And the chalice,' Agnes said. 'Was that on the mantel-piece too?'

'The Judas chalice?' A swift, sharp glance. 'No, that's been missing for years.'

'Andras Swift said you had it.'

'That man—' The voice was sharp. 'He never gives up.' She sighed. 'We did have it, yes. Gerard claimed to have promised it to someone. After his death, with probate, lawyers, there was an awful muddle. Then it was lost.'

'It's supposed to give absolution,' Agnes said.

A brief smile. 'Well, we could all do with that, couldn't we? And Andras Swift as he now is, as much as any of us.' There was a tightening of her expression.

'But what happened to it?' Agnes pursued.

Orla smiled. 'My family — we have lost a lot over the centuries. Paintings, property, land . . . Our wealth has shrivelled with the years.'

'And do you mind?'

'Oh, what good would it do to mind?' She touched Agnes's hand with her own. 'When my brother died, I learned something about the value of things.' She shook out her umbrella, closed it carefully. 'This life — this time allotted to us. That is all we have.' She got to her feet, leaning on the umbrella like a cane.

'You see, I gave up on Heaven because I realised this is enough.' She gestured to the space around them, the branches clustered low in the twilight, the distant tolling of church bells. 'This. If this is the best it gets, I'm happy with that. I've had a ball, being here, being alive. Being human.' She stepped on to the path. 'It doesn't need to mean more than that, does it?'

'No,' Agnes said, as they walked, side by side, towards the gate. 'I suppose it doesn't.'

Under the lamp light, Orla turned to her. 'I realise I have not been much help. You should speak to Iris. We still have the old place in Suffolk. Keld House. The old pilgrim route.' She laughed. 'Before all those Roundheads took it over.'

'Anglicans,' Agnes said. 'Hardly Roundheads.'

'Hmm.' She smiled. 'I'll give you her phone number.' She delved in her handbag, fumbled to produce a pen and paper, scribbled down the details. 'Here you are. She might be able to be more help than me. What with things being in the way.'

'And what is in the way?' Agnes took the paper from her. 'Julius?'

'He unites us. And divides us.' A small smile. 'It's been nice talking to you.'

She tapped her way along the pavement. The streetlights sparkled under the dripping trees.

Agnes walked towards the hostel. Across the river, the city bells chimed the ending of the day, the dawning of the Sabbath.

As she reached the hostel, her phone rang in her bag.

'Ezra,' she said. 'Hello.'

'Where are you?' he said.

'I'm at the hostel.'

'I'll be right there.'

CHAPTER ELEVEN

'It ain't just that one bro kills another bro.'

They sat at the hostel table in the quiet of the night. Most of the residents were in their rooms. There was the occasional beat of footsteps on the upstairs landing. 'No, Sister, it ain't that at all.'

'But everyone is saying Aidan killed your father.'

'They are?' He looked at her. 'That ain't my business.'

'Which means, doesn't it, that maybe you're not safe while Aidan is missing.'

'I can look after myself, Sister.' His thin fingers wrapped around his mug of tea.

She looked at him. She wished it were true.

'I had a chat with Orla St Fleur earlier,' Agnes said. 'She was once very close to your grandmother, spoke very highly of her.'

'She did?' He gave a shrug. 'Bet she went on about owning all the land round here too.'

'Well . . .'

He nodded. 'Won't let it go, man. Won't give it up. It's always the way. Men come, they say, this is our land. They lay claim to it and people, they have to load the carts, strap their little ones to their backs and walk. All through time,

Sister. And the ones left behind, what they going to do? You fight, or you die.' He took a sip of tea. 'And worse — the ones that take the land, they get rich from it, they sail the seas, they steal from other lands. You read it in the old stories. Like in my nan's book. They take the gold, the precious stones and then they take the people, load them on to ships, make them work on the lands they've stolen. You look at that woman's face — she knows, man, *she knows*. That's why she has to keep telling you that this is her manor. Cos, Sister, it ain't. Not now. You tell me I don't need the big stories? Sister, the big stories is all there is. When I read them tales, I can hear that truth ringing in my ears.'

Upstairs, there was laughter. A door slammed shut.

'Ezra, why do you think Jay died?'

He looked down at his mug on the table. He shook his head.

'He was in that church for a reason,' she continued. 'There were treasures in the safe — he wouldn't have known they'd been removed a day or so before. Did he go in search of them? Was he meeting someone?'

Ezra raised his head, he was silent for a moment, then he said, 'I don't owe him that. What I owe him is for my nan, that's all. And she's gone.'

'Meaning what?'

'I mean, I can't owe him what a son owes his father because that was a destiny he never took up. His choice, Sister, his choice.' A sudden blaze of anger. 'Pretty girls, that's all he saw. He'd be looking over there, man, when his own child was standing right in front of him. I called to him, and he didn't hear my cry. And when you do that to a kid, after a while something shuts down. They may still be crying, but they don't expect anyone to hear.'

'And your mother?'

'She tries. God knows she tries. But in her mind, what she's been put here for on God's earth, being a mother ain't at the heart of it. At the heart of what she's for is her great quest for love.' He smiled, as if it was funny.

Agnes went to the kettle, topped up their mugs of cooling tea.

'Your father, Jay,' she began, settling back at the table, 'he was scared of the church, and of someone connected to the church. But that night, he was there. Something must have pulled him back there.'

Ezra stirred a spoon of sugar into his tea. 'I think about that too. What made him go there, that night? But you know, my dad, we weren't best mates, it ain't like he told me all his hopes and dreams.'

'So — what made you ring me? What brings you here tonight?'

He leaned against the back of his chair. 'I been thinking, right. Aidan, I don't care nothing about him. But when I was little, and Reece was being my dad, Aidan was, like, my uncle. And he was kind to me. And now there's chat, right, that Aidan wanted my dad dead, my biological dad. And I don't think it's right. My mum, she's angry, she's raging — but she's always raging, people are always letting her down, always someone else's fault but never her own . . . But this time, she's saying she wants Aidan behind bars and never coming out. And I'm thinking, I know that man. And I don't hold great love for that family, but if they clap handcuffs on Aidan, it ain't right.'

'Ah.' Agnes nodded. 'Okay.'

'There was one of the feds. Years ago. An old bloke. Knew my dad, Jay, from the youth club before it closed down. Knew all them youth. He knows that family too. The old one. You know, like, they had a brother who died, well, that police knew them during that time.'

'What was his name?'

'DS something — DI? I keep thinking, if I could ask him about it, he'd know.'

'Is he still alive?'

Ezra nodded. 'I seen him, man. Along by the vape shop. He don't know me, though. But I've always liked him. My nan said he was a great strength to them, and there ain't nothing my nan didn't know about being strong—' There was a burst of music from his phone. He looked at the screen, put it back on the table. 'My mum.'

'Hadn't you better—'

'Hadn't I better answer it? And get an earful about where I am, what I'm doing, who I'm with? Nah, man, it makes me tired. Ain't got nothing to say to her.'

'Perhaps she's worried about you,' Agnes said.

'Funny way of showing it. But yeah, I'm going home now anyway.' He got to his feet. 'Thanks for being here. I just wanted to say that if Aidan Preedy is the answer, then someone is asking the wrong question.'

In the narrow hallway, he offered her his hand, towering over her.

'Ezra,' she said, 'when you say you can look after yourself—'

'When I say it, I mean it.'

'People only say things like that if they feel unsafe,' she said.

He dropped his hand to his side. 'Thing is, Sister, I don't know what it is to feel safe. Like, what I said, about my dad — that little kid, crying, wanting to be held. That was me. And when someone picks up that kid and takes him in their arms, then they feel safe. But if they learn that, like, ain't no one going to do that, then you just get used to it. That feeling that you're on your own.' He pulled his collar up around his neck. 'You're different, maybe. Like, you're held by your community.'

'Well, up to a point.'

'I bet people think you've run away from life,' he said.

'Sometimes.' She was aware of the chill in the hallway, the lateness of the hour.

'I don't think that. Because we can't run from ourselves, isn't it. Even in the old stories, those women who wall themselves up in a cave and speak only the truth. That weren't no escape. Just them and their God. Stuck there together.' He laughed, opened the front door, gazed out into the night.

'You'll go home now, will you?'

'Yeah. Nowhere else to go.'

'Promise?'

He laughed again. 'Promise.' Another touch of her hand. 'Laters, Sister. Let me know if you meet DS No Name.'

Agnes closed and locked the door, turned off all the lights and went to her room. She lay in bed, hearing the hostel settled around her, the cares of the inmates soften into sleep. *Just me and my God*, she thought. *Stuck here together. Walled up in my cave and speaking only the truth.*

If only it were that easy.

* * *

The 38 bus made its way to Hackney through empty Sunday streets and the slanting light of the dawn. In the chapel the sisters gathered, silent, yawning, flicking through the service books. Psalms were chanted, prayers were said, for the suffering of the world, for the mercy of the Lord.

'. . . the sacrifices of God are a broken spirit . . .'

And what if it makes no difference, Agnes thought. She imagined a young Ezra, crying for his mum, his dad. And after a while, getting used to no one hearing.

But we still cry.

* * *

At coffee she sat in a corner of the refectory.

She was aware of someone standing beside her, blocking out the light. Sister Winifred, of course, with her overbearing height and her untidy wisps of pale hair.

'Ah, Agnes. There you are. They said I'd find you here.' Winifred threw herself into a chair in an angular tumble. 'How are the mean streets? I do miss them, you know.'

Calais must be even meaner than South London, Agnes wanted to say.

'There was a centre for addicts,' Winifred went on, 'over near where you're based, in the south, years ago. It was run by the Methodists but I'd do the odd shift there. In fact, I loved it, I was there whenever I could be. Oh, I loved it.'

Agnes surveyed her.

'That's why they sent me to the school in Yorkshire. I gather you've been there too.'

Agnes gave a brief nod. 'A long time ago,' she said.

'They were right, of course. One shouldn't get too comfortable. We do as we are told. And now I'm in France at the camp, following orders again.' She smiled her warm, bright smile. 'You and me both.'

'Mmm,' Agnes said.

'Do you know when you're due to set out? I'll be back there next week, of course. I'll await your arrival.'

Agnes looked at the glow of happiness with irritation. I'm not going to go, she wanted to say. My friend Athena says it's out of the question, and she's always right . . .

'Oh, God, I felt just the same as you. Couldn't stand the idea when they said that's where I was going. I mean, babies? Children? Oof. Not for me. I was absolutely furious. But then I often am. You'll learn to avoid me at times, people do.'

It wasn't a glow, Agnes realised. There was no smile now. It was just a very good skin tone despite her age. Athena would want to know what face cream she uses . . .

'When I got there I was in a terrible state. I used to avoid the mothers,' Winifred was saying. 'And it rained all the time. I spent all my days in the kitchen tent, at least it was dry there and I could peel potatoes in peace.'

'What changed?' Agnes asked, in spite of herself.

There was a moment of thought, as Winifred screwed up her grey eyes. 'I'm not sure anything changed, but gradually I began to listen to the women instead of avoiding them. It was very hard.' She studied Agnes, then went on, 'It's when they tell you what they've fled. Stuttering, hesitant accounts of pure evil. No other word for it in the end. The way that men behave in war zones . . . young men, brutalised, wired . . .' Her gaze was direct now. 'Why do they do it? Why take it out on the women?'

Her fingers working now in her lap.

'I used to think goodness outweighed evil in God's creation, but it made me doubt it. I found my mind circling all those prayers of lament. "The sacrifices of God are a broken spirit."' She bit at the edge of one of her nails. 'It's difficult to see any redemption. Because, these women, they're carrying the burden of history. The cycle of violence. I tell the women there's hope, there's new life, there's a future . . . but in my heart there's only emptiness. I look into their troubled faces and all I can see is that they're carrying that anguish in their bones.' Her voice cracked. 'All I see is the evil of men, not the love of God.'

They fell silent. The refectory had emptied, and they could hear from the kitchen the clink of washing-up.

Winifred was sitting very still, her long fingers stretched out against her skirt. 'Obedience, you see. Always tricky in my view. I mean, I know it's at the heart of what we've chosen, being in monastic life, but — how do we know? When we give up our lives to God's will, when we trust our superiors to dictate our next move . . . what if it's wrong? It's an argument I'm always having.'

'And what do our superiors say?'

Her fingers pinched at the grey woollen fabric. She shrugged. 'That we have to be wary of resistance. That the self asserts itself, creates new things to do, puts illusory things in the way of truth. You know the stuff.'

'Yes,' Agnes said. 'I do.'

'That's why I get angry. Because doing as you're told can seem so utterly pointless. And yet — when I think of the alternative — what then? There'd just be me, shouting at the wind. All on my own.' Her fingers scrunched on her lap. 'And God knows there's enough wind to shout at over on the beaches there.'

Agnes smiled.

Winifred looked up. 'I wish I could be more encouraging,' she said.

Agnes took a breath. 'Before I join you,' she began, 'I have to finish something. There's a young man I've encountered,' she said. 'There's some kind of threat that he's facing . . .' She realised as she spoke that it sounded thin. 'And I think it's something to do with something from the past, as if something bad has come back.' She fell silent.

'Unfinished business,' Winifred said. 'Resistance. The self asserting itself. Just what I was saying.'

'But—'

'But you're right, of course. That's the whole bloody trickery of it. How do you tell what's the right thing to do? It sounds like this young man needs you.' Winifred drained the dregs of coffee from her mug. 'And that's another thing that makes me angry. Pain erupting from the past, passing itself on. Nothing changes.' She frowned at her mug. 'Not even this coffee. You'd think the sisters would manage something better after all these years.'

Agnes smiled, again.

'I'll be going back on Friday, they tell me. Maybe sooner. I'll expect you some days later.' Winifred touched Agnes's knee as she got to her feet. 'They speak very highly of you here.'

'Me?' Agnes shook her head. 'I doubt that. I expect they just can't wait to see the back of me.'

Winifred laughed, a sudden warm laugh. 'Perhaps they know you're good at peeling potatoes.'

'Perhaps it will have to do,' Agnes said.

Winifred leaned her hand briefly on her shoulder. 'We'll be okay, you and me.'

* * *

On the bus, Agnes looked out of the window at the familiar streets, the old brick terraces, the tower blocks looming behind. She thought about tents and rain and potatoes. She took her phone out of her bag and texted DS Rob Coombes: *I know it's Sunday, but when you get a moment, could we talk?*

She got to the hostel in time to help Eddie with the cooking. 'Sunday lunch, Sister, got to be extra special, got a load of free aubergines, very small, so I'm roasting them with cumin, and tofu, all vegan . . .'

The doorbell rang. DS Rob Coombes was standing there. 'I know it's Sunday,' he said. 'But I had Neave Sorrell on the phone just now. Ezra didn't come home last night.'

CHAPTER TWELVE

Rob Coombes had a lot to say. Ezra had gone out yesterday afternoon and Neave hadn't seen him since. He hadn't packed anything, just went out in his jacket, and the football scarf he always wears. 'But there's this crate in his room, been there ages, filled with stuff from his dad, from Jay — it seems he'd gone through it, she said, papers all over the floor . . .' Was it in his character, Rob had asked, to go missing. No, she'd said, though Rob had added to Agnes that he wasn't sure she'd notice much if he was there or not these days so that wasn't anything to go on, and did she, Agnes, know anything?

So Agnes recounted the conversation she'd had with Ezra. 'Only last night, I told him I was worried for his safety. He assured me he would go home. Promised me.'

'He never kept his promise, did he? Could be anywhere.'

'Ezra mentioned an old policeman,' she added. 'He called him DS No Name. He said he'd seen him around recently.'

'Len Wharton, maybe,' Rob said. 'The guy I told you about.'

'Ah. Yes.'

'Weird,' Rob said. 'Why would Ezra start talking about a retired copper?'

'He said that his grandmother had had a lot of respect for him.'

'Everyone did.' Rob sat at the hostel table in the pre-lunch clatter. 'But he retired, ages ago. His sister, Ivy, died, couple of weeks ago, she was in that care home. He called in after her funeral.' He checked his phone, put it on the table. 'So, Sister. Here we are, with the Sorrell murder. All sorts of tales swirling around about that one. And now his boy goes AWOL. And as for you . . .' He looked up, smiled.

'Me?'

'Don't know quite how to put this.' He fiddled with his phone, suddenly shy. 'I mean,' he went on, 'I know they always talk to you. Everyone does. One word from you about being a nun and you get everyone's previous in about five minutes, stuff it would take us a whole week in the cells to get anywhere near.'

She laughed.

'But — Agnes . . .' He seemed young, uncertain. 'This is a murder case we're dealing with. These old families, think they own the streets round here. And in a way, they do. And I know what you're like, 'cos I've seen it before with you. Once you get a sense of something, like a mystery, like something hidden . . . you turn detective. You're off, chasing after it. I'm sorry . . .' He blushed, and Agnes felt the gap of years between them.

'Don't apologise,' she said. 'Julius says exactly the same.'

'He does?' Rob brightened. 'Then you'll know what I'm trying to say. Don't put yourself in danger. Just because there's always someone who knows more than we do in the Job, doesn't mean you have to go down that path. Young Ezra will reappear, I'm sure. And when he does, just let me know, OK?' He checked his phone, got to his feet. 'I've gotta go.'

She followed him out into the hall.

'As for the Preedy boy,' he said, 'no one seems to have seen hide nor hair of him for days neither. So maybe that's another one you can tell me all about when you hear.' He hesitated. 'What I mean is,' he said, doing up the buttons on his jacket that seemed suddenly too big for him, 'what I mean is, you may be a nun, but you don't need to carry the burdens of the world upon your shoulders.'

She smiled. 'That's just what Julius says too.'

'See,' he said, smiling too, opening the door, 'I must be right, then.'

* * *

The hostel office was quiet in the post-lunch lull. The odd snatch of music coming from the lounge, faint laughter here and there. Agnes pulled out her phone, clicked on Neave's number.

'Yeah?'

'It's Agnes.'

'Oh.' There was a silence. 'He rang me. Ez did. Just now. Was about to call you.'

'What a relief. Is he back?'

'Nah.' Her voice was shaky. 'He said he was at his friend's. Him and Mosh were out late so he'd stayed there. He's lying, Sister.'

'He told me he'd go home.'

'Putting you off the scent. He's changed, y'know. Never used to be like this. Since the fire, and his dad and all that . . . and I've been saying to the feds, "What about a funeral, when can we lay him to rest?" "Soon", they say, "soon" . . . It's making me ill, Sister. I can't sleep, can't eat. And now, there's my boy. He's doing something. Chasing something. Up to no good.'

'Did he sound OK?'

'Yeah. Like, how am I going to know?'

'Did he say he'd come home?'

'I asked him. He got angry so I shut up.'

'I'll tell the police, OK?'

'Yeah. OK.'

'I'll do that now,' Agnes said. 'And you could contact his friend, maybe?'

'I tried. No answer so far.'

Agnes asked Neave to keep trying, keep in touch, to let her know if she heard anything, told her she'd keep the police posted. 'Like that's gonna help . . .'

* * *

She'd called Rob Coombes, told him all she knew, promised not to turn detective. At least, not yet, she'd added, and he'd laughed.

Now she sat on the wall outside the ruined church. Sunday afternoon. She'd knocked at Julius's door, the side door of the church, twice now, once at two, and again at half past. She'd tried the clergy house too, hearing the locks being drawn back until the door was opened by Yulia the house-keeper. *No, Madam*, she said, *not here, it's Sunday, madam, he'll be at the church.* The door shut firmly and politely in Agnes's face.

The air was warm and quiet, threatening summer rain.

Agnes could feel Winifred's touch against her knee, could see in her mind the Calais mothers, hear the squalling of their children.

We do as we are told.

Agnes stood up, brushed damp brick dust from her coat and set out once again for St Simeon's.

This time there was a light on. This time, as she pushed against the door, it opened. Julius was sitting at his desk, a mug of tea at his elbow, his face illumined by the soft glow of his computer screen, and he looked up and smiled and for a moment it was just like old times, as if nothing had changed, as if she wasn't just about to shatter the peace that settled between them with a granite-hard blow.

'Agnes,' he said. 'How grand.'

He went to the kettle, switched it on.

He sat down, and waited. Outside there was birdsong, a soft warm drizzle against the window panes.

'Oh, Julius.' She felt like crying. She looked at his quiet attention, and spoke again. 'I've had a long chat with Sister

111

Winifred,' she said. 'About Calais, the project there with the refugee mothers. They want me to go there quite soon.'

His face clouded. 'Ah,' he said.

'She is very tested by it. Evil, she said. The brutality of war, being passed on. Difficult to believe in God's love surpassing it all, that kind of thing, Winifred said.'

'Yes, I can see that.'

There was a silence, then he said, 'It's not very you, is it?'

She smiled. 'You could put it that way.'

'Mothers, babies. Tents . . .'

'Exactly.'

'I expect Athena has said the same sort of thing.'

'She has, yes.'

The kettle boiled. He went over and made her a mug of tea, added just the right amount of milk and handed it to her with a smile. 'What will you do?'

'I will do as I am told.'

'Ah.' He nodded. 'Yes.'

'But, in the meantime,' she began. 'I need to ask you—'

'What,' he said, oddly loud. 'What do you need to ask me?'

'Jay,' she began. 'You recognised his photo.'

His voice had a sharp edge. 'I've told you before. I can't help you.' He sat at his desk and turned back to his computer. The light from his screen threw harsh lines across his face.

She took a deep breath. 'This is what I know,' she said. 'Gerard St Fleur carried some terrible guilt that caused him to take his own life. The two sisters, Orla and Iris, are living with the pain. The guilt was about Father Anselm, now Andras, and Father Darius who moved away, and something to do with the youth group that used to meet in the old church before it became disused. And a boy, maybe called Albert, a troubled boy who sang in the choir and who went missing. And something triggered the return of all this now, centred around those objects that you had in your safe, that someone tried to steal, and were given to you by Orla. Who,' she added, trying to keep her voice level, 'told me that you helped her in an hour of need.'

Julius was gazing at his computer screen, unseeing. 'And why are you telling me this now, Agnes?'

'Because something bad is going to happen. Last night, Ezra, Jay's son, came to the hostel and we talked. He said he was going home but he never went home. He's lying to his mother. No one knows where he is.' Agnes looked at Julius's pinched face, knowing she was causing pain, knowing he was curious how much she knew. She ploughed on. 'Andras Swift is circling those objects you have as if he's been deprived of his birthright. But what I can't work out is why Orla had them, nor why she gave them to you. It's as if something dark from the past has been brought back to life, all these reappearances . . .' She stopped to catch her breath.

Julius's gaze was flinty. 'Andras Swift knows nothing about it. Nothing.'

'He's obsessed with it,' she said.

'I don't care.'

'Andras is insistent it was a betrayal, and that he should have them. And meanwhile, the police are about to arrest Aidan for murder and safe-breaking and God knows what else. And now there's Ezra, lying to me, lying to his mum . . .'

Julius spoke loudly. 'Well, then, perhaps you should look after Ezra rather than worrying about a time in my life that's over.'

'I would stop worrying, Julius, if it was over. But it clearly isn't. It's very much here and now, looming over you, and I worry that whoever set fire to one church to get the Judas chalice will set fire to another . . .' She looked at his strangely blank expression and bit back tears. 'I don't have long. I'm expected in Calais in a matter of days,' she said. 'And there's Andras Swift going on about grains of sand counting out the heart beats of a life—'

'I don't want to hear about that man,' he snapped.

'Julius, I want to help.'

'And what if you can't? What if the trace left by the past is indelible? All one's actions counted out. For good or for bad.'

'I refuse to believe it. Whatever this darkness is that circles the missing chalice, that explains why Jay died in the church that night. I refuse to believe that your agency is at the heart of it. You may be a victim of it, Julius, but you are not the cause of it.'

The sky outside had darkened, and distant thunder rumbled. He lifted his head. 'If only you were right, Agnes.'

'And Orla St Fleur?'

He breathed out, his shoulders bowed. 'Her brother died, as you said. Suicide. I tried to help. I failed.'

'Why, Julius? Why did he die?'

'What was it you said? About evil being passed on? About God's love not being sufficient?' His voice was tight, and Agnes wondered if he, too, was on the verge of tears.

'I have to know,' she said.

'No, no you don't.'

'But—'

'Obedience,' he said. 'Doing as you're told.'

'Leaving Ezra in danger?'

There was a flare of rage in his eyes. 'Hasn't it occurred to you that if all these events of the past have been carefully laid to rest, it was for very good reason? To spare certain people further pain? And that you poking around where you're not welcome, asking questions, keeping company with very distasteful persons, for no reason other than to delay the moment when you have to bow to the inevitable and do as you're told by your Order . . .' He was breathless, but continued, 'Hasn't it occurred to you that it might be you who's in the wrong and not everyone else? For once?'

It was as though he was someone she'd never met before, a raging, red-faced stranger. She stood up, gathered her coat as fast as she could, hurried to the door. On the threshold she turned back. 'When I am on that beach in Calais, contemplating a world on which the Lord has turned His back — I will still love you, Julius.'

She slammed the door hard.

Out in the street she walked fast, the traffic loud in her ears, her face wet with rain, with tears.

CHAPTER THIRTEEN

'How long were you crying for?' Athena placed a cup and saucer in front of Agnes.

'All afternoon.' Agnes settled back against Athena's cushions, still dabbing at her eyes.

'It looks like it, sweetie. Oh, you poor darling. At least you nuns don't wear mascara, that would be a disaster.' Athena poured a drop of milk into a cup of Darjeeling tea. 'You poor love. I can't believe it. He's definitely an alien. A Julius body-double. How dare he speak to you like that?'

Agnes took a sip of tea. The room was tidier than last time, more boxes cleared away, more books on the shelves. On the windowsill there was a vase of white roses, tinted pink with the ending of the day, the lifting of the rain.

'I was going to come here all jolly and laughing,' Agnes said. 'I had such a good coincidence to tell you, about Orla St Fleur appearing in the churchyard yesterday just as I was thinking of her.'

'Orla — ah, the one who was in love with Julius — that one?'

'Apparently not in love with him, she told me.'

'Who knows, eh? And she just appeared? Oh God,' Athena said, 'another ghost or alien or someone . . .' She stirred her tea in its dainty cup. 'I bet not a coincidence,' she said. 'I bet she's been wanting to talk to you and she just chose her moment.'

'That's more likely.' Agnes felt the despair of Julius's rage begin to lift. 'That's what I thought.'

'So,' Athena said. 'The wealthy Catholic bird. What does she look like? Old? Young? Looks after herself?'

'Ageless,' Agnes said, 'but she must be in her late sixties at least.'

'And did you like her?'

Agnes sipped her tea. 'Yes,' she said. 'Yes, I did. She's very guarded, but if your brother had died the way he did, I imagine it would make you a bit ringfenced like that.'

'And don't tell me, there was loads she wasn't saying.'

Agnes looked up. 'Yes. That's true.'

'Same for all of them. Everyone involved with this mystery that you're chasing. Weird art dealers and poor neglected kids, and old-money Catholics who knew Julius a long time ago, and whose very mention causes him to change personality . . .' Athena pushed her cup away from her. 'I've said it before, but might life not be simpler if you just stepped away?'

Agnes shifted on the deep, soft sofa. 'Athena, I can't.'

'But—'

'There's something very wrong about all this. Jay was connected to the death of another young man, Reece, a few years ago. Then he was lured to that church, a building he was known to avoid, and killed after a struggle, it seems, a blow to the head. Then the safe was raided and the church was set on fire.'

'And what is it to you?'

'Now Ezra has gone missing. Lying to his mum about where he is.'

'The kid — the lovely young man?'

Agnes nodded.

'Ah. I can see why you can't let go.'

'And more than that — Julius has never been like this before. It's as if he needs rescuing from himself, and up till

117

now—' Agnes felt tears welling again, 'up till now he's always been the one to rescue me from myself.'

'And now it's your turn?'

Agnes managed a smile.

Outside the sun was low in the sky, rosy in the urban haze.

'Oh, for God's sake — it's far too late for tea.' Athena jumped to her feet. From the kitchen Agnes heard the clink of glasses, the clunk of a fridge door, the chink of ice cubes.

'There—' Athena came back with two wide-brimmed glasses on thick crystal stems. Agnes could see ice, syrupy gold liquid, slices of lime.

'I read about this in a magazine. Don't worry, not alcoholic. But cocktails all the same.' She passed Agnes a glass. 'We just have to pretend to get tipsy.'

Agnes laughed.

Athena took a sip, frowned at the glass. 'Well, if they weren't in love, and let's assume that's true — Julius and your posh old bird have some dark secret in common. It's the only explanation.'

Agnes sipped her drink. 'Are you sure this isn't alcoholic?'

'Angostura bitters — is that alcohol?'

'I'm not sure.'

'Me neither. But nice.'

'It's all about the chalice,' Agnes said. 'Before the church safe was raided, she'd gone in and removed those things, as if she still owned them. Which she probably does. And then she gave the lot to Julius, and that's what changed him. Everything except for the chalice, which is missing, and which everyone seems to be after. It's like something triggered all this activity. Orla appears, gives stuff to Julius, who she claims not to have seen for ages until now. Dr. Swift starts lurking. It's like there was a rumour or something that brought them all back suddenly. Andras Swift in particular.'

'The creepy art dealer?'

Agnes nodded.

'I bet he's a Virgo,' Athena said. 'Or maybe Capricorn.'

'How on earth . . . ?'

'Next time, ask him.'

'I couldn't possibly.'

'Never fails. A nice person will laugh, and a horrible one will be wrong-footed, and then you can lead them where you want. And in this case, you can find out why he wants this chalice. Although, I can't help thinking that the old Catholic bird must know where it is.'

'She says it's lost. But Andras Swift told me she showed it to him only a few years ago.'

'Well, one of them is lying.'

'Orla told me to go to talk to her sister, Iris. She lives in Suffolk.'

'Suffolk?'

'It's the old family home. Iris still lives there. She said Iris could tell me more.'

'Oh God. And don't tell me, that's where you'll go next? Couldn't you just call her?'

Agnes crunched on an ice cube. 'I'd have to drive. I'd have to ask the Order to borrow the car. And Sister Christiane will almost certainly say no. I'm supposed to be concentrating on getting ready to go to Calais.'

'Hmmm.' Athena kicked off her mules, tucked her legs under her.

'What?'

'I'm just thinking about the big family house. I mean, it's nicer than a rainy tent on the French coast, isn't it? And you wouldn't be away long. I bet there's staff. And a lovely bedroom with a huge en-suite bathroom, you know, lots of marble . . . and a view over the estate, all those rural fields. And maybe horses, you can ride again after all these years . . . Where is Suffolk anyway?'

'Kind of east. Up the M11 and then turning off.'

'Hmm. Maybe it'll be one of those large old houses, with a long, long drive, even rhododendrons, you know, sweetie, like that book — you can walk up the drive with all those gorgeous purple blooms, and then inside there's a spooky housekeeper and a melancholic husband, and something awful happens with an evening gown and you appearing at the top of the stairs, I'm sure you could manage that too . . .'

They laughed, clinked glasses, laughed again.

'No one is telling me the truth.' Agnes sighed. 'The only true thing Orla said to me was that she doesn't believe in Heaven. Or God. She said, to be here is enough. She said, "I've had a ball."'

Athena glanced up at Agnes. 'I think two things about that. One is that I can't help but agree with her. And the other—'

'What?'

'It sounds like she thinks it's over.'

'What do you mean?'

'In the past tense like that. As if she's dying.'

Agnes met her gaze. 'Are you sure?'

'Don't you think . . . ?'

A flicker of memory. The thin hands, the sharp glances, brief smiles. 'She said, "running out of time,"' Agnes said. 'About the sand timer. But that doesn't mean . . .'

'Don't you see? If it was me, I would say, "I'm having a ball. And I don't intend to stop any time soon." Whereas this bird said, "I've had a ball." It's very different.'

Agnes drew a breath, exhaled. 'I see what you mean.' She sipped her drink. 'And are you?'

'Am I what?'

'Having a ball?'

'Oh. Um — suppose so. This money from Greece is a burden, to be honest. Nic is making endless plans, all this talk of investing in property and doing up the loft apartment and ditching our old car. I don't want plans, I just want to have fun.' She drained her glass. 'What I want is for Nic to take me away on a cruise, and we can spend all the money on champagne, and some decent clothes to match. Then I can say, "I'm having a ball." In fact, now I come to think of it, that's exactly what I'm going to do.' She picked up her empty glass. 'Well, whatever Angostura bitters is, it does the trick.' She looked at Agnes. 'Nah, she's definitely on the way out. It explains it all, her coming back to see Julius and giving him those things. Anyway, that's all sorted. You take the Audi to Suffolk.'

'Really?'

'Yes. Of course. It'll get Nic off my back, and anyway there's no point you trying to steal the old Vauxhall from your Mother Superior.'

'That's true.'

'In fact, it's the ideal solution. You can even keep it on long-term loan. And if your Order are still insisting on exiling you to live in a tent with a load of inspirational nuns, you can just hole up in this gorgeous manor house instead. I mean, I'm not saying I approve of all this investigating, but this way you can leave poor Julius alone, or his body double anyway, and you can put this mystery to rest. If you must.' She raised her empty glass. 'Doc Mitch says sometimes we collide with stuff that seems to be bad for us but turns out to be the lesson we need to learn. And I thought about how you always do it, and you always emerge in one piece. I just worry that one day you won't.' She uncurled herself from the sofa. 'And now let's have another of these, seeing as they're just fruit juice, really.'

* * *

Agnes walked back towards the hostel in the damp twilight, in the puddled streetlamp glow.

Orla knows she is dying, she thought. *Julius will know. It explains . . .*

What exactly?

Nothing at all.

* * *

The hostel was quiet. Agnes read Eddie's handover notes, warmed up the pasta from supper, the tomato chilli sauce

— Aysha's cooking, she thought, always something special about it . . .

Eddie put his head around the kitchen door. 'Someone at the front door for you, Sister.'

'Again?'

'I mean,' he said, following her out to the hall, heading up the stairs, 'the rest of us don't use this address for social stuff, but then maybe it's easier for you than your nunnery.'

Bridget was standing at the door. She walked past Agnes into the lounge.

'I wasn't going to come back,' she said, perching stiffly on one of the chairs. 'But Aidan is hiding at my house now, terrified he's going to be charged with killing Jay Sorrell. And he didn't do it. Any more than Jay killed Reece but that's another story.'

Agnes brushed crumbs from the arms of her chair as she sat down. She looked at Bridget, who was brisk and pinched.

'You won't tell, will you?' Bridget said. 'I'm trusting you.'

'I won't tell,' Agnes said.

'I knew you wouldn't.' Bridget softened slightly, undid the belt of her coat, settled in her chair. 'One of the few advantages.'

'Another one in hiding,' Agnes said. 'Ezra, Neave's boy — he's lying to his mum, saying he's with a friend, when she's sure he isn't.'

'It's been a lot for him, all this,' Bridget said. 'I reckon, being told you've got two dads and now both of them are dead . . . it's a lot for a kid to deal with it.'

'The thing is—' Agnes began. Bridget was all quiet attention now, and Agnes went on, 'It was me. I was the last one to see him. He promised me he'd go home. And now no one knows where he is. He said he was okay, but — he isn't.'

'Doesn't mean you're to blame,' Bridget said. 'A limit to what you people can do, isn't there?'

Agnes rearranged a mat on the side table by her chair. 'I'm thinking of going to Suffolk,' she said.

'To Keld House?'

'Yes.'

'Ah.' Bridget eyed her. 'You'd better give Iris a ring first.' She placed her bag heavily on the table. It was worn and brown like her raincoat.

'I don't want to be intrusive.'

Bridget considered this. After a moment, she said, 'You know what you're searching for, I suppose.'

'I don't. That's the problem.'

'She's different from her sister,' Bridget said. 'Nip is.'

'Nip?'

'Iris. It's an old name, I've always called her that.'

'Why?'

'Why?' Bridget echoed, amused. 'No idea. Lost in the past. You must have names from people around you when you were a kid?'

Agnes hesitated. 'No, not really.'

'Oh well. Perhaps that's what's made you what you are. The stony path to sainthood, eh?'

'I'm a nun, that's all.'

'Mmmm.'

'So, Iris,' Agnes prompted. 'Different from Orla in that—'

'Iris tolerates me. Her sister doesn't.'

'Orla spoke kindly of you. She said their mother preferred you to her own children.'

Her face thawed, a warmth in her eyes. She smiled. 'That's certainly true.'

'She said you played together as children.'

'I liked it there. I felt at home. Our father . . . well, he had disappeared again, and my own mother . . .' She looked up. 'She did her best. But there . . . there were games, all that space, trees to climb, ponies — mind you, I was that scared of them I was, still am to be honest, old Duchess out in the field still won't come near me . . . There was cake and cordial, raspberry, can you imagine? I mean now you can buy it at the corner shop but in them days . . .' She fell silent, sipping at her tea.

123

'I saw Reece's mother,' Agnes said.

'Connie. How is she?'

'Angry.'

She nodded. 'Well, you would be. That's why I said I'd help with Aidan, at least.'

'He can't stay in hiding for ever.'

'He'll stay with me as long as he needs to. I won't have another injustice.'

'Another?'

Bridget took a handkerchief from her pocket, a neat folded square. She shook it out and laid it across her lap. 'I might as well tell you.' She took a deep, reluctant breath. 'I was there. When Reece died. Outside his own house it was, Connie and her daughter, they was away, he was alone in the house, Jay was paying a call the way those boys do. Someone came knocking at my door, a wee lad from the corner flats, shouting for help. I ran.' She smoothed the white linen on her lap. 'He was calling for his mum, Reece was. I'll never forget the sound. Blood gurgling up in his throat, and him wanting his mum, calling out for her.' She looked up. 'Do you think we all do that in our dying moments? I can't imagine I'd bother when it came to it.'

Agnes smiled. 'No,' she agreed. 'Me neither.'

'But the thing was, Jason Sorrell was at his side, begging him to stay, begging him not to leave him, his hand over the wound, trying to slow the bleeding, calling him "brother" . . . And I thought, no one does that if they're guilty. They run, that's what they do. Or they pretend, but that boy was incapable of lying.' She smiled, softly. 'I remember when Ezra was little, when Jay was still in his life, and Ezra asked him why did God make the world and Jay just took him in his arms and said, "I don't know, son. No one knows."' She laughed. 'He couldn't lie, could he?'

Agnes studied her. 'Why did they come to you, the wee lad on the corner? I mean, when there was trouble?'

'Me?' She sighed. 'I'm the one they come to. I think maybe not having my own children . . . it means if there's a spat I don't take sides.'

'The peacemaker?'

She fiddled a corner of the handkerchief. 'I don't see it that way. I'm just Bridget O'Leary. People think I'll rescue them, and so then I'm obliged, aren't I? Sheltering other people's trouble, other people's children. Like little Arthur, I was thinking about him the other day, the one who vanished.'

'Arthur?'

'Arthur Cowell. He was a kid from the children's home, kept absconding. He ended up with me for a bit. Older than the usual kids, but needing a home. A lovely boy, but he had no understanding of family life, he'd never known it himself . . .' She smiled. 'We had fish in a tank, people did in those days before we found out that they could think and so it was cruel after all. He'd stare at them, tracing the little swimming journeys they made with his finger on the glass.' She picked up her handkerchief and dusted the end of her nose.

'Connie Bennett mentioned him, I think.' Agnes looked across at her. 'She said that soon after he vanished, that was when Gerard died.'

There was a brief clouding of Bridget's expression. She nodded. 'They were close, Arthur and Gerard. Not what you'd think, none of that wrongness, a big age gap between them. But they were like kindred spirits.' She looked up. 'Arthur didn't have boundaries, didn't know how to ask for love. He needed protecting. I think that's what Gerard did for him. Then Arthur disappeared. But—' her voice was louder now — 'that's not why Gerard died. No one knows why he died. I think life was always too much for him and one day he'd had enough.'

She fiddled with the silver bracelet on her wrist. Upstairs there was shouting, laughter, the thump of trainers on the staircase.

She spoke again. 'I used to ask Orla about Gerard and why he died, across the way there, it was, in the old church-yard. I was fond of him. There's a plaque to him, in the crypt, no one goes in there now . . .' She shifted on her chair. 'But Orla would change the subject and Iris just cries if you ask her, so I gave up. No point upsetting her after all this time. I just thank God their mother wasn't there to see it.'

'And your father, Ralph?'

Bridget sighed. 'He'd left by then. A new love. But he was old, the new wife had become his nurse, not that that was her plan, serves her right, if you ask me.'

'Bridget — what went wrong? What happened with that priest, the one with the Greek name who wasn't Greek? And with Gerard, and with the youth group, that no one will tell me about, not even Father Julius . . .' Agnes's voice tightened, and she wondered why it always made her want to cry, the thought of Julius turning away from her.

Bridget looked up. 'If people won't talk to you about it, it's because they don't know. Or, because they don't want to know.'

'And you?'

Bridget shook her head. 'If I could save Aidan . . . if I could protect Ezra, Francie's little lad . . .' Another turn of the bracelet on her wrist.

They sat in brief silence.

'A cross,' Agnes said.

'What?'

'On your bracelet.' She hadn't meant to speak out loud.

Bridget looked at her wrist, as if surprised. 'Suppose so,' she said. 'It's old.' She stared down at the table, the stained rings of tea.

'Andras Swift is after the chalice,' Agnes said.

Bridget gave a scornful sniff. 'Andras Swift? I'm not surprised. Always claimed he was a "connoisseur". He's been after that stuff for years. He visited Iris soon after Gerard died, we'd only just had the funeral, back at the old house. He told her that the chalice is worth over a million quid, and that none of us know how to look after it. He accused us of stuffing it away in a box in the attic, leaving it to tarnish. That was the word he used. Tarnish. Iris got very angry, she told him to go up to the attic and look for it himself if he was that concerned, and the funny thing is, he did. We were all sitting in the upstairs parlour, a grieving family, neighbours were visiting to pay their respects, people down in the kitchen making endless cups of tea — and there was Andras up in the attic, moving stuff; we could hear him, scraping crates across the joists, pulling the string off cardboard boxes . . .' She gave a thin smile. 'At length he reappeared, all dusty, cobwebs in his hair. Empty-handed. He exchanged a few words with Iris and off he went. But he never gave up. He's obsessed with it. But there's more to it than that, something about that other priest, the Greek one, but if you mention it to him he just shuts down, then gets really cross.'

'Connie Bennett said he got stuck in the church loft looking for it too.'

She smiled. 'I'm not surprised. Mind you, he has a point. He probably does know its value, probably the only person who does. It's part of his job, isn't it, going around galleries, authenticating. That's what he said to me once, "Bridget, it's all about authenticating . . ."' She huffed. 'Silly man.'

'It's supposed to give absolution,' Agnes said.

Bridget gave a shrug. 'It'll take more than a few sips of plonk from an old cup to give him time off from Purgatory.'

'You think he's that bad?'

'I don't like him,' she said. 'But not Hell, at least. Just the waiting room for Heaven.'

'What I don't get,' Agnes said, 'is that Gerard died where he did — right at the heart of that neighbourhood—'

'No.' Bridget's voice was loud. 'You don't understand. It wasn't the neighbourhood. Not the streets, the blocks of flats, the pub on the corner, not even that old churchyard . . . He died there because of the fields beneath. It was his family's land — that family's land — not mine, I won't ever say mine, because I never felt I belonged and I'm happy that way . . .' Another deep, drawn breath. 'Sometimes I think that was why he strayed, my father, because in some way he never belonged neither, not that I'm making excuses, he behaved badly . . . Where was I? Oh, yes. Gerard.' She traced a circle on the table in front of her, her fingernail nicotine-brown like the grain of the old wood. 'He was a good man, Gerard. Sensitive. An artist, you know. Depressive, I suppose you'd say these days.' She raised her eyes to Agnes. 'And when he died, he placed himself at the heart of things. So that they couldn't forget.'

'Who?' Agnes said. 'So that who couldn't forget?'

Bridget turned her head, as if listening out for something. 'What?' she said. 'Oh. People. People who'd harmed him. His family. Your church.'

'My church?'

'You people, I mean. Not you personally. Nor that other one, the nice Irish one, not him. But the others . . .' Another twitch of her head, and now there was a sound, a slam of a door from the kitchen, loud conversation, the cry of a baby.

Bridget stood up, gathered up her handbag. 'Go to Keld. Why not? It'll be company for Iris, she'll like you, I know she will. You've got her number? Give her a ring first. Tomorrow? You've got a car? I didn't think they let you drive, those women.'

Agnes showed her out, murmuring about a friend lending her a car for a day or so, thanking her for her visit, promising not to breathe a word about Aidan.

Now she cleared up the kitchen, washed up the saucepan.

She picked up her phone to Rob Coombes, she left a voicemail — 'Any news of Ezra, tell me at once, please.'

She thought about Gerard's death and tarnished silver. She thought about marble bathrooms and wide staircases, and views over the countryside. She found herself hoping that Duchess would still be out in the field.

CHAPTER FOURTEEN

A huge old house with a long, long drive. But the rhododendrons had finished flowering, their leaves brown-edged, their overgrown stems drooping with neglect.

At the end of the drive Agnes could see the house. It was wide and white, with extended rows of elegant windows. But as she approached, she could see the peeling paint, the ivy taking hold around the door.

Spooky housekeepers, Agnes wondered. *Melancholic husbands.*

The Audi slowed to a halt by the rusted gate. The engine purred softly under her foot, despite the hour or two spent weaving in and out of lorries in the diesel haze of the London sprawl, then the gradual widening of the motorway, the freedom and speed as the tower blocks and warehouses gave way to farms and fields, and finally the winding roads with timbered houses and thatched villages nestling under the clear bright sky.

She parked next to a battered Volvo, switched off the engine, and got out of the car.

The front door had a wooden painted porch, some of which was missing. The bell was a large black button in a round white base. A cardboard sign read: *Press Hard. May Not Work.*

Images began to fade. Lovely huge bedrooms, marble en-suite bathrooms.

Agnes pressed the bell, twice. She could hear footsteps, the heavy click of a lock. The door opened.

'Hello,' said Iris St Fleur. 'How nice of you to come.'

* * *

Later, Agnes would try and describe it all to Athena, the huge chilly rooms with cobwebbed ceilings, the Victorian paintings hanging on walls of cracked plaster, the bedroom with its worn, once-beautiful rug spread thinly over uneven floorboards, the bathroom a dark tiptoe along a damp corridor, the casserole from the freezer, surprisingly good, a very decent Beaujolais too . . .

But now there was just this. This thin, graceful woman standing at the door, like a softer version of Orla, taller but somehow less definite, with longer hair tied back, a soft baggy jumper over jeans, muddy boots, and a warm smile.

She led the way into the hall.

A dark staircase curved away towards a landing. An arched window shed a speckled light across the tiled floor.

The kitchen was taupe, smart and bright.

'It's the only room we ever did up,' Iris said, gesturing her to a sleek pale wooden chair. 'Let me make you a coffee. How was your journey? It can be hell on the M11, although I see you have a very nice car, rather surprising I thought for a nun but I know it's all changed since my boarding school days . . .' She placed two mugs on the rose granite worktop.

Outside there was birdsong, a distant tractor.

Iris turned to her. 'So,' she said. 'Welcome to Keld House.'

Agnes looked up at her. 'Thank you.'

They sat over coffee, then bread and cheese. 'It's my habitual lunch, I'm afraid, rather set in my ways . . .'

Iris talked about the history of the house. 'Of course, I've never really lived anywhere else. I expect Orla managed to convey what a stick-in-the-mud I am. You know what sisters are like . . . An only child? I imagine that's a huge relief, isn't it, although no doubt the nuns make up for any lack of family dysfunction . . . and as for dear Bridget, what did she say? Oh Duchess, such a sweet old thing. Bridget's still scared of her and she wouldn't hurt a fly . . . You used to ride? How lovely, we'll go and say hello to her after this. I keep her as a pet these days, she's nearly fourteen, spoilt to bits, she doesn't get exercised enough. There's a lovely girl in the village who adores her, comes up after school as much as she can, but if you wanted a canter across the fields I'm sure she'd be happy and I'd be delighted. We can find you a hat . . .'

Iris cut a small piece of Stilton. 'So, it was Orla who suggested you come here? That's what you said on the phone, I think?'

'Yes,' Agnes said.

'How is she? I worry about her in London. She has a nice big house out near Harrow, but she kept the London flat too, always was drawn to the place, much more of a culture vulture than I ever was . . .' She laughed. 'And at least she doesn't have to look after all this.' She gestured around her. 'Oh, look, have an apple, we'll keep one to one side for dear old Duchess.' Iris began to peel one. 'So — why did you really want to talk to me?'

A shaft of sunlight fell across the wooden cheeseboard, the terracotta fruit bowl, a small jug of wildflowers, blue and yellow . . .

Agnes looked up.

Iris spoke again. 'It's about Gerard, isn't it?'

The grinding of the tractor seemed to get nearer.

'He . . .' Agnes began. 'I don't wish to pry, but . . .'

'A life cut short.' Iris's voice was loud. 'But why come here now?'

'Something has happened,' Agnes said. 'A man was killed, his son has gone missing, I'm worried he's in danger of some kind . . .'

'Francie's grandson. Bridget told me.'

'Did you know Francie?'

'No,' Iris said. 'But Orla would often talk of her. Even after her disappearance.' She looked up and there were tears in her eyes. 'My view is that Francie betrayed us.'

'Betrayed?'

'Oh, I know. No one speaks ill of her. I'm alone in my views, I fear. But when Gerard was . . . What you have to know is, his death didn't come from nowhere. There were many cries for help. Many. But no help came, and so it ended as it did.'

The tractor noise stopped suddenly, and the silence hummed in the space around them.

'He was a real artist. He was just getting established. He had exhibitions and things. Venice, even. But it was hard won, his talent. A lot of him went on to the canvas. His heart and soul . . .' She sighed. 'He chose his friends unwisely, in my view. People wanted to exploit his talent. And it was more than that. His faith, he was deeply, deeply Catholic in a way that probably you can understand better than me. But it meant he trusted people, men who wore the carapace of faith but lacked the heart of it.' She looked up. 'I'm not sure if that makes sense . . .'

'It makes a great deal of sense,' Agnes said.

'There was a boy.' Her face shadowed. 'Arthur. Gerard looked after him like a son. He disappeared. He was a difficult young man, but Gerard gave him work to do in the studio, mixing paints, things like that. He sat for him too. But there were rumours, and then when he disappeared, the rumours got worse.' She sniffed, reached for a piece of kitchen roll. 'That wasn't the reason he died, but it kind of added to the sense of guilt that he'd had since birth, I think. Born with it. Your people's idea of original sin . . .' She blew her nose. 'He had made various attempts on his own life, over the years. And then, one day, he succeeded.'

'How awful.' Agnes felt her words hanging thinly in the empty silence.

Iris looked across at her. 'His work, that's all that's left of him. Stacks of it. Nowhere else for it to go. They're out in the garage. I had it totally refitted, it's the only dry space, why else do you think my car is out on the drive the whole time?' She dabbed fiercely at her eyes. 'Come on, let's go and say hello to Duchess.'

CHAPTER FIFTEEN

After dinner, Iris topped up their glasses with what was left of the wine and led the way along the corridor.

'We'll go to the sitting room,' she said, 'it's cosier.' She sat on a dark red sofa and reached along the low coffee table for a bowl of fruit, a plain cream ceramic dish with a patina of age.

Agnes took a tangerine.

They talked some more, about the lovely afternoon, the sweet nature of horses; about childhood, Provence and vocations and faith.

'Each to his own,' Iris said, 'I mean, I don't call myself church-going but at my funeral I want the whole lot, hymns, the Lord's Prayer, all of it . . .'

And that was when Agnes said, peeling her tangerine, 'Orla seems very keen not to believe.'

'Orla?' Iris placed a curl of peel next to the bowl.

'Yes,' Agnes said. 'She said, it was enough, to be here on this earth. She didn't need to call anything God.'

'Ah.' Iris nodded.

'It's not a position I would argue with,' Agnes added, and Iris softened slightly.

'The thing is,' Iris said, 'she's not very well. She's —
been given a few months. Started in her stomach, but it's
spread . . . She's having to make her peace with things.'

Athena's words. *People don't talk like that unless they're not
long for this world.*

Agnes looked at the mantelpiece, with its dusty paperweight and its old tobacco pipes.

'It explains why—' Iris hesitated. 'It explains her reappearance in your part of London, I think. There is work she
has to do.'

'She gave those things to Father Julius,' Agnes said.

'Yes, exactly.'

Iris picked a grape out of the fruit bowl and looked at
it between her fingers. 'We are broken, you see,' she said.
'Broken by the death of our brother. It is as if he is still there,
swinging from that tree in that churchyard.' She replaced the
grape in the bowl. 'The way we were raised . . .' She looked
up. 'All this. Space and land, ponies and piano lessons . . . but
no real family life. My friend Phyllis, she's a therapist, lives
in Hampstead. You get her on the subject . . .'

The ash settled in the fireplace. Outside there was the
hoot of an owl.

'Orla fell in love, to escape,' Iris went on. 'He was
French, into racing cars. I think she imagined a whole new
life, a different one. She was only nineteen. But he was someone who thought love just happened to you, as if he had no
agency over it, and after a while a different woman "happened" to him, an older, married woman, and he disappeared
to Geneva, or Bologna or somewhere . . .' She pulled her
cardigan around her shoulders. 'As the oldest, I think I felt it
wasn't worth the risk.'

'And Gerard?' Agnes asked, into the silence.

Iris fiddled the grapes against the edge of the bowl.
'Gerard. The middle child.' She looked up. 'There was a very
thin membrane between Gerard and the rest of the world.
That's how Phyllis described it, and she was right. He hated

the country. He'd get upset for the animals. He'd hear the cows — there's a sound they make when the calves are taken from them, too early in my view, much too early . . . it's a kind of bellow — pain, rage, I don't know . . . It would upset Gerard terribly. Once when he was about sixteen he was found out in the fields at dawn with our father's shot-gun, shouting about how he was going to save the cows. "Let them keep their babies," he was shouting, all set to threaten the farmer . . .' She was pink-faced, her voice strong in the shadows of the room. 'Shots were fired, but he was aiming at the tyres of the trailer, so that they couldn't drive the calves away. And it worked, that day anyway. But after that . . . that was when they decided to send him to school in London. Thought he'd be happier there.' She stopped, breathing hard.

'And was he?'

Iris sighed. 'The thin membrane — it was about all of creation. He would say, about the animals, not just the calves, the sheep out on the fields beyond the farm, again, when the lambs were taken away . . . Don't you feel it, he'd say. "Where there is suffering, we all feel it. It resonates within us all." It was worse when anyone pointed out humans suf-fered too. He'd start talking about people being tortured in prisons in wherever they were discussing on the news, Iran, perhaps, how that suffering vibrates, around the world, how we all carry that pain. And I would say, what about kindness, doesn't that balance it out? And he would tell me that the problem is that one is much heavier than the other.'

A rattle of wind caught the chimney, showering ash into the grate.

'So — in London . . .'

'It was just as bad. He came back here after a while, tried to live quietly. But, in the end, he was defeated by it.'

'Yes,' Agnes said. After a moment, she said, 'And Bridget?'

'Oh, Bridget survives. Our mother was very fond of her. I think because she didn't remind our mother of herself. Also, Phyllis said it was a way of getting back at our father, to be kind to the child he never wanted, and I think that was true too. Bridget's mother, Anne, stayed in touch, they were quite close, particularly after our father had moved on to another wife — poor old Hilary, she thought she was getting an international lifestyle and she ended up nursing him in a dreary semi-detached house in Eastbourne.'

There was a rumble from the old radiators, and Agnes realised that somewhere in the house a boiler had creaked into life.

Iris took another grape and ate it. 'And you? What makes someone become a nun?'

Agnes wondered what to say. After a moment she answered, 'I don't know.'

Iris gave a small nod.

Agnes went on, 'There are as many paths as there are monastics,' she said. 'Sometimes God just calls, perhaps.'

'And did he call you?'

'It was more that he shouted very loudly for some years while I covered my ears.'

Iris smiled. 'But you listened in the end?'

Agnes reached for a grape, held it in her hand. 'It's a leap into the dark. It's not that I have any certainties at all. I'm not sure any of us really do. But — at some point it seemed clear to me that it was the only path to take. And to turn away then, that would have been an act of wilful self-destruction. Does that make any sense?'

'Oh yes,' Iris smiled. 'I was raised a Catholic too.'

Agnes laughed.

'But,' Iris went on, 'your family were religious?'

'My family was very much like yours.' She felt her throat tighten. 'My mother made it clear that marriage and a child was not her choice,' she said.

Iris nodded. 'And the house in Provence? A burden too?'

'It was. But as a nun I had to give it away.'

'That must be a relief. All this . . .' She gestured with a sweep of her fingers which took in not only the room, the grit on the grate, the radiators which clicked and shifted with unaccustomed warmth, but the darkness beyond, the garden,

the beech trees, the fields still imprinted with the generations. 'My father's surname, St Fleur, it was a conceit,' she
said. 'A device, invented in the eighteenth century. It was my
mother who carried the ancient bloodline, she was Norman,
she could trace herself back to William the Conqueror, or
so her mother said, in a tone that would always imply my
mother had married beneath her, a Johnny-come-lately . .
. And this land, and that large chunk of what is now South
London, that was settled on my mother's side about a thousand years ago. My grandmother would behave as it had all
been recently stolen, as if somehow we should all still be
ordering the peasants to bring in the harvests.' She pushed
up her sleeves. 'It was another thing that upset Gerard. He
claimed he'd found manacles from keeping people enslaved,
but when he showed me, it was just the old brass rings in the
barns for the over-wintering cows, not manacles at all. But
when I said this to him, he got very angry. "It's the same,"
he'd said, "it's all suffering, the wealth of our family, where
do you think it came from?"' She looked up. 'Perhaps he was
right. Certainly, on our father's side, there was trade, right
across Europe, textiles . . .' She looked towards the windows,
the silence of the night outside.

'When Gerard died—' Agnes began.

Iris got to her feet. 'Come with me.'

* * *

Iris strode through the darkness on the slippery damp path-
way, its every uneven dip and crack familiar. Agnes picked
her way behind her.

Iris pointed towards a copse of trees in the distance,
haloed in the moonlight. 'That's where he is, dear Gerard,
resting in peace by the old apple tree there. Took a while for
the Old Bill to allow us a funeral.'

She led the way past outbuildings, a half-restored barn,
out to the front drive. The garage was sleek and grey, sprung
into sharp relief in the beam of the security light. A pad

beeped at them as Iris typed in the security code, and the metal shutter lifted with electronic grace.

The first thing Agnes saw, as the interior was flooded with light, was a crucifixion. A huge red canvas, a black cross slashed across it, a drooping, cream-white corpse.

'They sold for hundreds, very occasionally thousands,' Iris said. 'And then he died, and was forgotten. There are others, look.'

On one wall, another work, smaller, but with the same angry red, the slash of black. On this one, the cross was empty. At its foot, a woman, a gentle curve of blue paint, a resting, female face. The grey-white male body was draped across her knees, held in her embrace.

'He'd say it was about hope.' Iris's voice came from behind her. 'That death isn't the end.' There was a catch in her voice. 'But what he didn't know was that a death like his breaks something. It makes things irretrievable . . . I'm sorry, I always do this . . .'

Her face was wet with tears. Agnes touched her arm. 'He was your brother,' she said.

'And the stupid thing is he didn't believe any of it. All our childhood we were told that Christ died for us. Finally he started to question it. He was only fifteen, sixteen, but he used to shout at the priest, "What good did it do?" Raging at the poor man who wasn't used to being challenged.' A small smile through her tears.

'But these were the images he painted?'

Iris touched the edge of the canvas. 'I think it was rebellion,' she said. 'Also . . .' she hesitated. 'He understood suffering. I don't know how.'

'You loved him.'

'I loved him very much. He was a good person. Not many people are.' She dusted off an old high stool with her fingertips, leaned against it. 'Gerard was someone that everyone loved. Everyone. But there was something about him that couldn't commit. Men, women . . . He drove people mad. He didn't mean to. His art was what he loved most of all. It was like a strange kind of self-obsession, and yet always about something beyond himself.'

There were paintings leaning against the wall. Agnes bent to look at one. She pulled out a small, framed canvas. It showed two men, standing by a window through which was a sunlit vista of trees. The room had yellow walls, the men were in blue jeans, facing each other. One was handing something to the other, as they locked eyes. It was a chalice, painted in silvery detail against the broad bright brushstrokes.

'The Judas chalice,' Agnes said.

'You know about that?'

'Only that it belonged to your family and is now missing. And that various people seem to believe they have a claim to it.'

Iris took the painting from Agnes and studied it. 'A self-portrait,' she said. 'Both the images are him, see?'

Agnes studied the two faces, like identical twins.

Iris placed it carefully back with the others. 'There's something I want you to see, a photograph.' She made her way through the various artworks until she found a glass-framed, black-and-white square. 'It was taken in one of Gerard's last shows at this gallery in Chelsea who always supported him, run by an American woman. I can never remember the name . . . I always want to say Finkelstein but it wasn't that . . .'

In the photo, three men stood in front of a wall draped with a long, wide cloth depicting a cross, another slash of black against grey.

'That's Gerard.' Iris pointed to the middle of the three. Dark-haired, even-featured, intense dark gaze, a floppy fringe.

'And that's—'

'Andras Swift,' Iris said. 'He'd just reverted to that name, having given up the priesthood.'

'He looks no older now.'

'You've seen him? I'm not surprised, he has a sixth sense for our things being back on the market.'

'And is that Darius?' Agnes pointed at the other man. He was short and pinched, with narrow features and a tight, peering smile as he gazed outwards at the camera from under the brim of a straw hat.

'Yes, that's Darius. He was a priest, too, he remained a priest until he retired.'

'They knew Father Julius,' Agnes said.

'Yes. Through Orla, I think.' Iris placed the photograph carefully back with the other frames, leaning against the wall. 'He's a friend of yours, Julius?'

'Yes. At least . . .' Agnes wanted to tell her, he's changed, he's angry, something's happened, 'it's all about this—' as if buried in these anguished splashes of paint there might be a clue. But Iris was looking at her with concern, and instead Agnes said, 'He's a very good friend,' and turned to the art-work in the photograph. 'Can you tell me about that piece?'

'Gerard called it *The Keld Shroud*. He worked on it for a long time. He got local weavers to make the linen for him, and then he painted it. He set up the old barn across the way there as his studio, with a great big table for all his paint. It took years. He said it was his best work — another pieta, of course, but there are other scenes too, like a story told in pictures.'

'Where is it now, in a gallery?'

'No one knows. Like the chalice, it has disappeared.'

Iris turned to go, and Agnes followed her outside. They stood in the muted dampness of the night, while the metal shutter clattered to the ground.

'It is all a burden,' Iris said. 'I have no idea what to do with any of it. The kind American woman, she's dead now. Andras pretends to be helpful, but he only knows about medieval church hardware, not modern painting, and any-way what he really knows about is money, not art. Darius came to visit not long ago, but I sent him away.'

'Darius? I thought he was abroad. What did he want?'

'No idea. He was going on about trying to sell the Judas chalice, he was very angry. He said Gerard had entrusted it to him. It was all nonsense and I told him so and off he went, thank goodness. Gerard never liked him either.'

She glanced back at the garage door. 'Arthur helped him with the shroud. The boy.'

'From London?'

'Yes. He came here and stayed. I wasn't around much, as we had an elderly cousin in Aldeburgh who needed looking after. They had a golden summer, Gerard said. During the day they'd work in the barn. We were keeping a Welsh cob for a neighbour, and Arthur learned to ride. They adored each other, the boy and the horse. I used to ask Gerard what Arthur made of it. He said Arthur had had to make his own sense of the world. He'd had no one in his life to tell him how it all worked, so every day was new to him. Arthur was good as gold here, which is odd because he was thrown out of every school he'd ever attended, apparently.' She shivered in her thin cardigan. 'Arthur went back to London that autumn. Bridget looked after him for a bit, but then he disappeared. Gerard tried to find him, he'd get angry that no one else was bothered, he'd talk about how some people just fall off the radar, the injustice of it, how Arthur's coming into this world had been so chaotic that he could disappear without anyone noticing. He was furious. He took the shroud down from its frame and we never saw it again. I think the chalice went missing at around the same time.'

'Do you have any idea where it went?'

'No idea. If it was stolen, we'd have heard about it, that's what our solicitors say. Gerard ended up with a lot of our old family treasures, and after he died, Orla got quite a lot of it. Some rare books, antiques, old tobacco tins — our father collected them — I don't know why . . .' She looked up at the moon, sharp against the chilly sky. 'We should go in.'

* * *

Iris cleared away the dinner things, stacked plates in the dish-washer, placed glasses by the sink. Agnes sat in the warm kitchen and watched her, her slender grace, her brisk, quick movements.

'When you said that Francie Sorrell betrayed you . . .'

'Did I say that?' She paused by the sink, glass in hand. 'What I meant was she could have helped. That's my view, in any case. A death like his, it doesn't come from nowhere, there are warning signs. And we all missed them.' She rinsed the soapy glass under the tap, placed it on the draining board. 'There were people who were bad for him.'

'Francie?'

'No, not her. But people in their circle. I think.'

'Did he have close relationships?'

She paused, a tea towel in her hand. 'Not really. He would fall in love, sometimes with a man, occasionally with a woman. But it never lasted. Either they would tire of it, or he would decide that love was an ideal that a mere human could not attain.' She dried a glass, placed it on the shelf. 'I think there was a love affair just before he died. I only know fragments of it, he wouldn't talk about it. But after that, Gerard went downhill.' She blinked back tears. 'Survivors' guilt, that's what Phyllis said. I asked her, surviving what? And she would say, Gerard is someone who wonders why he's still here when all around him he sees such suffering. I think she was right.' She rinsed another glass under the tap. 'A death like that, you see, it casts long shadows. My sister and I, we took a while to heal.' She smiled. 'It was Bridget, with her rough anger, who helped me see it was acceptable to rage. She would come here and together we would shake our fists at the heavens.' She bent to the dishwasher. 'We still do, sometimes.' She pressed a button, straightened up. 'We should go to bed,' she said. 'It's late, and I've drunk more than I'm used to.'

* * *

The bed was comfortable, with its old eiderdown quilt and crisp linen sheets. Agnes lay in the velvety darkness and listened to the rural silence.

It's that photo, she thought. *Something about those three men. And the shroud, the way it seems to tell a story — the crucifixion in the middle, but with that sense of scenes leading up to it and away from it too, a glimpse of the Annunciation, some kind of Resurrection too.*

It had taken years, Iris had said.

Agnes wondered what story he was trying to tell, the non-believing brother of this troubled family.

She put on the light, grabbed her phone. Nothing from DS Rob. She scrolled through contacts, hesitated, then tried Ezra's number which went straight to voicemail. She hoped he at least had a roof over his head.

She lay back down in the darkness. Francie Sorrell betrayed us, Iris had said. There were warning signs, we should have known . . .

But known what?

The shroud, created in a golden summer.

In the photograph, Gerard is standing between two men. Andras, once Father Anselm. And this man called Darius.

Tomorrow I will go back to London, she thought. And then she turned over and went straight to sleep.

CHAPTER SIXTEEN

Agnes carried her bag out to Athena's car in the morning sunshine. Iris had made coffee, laid plates, putting out toast and jam with brittle chatter, as if to deny the confidences of the night before. 'Hope you slept well. Oh, no breakfast? Just coffee? Don't you get nagged by the nuns? It must have changed since I was at school. I was never hungry, it was part of the tyranny, forcing me to eat . . .'

Now they stood by the car. Iris touched the engineered curve of the passenger door. 'Perhaps your friend will let you keep it,' she said.

'Ooh, let's hope so,' Agnes said.

'Well.' Iris looked at her. 'I hope you find the missing Sorrell boy.'

'Thanks. And maybe — maybe the chalice too,' Agnes said.

'Oh, I don't know about that.' Iris wrapped her arms in front of her, as if chilled. 'Might be best if that thing stays unfound. If it comes to light it will only awaken the sleeping vultures.' She smiled. 'And will you see Orla? Please try to persuade her to visit.'

'I will, if I see her.'

Surprisingly, Iris stepped towards Agnes and hugged her. Agnes felt the thin, hesitant arms wrap around her as if she wasn't used to such a thing.

'Thank you,' Iris said. 'Thank you for coming. I — I don't usually go into the garage. But showing you those things . . . it was — it was helpful.' She dabbed at her eyes. 'It's good to remember him as he was, an artist, very much alive, rather than just my own puddle of grief.' She hugged her again. 'Good luck.'

* * *

The weather darkened as Agnes reached the motorway. A few drops of rain smeared the windscreen.

She put on the radio, and the windscreen wipers beat time with a loud, angry drumming and a girl's voice shouting vengeance in wispy rage.

Hours later, she parked the car at the hostel, tucking it away on the littered drive behind the bins, texted Athena, *I'm back but I'm keeping the car*, with a smile emoji.

She walked into the hostel, glad of the post-lunch lull where only the ringing of the office phones broke the dulled silence.

She sat in the empty kitchen and phoned Neave.

'Nah,' said the sleepy voice. 'No sign at all. I called Mosh's mum. She'd seen him that night, but he didn't stay and she's not seen him since.'

'The crate in his room,' Agnes said. 'Do you know what he was looking for?'

'It's all old stuff from Jay. Hats and things, all over the fucking floor.'

'Letters? Photos?'

'How do I know?'

'You don't know what he took?'

'Course I don't. Cos it ain't here now, is it? Did you talk to the feds?'

'I told them he'd called you.'

There was a dry laugh.

'We need to find him,' Agnes said.

There was a pause, then Neave said, 'What I'm scared of, Sister, is that he's just like his dad. First sign of trouble he walks towards it, not away.'

'No,' Agnes said. 'From what he said to me, he's the opposite. Talked about how you have to lay down your sword.'

Neave laughed, briefly. 'Got that from Francie, I bet. I just wish he'd been old enough when she was around to understand even the tiniest bit of that wisdom.'

'Do you think he's come to harm?'

'Sister, I ain't slept since he went. But you ask me if he's in danger? My fear is, it's danger of his own fucking making.'

Agnes heard a female voice in the background, then Neave again. 'Listen, babe, I gotta go. I appreciate what you're doing. Keep in touch, yeah?'

The call ended.

Agnes thought about the crate in Ezra's room, the sense of a hurried search for something. A clue? An object?

Laying down of swords, she wondered.

A text from Athena. *Rhododendrons? Ballgowns?*

I'll tell you later, she texted back.

Is my car safe, seeing as you say you're keeping it?

As safe as any Audi on a disused drive in SE1.

At least I'll get the insurance. Catch you later.

Agnes borrowed a spare umbrella from the hostel, wondering, as she opened it against the rain, how they'd ended up with this patriotic flag of red, white and blue. She caught the bus to the convent house.

* * *

The Order's library was in a wood-panelled room with green leather chairs, as if resisting the brick-and-glass modernity of the rest of the building.

She began to take books from the shelves: *Medieval Embroidery in Northern France, Iconography of the Eastern Churches 1450–1600* . . .

She wondered what she was looking for.

Cultural Dissolution: Monastic Art in the Counter-Reformation.

She sat down at a desk and opened the book.

She saw paintings, Our Lady, the Stations of the Cross, the Raising of Lazarus from the Dead.

Judas with Our Lord. Agnes stared at it. One man leaning to kiss the other. Two faces, china-pale in the red-draped darkness; one gazing outwards, all equanimity within his haloed glow, the other facing his friend and victim, his eyes dark with anguish at his pre-destined role. Thirty pieces of silver. As Julius had said.

The door opened, quietly.

'They said you were here,' Sister Winifred said.

'Tracking our movements now, are they?'

'They allowed you to go to Suffolk, though.'

'Not sure *allowed* is the word.'

Winifred sat down next to her. She glanced at the book, open on the painting, the two men, the visceral embrace. She looked up at Agnes.

'You'll be okay in Calais. A woman like you. I've been thinking about it.'

'You reckon?'

Winifred's gaze fell on the book again. 'At least, when you've finished with—' she touched the edge of the book — 'all this. Whatever it is.'

'I wish I knew,' Agnes answered.

Winifred sat silent, her hands tucked into her sleeves. After a while she spoke. 'I am not as I appear. Sometimes people get the wrong idea about me. I don't want you thinking that I'm . . .'

'That you're what?'

Winifred met her eyes. 'You know what you were thinking about me. And I'm not that.'

'Ah. Okay.'

After a moment Winifred went on, 'What I mean is . . . I had a breakdown, you see. A long time ago now. I was in my previous Order, up north. I thought that God had called me to be a better person. I was gripped by the sense of falling short. So I worked harder, prayed more, slept less, ate less — you know the kind of thing.'

Agnes smiled, nodded.

'But it wasn't really that. You see, in the middle of all that, I encountered a former priest. He'd been moved on, from somewhere. He was a dreadful man. He'd spent his career abusing children, boys, you know. The Church authorities had scooped him up and moved him on, time and again, until he could be retired, and he was living out his days in this old mansion house. He attached himself to me, once he learned I was a nun. I think he thought we would be on the same level. He wanted me to know that it was everyone else's fault. He wouldn't say what he'd done, of course, but he had a huge sense of injustice about it all. He was quavering and feeble, and he wanted me to know about the great ingratitude everyone had towards him, how he'd made a huge contribution to his community, how no one acknowledged that.'

She pulled her sleeves down over her pale fingers. 'He had people looking after him, a very nice woman who ran the home, and he was appalling to her, issuing orders, unsmiling, as if she was some servant and he was lord of the manor. And I thought, How does someone like that preach the word of God? How do we let someone like that hold that role, for all those years, with that untold damage? He claimed to be religious, still said the Mass. And I would think, How could he say those same prayers as me, as if they had the same meaning? It challenged me. I thought of leaving, because of him, really. I mentioned it to my confessor, and all she said was, Human frailty knows no bounds. We are all in exile. It is for God to judge.

'I sat with this for a while but I decided it wasn't enough. One day, when he was visiting, which he did a lot even though we didn't want him there, I found him alone in the lounge. He started up again, telling me about how wronged he'd been. So, finally, I faced him and I said, "I know what you've done. I know why you're here. You're lucky they didn't press charges. You ought to be in prison."'

'What did he do?'

'His hands began to shake. He had a teacup and it rattled on the saucer, and he managed to put it down on the table next to him. And then he got angry. Really angry. Said I was just like everyone else, he'd thought better of me, how dare I come in here with tittle tattle, that kind of thing. So I waited until he'd finished and then I told him, "What you did was very wrong." And he said he was the wronged one, not other people, he'd had to take the blame, surely I could see that, "an intelligent woman like you . . ." So I asked, what happens when you die? We are people who believe in the next life — how will you account for yourself before God?

'There was more rambling accusation then. So I said, "What about your own victimhood? What pain are you carrying? You followed your warped desires because the alternative would be to hold them up to the light and see your own pain. And for you it was preferable just to pass it on."'

'What did he say?'

Winifred gave a small laugh. 'I thought I was so clever,' she said. 'But all that happened is that he said I sounded just like the psychiatrist they sent him to. "And he talked rubbish too." I said, "How dare you? Those poor children. You should be locked up." I was shouting then, and he was too. He told me to go. But I said, "Don't you think about them? They're adult men now, living with the legacy of your harm, your wrongdoing. Do you have no sense of the damage you did? What happens when you're in chapel and you're called to confess your sins?" He just said some kind of rubbish about how God would see him for what he was, unlike all the high-ups in the church who had accused him . . .'

She stopped, breathless, gathering herself. 'I got nowhere, Agnes. And it was all in the middle of me trying to be as sinless as I could be. And here I was, sharing God's earth with someone who had been so bad, and yet who claims to share my faith. My confessor said to hand it over to God, that it's up to God to judge him, not me. But there he was, living this comfortable life, absolutely believing he'd done

150

nothing wrong. I began to believe that whatever I did, evil would still triumph and that it was just wishful thinking that God's love triumphs.'

'What happened?'

'I stopped eating. I didn't speak. I hid from the community.' She took a long breath. 'The truth of it was, that I had decided to kill that priest. I started planning how to carry it out. I thought of stealing a kitchen knife and just doing it, you know, one day just turning on him — but that seemed fraught with difficulty. So then I worked out that the best thing to do would be to stockpile huge amounts of sedative and get them into a cup of tea. I was researching opiates, that kind of thing, we had links with a pharmacy and I lurked around there . . .' She managed a small smile.

'Then what?'

'They sent me away. I don't know if they knew my plans, or if they just knew I was in trouble. I went to the community we had in France, in the Alps. It's lovely there. Calm. Peaceful. Good people. I had a lovely spiritual director there, I'm still in touch with her. I began to heal. What I think now is that it wasn't that the man was evil that opened up the abyss, it was that there wasn't an answer. That's what tipped me over the edge.'

'What happened to him?'

'The priest?' She shrugged. 'He died. Old age. Drink. Whatever. I don't care, actually.'

The silence thickened around them.

'And now?' Agnes asked.

Winifred fingered the book on the desk. 'Sometimes it's the same. In Calais, you hear their stories, the victims . . .' She looked up. 'There are torturers who love their job. That's why they do it, because they like doing it. We share the planet with people who are capable of doing terrible things to other people and who love doing it. There is no answer about why they behave that way. Other than to say, we are so damaged, we human beings, that we carry pain in our bones. Some people, good people, allow themselves to call a halt to that pain. Some of them pass it on. In the end, what can we do? We pray for the world. We do what we can. And sometimes it seems that perhaps love does win out. Sometimes.'

In the corridor there was movement, passing footsteps, a clink of crockery, someone wheeling a trolley.

'I'd have tried to kill him too,' Agnes said.

'Yes,' Winifred said. 'I know.' She got to her feet, rested her hand on Agnes's shoulder. 'Good luck with your quest. I'll be leaving soon. I look forward to working with you.'

After Winifred left, Agnes sat in the silence of the library, turning pages, looking at church art. She looked at the image of the crucifixion and thought about the triumph of God's love. She thought about Gerard in the barn, painting the shroud, before he was overwhelmed and put an end to it all.

She wondered where the shroud was now.

The ringtone of her phone broke the silence.

'Sister?' It was Neave. 'Ez called.'

'Thank God. Where is he?'

'Fuck, I wish I knew. He told me not to worry and he'd be back soon. But he asked me questions, about Jay, about the time he did in prison, about what made his nan leave everything behind. I says to him, "Ez, this is the past, come home, you got your exams to think about," and then he laughs. "Exams," he says. And he tells me he's got better things to do. He says, "Mum, working hard all that time at school and we can't even pay our bills. You wait," he says, "we won't have to worry no more." What the fuck does that mean, Sister? And I'm saying to him, "Ez, come home, for Christ's sake, think about your future," and he's all the big man on the phone and he says, "Mum, this is my future. This is my inheritance." And then he hangs up.'

The voice at the end of the phone cracked. 'Inheritance, Sister. What the fuck does he mean by that? Like, following his dad? Is that what he means?' There was a loud sniff. 'Sister, I'm losing him. Like I lost his dad. It's me who's to blame.'

'No,' Agnes said. 'Not you.' *Thirty pieces of silver.* The thought flickered through her mind. 'I'll be right there.'

CHAPTER SEVENTEEN

Neave's house was in darkness when Agnes rang the bell. Neave answered, eventually. She was wearing large pink slippers and an oversized white shirt.

She led Agnes silently into the kitchen and flung herself into a chair. Her face was young and smooth and un-made-up. 'Look,' she said, her phone thrust into Agnes's face. 'I've been trying to call him back, but it don't answer now. Just voicemail. Where the fuck is he? And all that stuff from the crate in his room, what is all that rubbish, old photos and shit? It's typical of his dad, to leave a fucking unexploded bomb ticking away in our lives, and now it's about to go off and my baby has walked right off with it . . .'

Agnes sat down wearily.

The kitchen table was empty, apart from a half-drunk mug of cold tea, a small table lamp and a framed photo of Ezra. He looked young and bright and smiling.

'What was he searching for? That's what I don't get.' Neave looked up, waiting for an answer.

'I don't know,' Agnes said.

'Well, if you don't, we're lost.'

Agnes picked up the framed photo and studied it. 'What was Jay's connection to the St Fleur family?'

A shrug of dismissal. 'None. His mum hung about with that woman but I don't think he did.'

Agnes put down the photo. 'Who was Jay's father?'

Neave leaned back on her chair, shaking her head. 'I never got the truth of it. So, Francie Sorrell, she was Jay's mum. He never knew his dad. She raised him, on her own, just ordinary, like the people round here. But — he never wanted for nothing, Jay. Like, when he was a kid, always nicely dressed. New stuff. And their house, always a cut above everyone else's. Word was that Francie was doing laundry for someone and taking a cut, but it never fit with her community stuff, clean image, all that, you know.'

'When you took up with Reece . . .' Agnes began.

'What you gonna do?' Neave faced her. 'I had a baby with a bad lad. So, it was fun for a while — Jay chasing his dreams, me working nights to keep them dreams alive, and then . . .' her face clouded. 'The dreams got more chunky. Took him away from me and Ez. Still chasing, but it was like a mighty warrior through foreign lands, not someone with a little kid in a small London street.' She leaned across the table to switch on the lamp, but nothing happened. She fiddled with the bulb, which eventually flickered into life. She looked up at Agnes.

'And then Reece Bennett came back into my life.' She shook her head. 'And compared to Jay, he looked like what I wanted. So I said yes. I made a life with Reece, he was a good dad to Ezra, life was sweet.'

'What did Francie make of it?'

Neave gave a tight smile. 'While I was looking after her son, giving him a child . . . she was all over me then. But, you know, marriages go wrong. It wasn't her business. Francie never forgave me for turning out Jay into the night to face his demons. I just didn't want them demons in my house day after day.'

'And then Reece died.'

Neave gave a cold, pinched nod.

'Did you love him?'

154

'What kind of question is that?'

'I just wondered . . .'

'What can I say?' The lamplight cast its uncertain glow against her skin. 'About six and a half years ago. There was a fight. Outside Reece's house. My man ends up bleeding to death. Jay gets pulled in by the feds, charged with his killing. Then he pleads not guilty, and there's no evidence, and he's out again.' She spread her hands across the table. 'Which of them is going to be my baby's dad now?'

'Did you believe Jay?'

'I did,' she said. 'Because I ain't never seen him like that. "It weren't me," he kept saying, crying and that. And I'd say, then who was it, you were there, babe, there were knives, you must have seen, and he'd shake his head and say he saw nothing, he heard the shouting, he came upon his friend dying in the street.' She shook her head. 'What the feds said was that Reece had gone armed and whoever killed him used his own blade on him. But that don't explain nothing, does it?'

She breathed out, spoke again. 'People like you . . . you don't know what it's like.' She was wide awake now, all sleepiness gone. 'You ain't had the love and the rage. What do you know of that? That day when they lay that sweet baby in your arms and you think, I ain't never going to love anything or anyone the way I love this baby. And then life gets in the way.' She faced Agnes, in the mean pool of light. 'And that baby becomes an angry, wayward boy. And there ain't nothing you can do.'

Agnes felt large and awkward in the small space.

Neave softened. 'The thing is, Sister — I still love that boy the way I did when they laid him in my arms all them years ago.' Her eyes filled with tears.

'Are your parents still around?'

'Nah. My sister lives in Canada, she's got four kids. Four. Can you believe it? My mum's there with her, my dad ain't around no more. He went over there with her but he took up with a dancer in Vegas. Always was one for a cliché.' She picked up her phone, put it down again, chewing her lip. 'What you just said . . . that woman — the St Fleur one — she came round here to see Jay. About a week before he went to that church.'

'Orla St Fleur?'

Neave gave a small nod. 'That's the one. She was nice. Very polite. Respectful. But she asked to be alone with him, and they talked for a bit in the front room, and then she went.'

'What was he like after that?'

She shrugged. 'The same. He went out in the yard here and had a spliff. Needed to make a call.'

'Who to?'

She shrugged. 'Some priest. An old man.'

'Did he say which priest? Where he was located?'

She shook her head. 'No. Only there was a reckoning. That was the word he used. He wouldn't say more, and I didn't ask. He finished his spliff, then I made him dinner. Then he went out. But that was normal.' She fiddled with a button on her shirt.

'Do you still have the crate of stuff? I'd like to see it.'

'Yeah, if you want.' Neave pulled herself to her feet and Agnes followed her along the dark corridor.

'Here.' Neave pushed open a door, switched on a light.

The room was cosy, painted blue. There was a frieze around the top of the walls showing the moon, the sun, stars, all in bright yellow.

A single bed was covered with a blue-striped duvet, neatly tucked in.

'This is Ezra's room. Always has been.' Neave straightened a pillow.

There was a yellow plastic crate in one corner, papers strewn on the carpet around it. Agnes knelt down. She could see photos, envelopes, handwritten sheets of paper.

'Just photos of Jay when he were a kid. That kind of thing,' Neave said. 'Load of rubbish, knowing Jay. Don't know why he gave it to Ez.'

'So you don't know if Ezra took anything with him?'

She shook her head. 'He was in here ages, like, looking for something. Then he left.'

Agnes pulled out a sheaf of papers tied with string. Envelopes, letters, yellowed at the edges. A photograph of a woman holding a baby. She was wearing a long brightly coloured dress and a turban.

'Francie,' Neave said, 'with Jay as a baby.'

'This all came from Jay?'

Neave nodded. 'I ain't paid no attention to it till now.'

Another photograph. Black and white. Three men, in smart jackets, holding wine glasses, smiling. Behind them some kind of art, painted squares in large frames. 'This—' Agnes tapped it. 'I've — I've seen this before. That's Gerard , in an art gallery. The one with the long fringe.'

'Him. He was the brother, weren't he? The one who died.'

'And—' Agnes felt her breath quicken. 'Andras. And—' The third man was smiling outwards, a narrow-eyed, triumphant kind of smile. She looked at the slick-backed hair, the thin dark tie against the white shirt. 'And Darius. The three of them together.'

'Means nothing to me.'

'Why? Why is this photo here?'

Neave gave a shrug.

Agnes flicked through more papers from the same envelope. 'Here,' she said. 'Another one.' The same three men, in black and white. Same place, it seemed. Behind them a long skein of painted images. A crucifixion. Disciples, saints. A procession.

'*The Keld Shroud*,' Agnes said. 'Painted by Gerard St Fleur.' She grabbed some more photos, all black and white, with the same art gallery background.

'That one's a priest, look—' Neave was pointing at the photo in Agnes's hand. 'He looks sweet,' Neave said. 'What's he doing with those weird guys?'

Agnes stared at the photo in her hand.

'You look like you know him.' Neave seemed amused.

'I . . . I do know him. That's my friend Julius.'

'With them other three? All laughing and having a drink and that? Weird.' She yawned, turned towards the door. 'You want to keep that?'

Agnes studied the photo. 'Yes,' she said. 'I'd like to keep this one.' She put it in her pocket and tidied the rest back into the crate.

She followed Neave back along the darkness towards the kitchen. 'I'll tell the police you've heard from him, at least.'

'Up to you, Sister. Can't see my boy is going to be top of their to-do list.' Neave slumped suddenly at the table. 'I am so scared,' she said. Tears filled her eyes. 'So scared. What if what happened to his dad happens to my boy? He left here in a hurry, I reckon. His scarf was out there on the ground, by the lamppost. Look.' She bent to the back of a chair and retrieved a football scarf. 'QPR, he's always supported them which is weird for round here.' She placed the scarf on the table. 'He didn't even notice he'd dropped it.'

Agnes sat down next to her. 'Is it like him, to be secretive?'

Neave breathed a heavy sigh. 'You ask any of the mothers round here what their boys are doing, they won't have no answer for you. He's just like his dad, that's the problem. Jay was more frightened of being called a coward than he ever was of doing the wrong thing. I loved him for it, Sister. I still do. But maybe I was wrong. Maybe Ezra is going the same way.' She picked up her phone, scrolled, clicked, stared. 'I just want him back.'

Agnes was aware of a thought, just out of reach. 'Money,' she said. 'It's important to him?'

Neave gave an empty laugh. 'Like it isn't to everyone? Maybe not to you people, but the rest of us — man, I'm tired of it. Every time at the shops, checking the prices, comparing this with that. Ez always says, one day, Mum you won't have to worry.'

'So if someone had offered to pay him for something?'

Neave lifted her head. 'Like one of them little gangsters round here, you mean? Happens all the time.'

'I meant someone older. Higher stakes.'

'Like what?' Neave yawned.

Agnes took out the photo from the gallery, looked at Julius standing there in black and white, young and cheerful. She put the photo in her bag. 'I don't know. None of it makes any sense,' Agnes said.

'You as well? I thought you knew what you were looking for,' Neave said.

Agnes gathered up her bag.

Neave yawned again. 'I'm gonna try to sleep. Not that I will. Thanks for coming over.'

Agnes followed her as she dragged her slippered feet out into the hall.

Outside a gust of wind whirled the litter, and a figure on a scooter in body-tight lime green whizzed past. Neave brushed Agnes's arm with her pink-painted nails. 'Will you find him for me?'

'I'll do my best,' Agnes heard herself say.

'That's what I say too.' Neave peered out into the twilight. 'I do my best.' She reached for Agnes's hand. 'Thank you, Sister.'

The door closed.

* * *

Agnes stood in the street. The spire of Julius's church was dark against the red-tinged sky. She could see a light in the office window.

She walked towards it, stood there for a moment as the church clock chimed nine. Then she walked away.

At the corner, she sat on a wall and took out her phone. She scrolled to a number, clicked on it.

'Hello?' asked a clipped, evasive female voice.

'It's Sister Agnes,' she said.

'Andras isn't here,' the voice said.

'Actually,' Agnes said, 'it was you I wanted to speak to.'

CHAPTER EIGHTEEN

Ginny Adler was blonde and tailored, in a navy dress, knee-high white boots and chunky silver jewellery.

They were in the Brougham, a bar in Mayfair which she had suggested on the phone. 'It's Andras's club. He's out at the moment, but if I'm there he can always track me down,' she'd said.

Agnes looked at her smart white collar and her pretty nose and wondered why she was the kind of woman a man would track down.

Ginny leaned back against the dark blue bench. 'I was going to catch the eye of that waiter, only I've no idea what people like you drink. Their house champagne is very good.'

'I'll have that, then,' Agnes answered.

'Oh. Okay.' She cast a studied gaze at Agnes. 'Andras only drinks champagne. He's bound to find us. I'd better get a bottle.' She looked around to find the waiter.

Agnes felt underdressed and weary. She had caught the bus from Southwark Bridge Road, and now it was nearly ten.

The waiter approached, murmured approval, bowed and departed. Ginny settled back against the navy leather. 'So,' she said. 'You wanted to talk to me? As long as it's not about God or church or anything, I'm done with all that.'

'No, it's not about God,' Agnes said. 'Although Andras might say that it is.'

'I doubt it. He doesn't believe in God. He doesn't really believe in anything.' Her accent was London with a crisp Germanic hint.

'I wanted to know about Gerard St Fleur,' Agnes said.

'Ah.'

'Their friendship. Him and Andras, and Darius . . .'

'Oh, God. Him.'

'What was he like?'

'Darius Samaras. Father Darius properly, though I'm unconvinced he was a father to anyone, in any sense.' She smiled. 'I didn't like him. To be honest, I was so glad when it all fell apart and he drifted away.' She crossed her legs in their long white boots. 'He was a sort of shape-shifter. Whoever you were, he'd kind of reflect it back. Like now, if he was with us, he'd be joining in, admiring this necklace, talking about bargains you can find in Bond Street these days. And then, say, Andras joins us, he'd suddenly ignore us, and start talking to him about the cricket scores. They all three loved cricket.' She uncrossed her legs, fiddled with the zip on her boot.

'Your boots,' Agnes said. 'They're lovely. My friend spent all last year obsessed with boots like that.'

'I love them. Half price, luckily, given what they cost. I'm only size 4 and it gives you more options.'

'Lucky,' Agnes agreed, as their champagne arrived.

Agnes took a sip. 'I grew up in France,' she told her.

'Ah, I thought you were foreign. I always know. I grew up Zurich,' she said.'

'Both of us Londoners, then,' Agnes said, and Ginny smiled. 'Father Darius,' Agnes began. 'I mean, a priest . . . celibate, obviously. Except . . .'

Ginny twirled her glass in her fingers. 'Exactly. There was something very odd. Kind of predatory about him. Kind of like you didn't want him sitting too close to you. Not that he ever tried anything, but even so . . .'

'Did he desire men or women?'

'I'm not sure it was desire, exactly. What I felt in the end was that his only concern was himself. When he was interested in anyone else, it was like they were two-dimensional, and he was the only three-dimensional person in his universe. As if everyone else was a figment of his imagination.'

'Wow. You really didn't like him.'

She shook her head. 'No,' she said. 'I didn't. Didn't trust him. This obsession with the old church, the stuff that belonged to Gerard's family, Andras got interested in the provenance of it all, there were some old oil paintings that ended up in Suffolk at the family house, quite valuable, pictures of saints. There were a couple of Italian Masters but they got given to the nation in lieu of tax, Andras said. And Darius would go on about the vestry of the old priory church, like really weird. He'd talk about versicles or something, tunicles, silverware and ancient silk embroidery. Gerard would try and shut him up, telling him how the sisters ended up with all the family stuff. I'm sure he was telling the truth.' She sipped her drink. 'Darius wouldn't give up. It was this bloody chalice, the Judas chalice it was called. Gerard swore blind it had gone missing years ago, and he wouldn't lie about a thing like that. And anyway, as Gerard said, and Andras agreed, it was worth an absolute fortune, it wouldn't just be lying around.'

'Did he know what it looked like?'

'Yes, they had photos. Andras had traced it to the old priory, before it vanished. There was an inventory. The two men, engraved on the side of it. Judas and Christ. Darius was obsessed with it. Betrayal and redemption all in one cup, he'd say.'

'And Andras?'

'Oh, once he thought Darius was on to it, he got interested in it too. He's like that. You see him at an auction, he'll always bid more than he can afford just to win. And if he loses . . .' Her face clouded. 'I try not to be around on those days.'

Agnes had a vision of Andras climbing around the loft at Keld House.

'Andras told me he'd seen it once.'

Ginny made a face. 'When the women were laughing at him, years ago? That story again.'

'Was it the real chalice, do you think?'

'I've no idea. But if it was fake, Andras would know. That's his job, authentication. He's expert in counterfeiting. "Those priests and their fakery," he says. All that stuff destroyed by the Protestants all those centuries ago. He says the churches just recreated it.' She laughed. 'The funny thing is, he's so good he could make a fortune with fakery, I reckon, he's so well thought of, and he knows so much. But I said that to him once and he got cross. Not for the first time either.' She darted a glance towards the door. 'He hates not knowing where I am,' she said, with a small smile. 'He'll turn up and do a funny scowly kind of thing with his face, you'll see.' She took a large mouthful of champagne, turned back to Agnes. 'What you need to know about Andras is that he was raised in terrible poverty. Some people, when they get money, they can just relax and enjoy it. But him — there was only him and his mother, and he always says the poverty killed her. It's like as a small boy, he felt responsible, he wanted to make things better for her.' She crinkled her pretty nose. 'It's not a game you can win, that one. He still has it, this awful guilt about his mum, and actually, when you ask him, she had lung cancer, she smoked all her life, it's hardly his fault, is it?' A brief laugh. 'He goes on about things holding their value. Like houses — he scans property listings all the time, checking the value of where we live in Kilburn, and the little seaside cottage we own in Cornwall, oh, and the house in the Dales, but we have long-term tenants there . . . It's like he's afraid that, whatever he thinks has value, it might just trickle away and he'll be left with nothing again. I keep telling him we'll be dead before that happens, but that doesn't help at all. My German grandmother used to say, there are no pockets in a shroud.' She laughed. 'But he's not like that. Not like that at all.'

'Is he happy now?'

Ginny gave a small shrug, a smile. 'Is any of us happy?' She took a sip of her drink. 'He has me. He has our lovely home, his collections of books, of art . . . He has his expertise, he enjoys that. Being a clever-dick — is that how you say it? — he says he can spot a fake just by breathing in the air around it . . .' She smiled. 'He's a funny one.'

Agnes spoke, remembering the faded photograph. 'Darius — what was he like?'

'He was vain. He had this jet-black hair, I think he dyed it, and he'd always wear a hat, a kind of old-fashioned, men's hat, maybe a trilby, would you call it that? His suits were tailored too. That's what I mean about him — how he appeared really mattered to him.'

'Have you seen him recently?'

She shook her head. 'I mean, all the unpleasantness was years ago now. Gerard's awful death, it fractured their friendship. There's always guilt with a suicide, isn't there? Andras said they both loved Gerard, and it broke something. Darius moved away.' She put her glass down on the table. 'Although . . . he did come back. About five, six, six and a half years ago, it must be, it was autumn . . . He and Andras were closeted in the study for a while, and then he went on his way.'

Six and a half years ago.

She thought of Neave, earlier that evening, and her tight rage in the thin lamplight. The same phrase — six and a half years ago, when Reece was found stabbed and Jay was blamed.

'Do you know what they were talking about?'

Ginny shook her head. 'The thing about Andras . . .' She flicked her hair away from her face, then looked up. 'I don't know how much you know about men,' she said.

'I know enough,' Agnes said, and Ginny smiled.

'He needs to believe he's in charge. I have to — I have to behave in certain ways for the whole thing to run smoothly. And asking him questions . . .' She fiddled with the zip some more. 'I've learned that sometimes I have to leave him alone. Like now—' Her voice was nervous, her poise deserting her.

'He'll join us, soon, I know he will. He doesn't let me out of his sight for long and I left him a voice note to say where I was, otherwise there'd be trouble . . .' She looked up. 'You will be nice to him, won't you?'

How many of us are there, Agnes wondered, watching this woman, a classy bird as Athena would say, glancing nervously towards the door. *How many of us, checking our words, being careful with what we say, living in fear . . .*

I got away — you can too, she wanted to say, but now Ginny had turned back to her, with a bright, bleak smile. 'Still enough champagne, at least,' she said, glancing at the bottle. 'That will keep him happy.'

'How did you meet?'

'I'm an auctioneer. I've specialised in painting, Dutch Renaissance mostly, but I do all kinds of stuff. I love it. And I'd see him from time to time . . . and then one day we bumped into each other at an art gallery. It was my friend's show. She does these bronze sculptures. There's one on the South Bank, near that bridge . . . Ah, look, there he is.' She gave a cheery wave.

'Ladies.' Andras approached the table, bowed to Agnes. 'Delightful to see you again, Sister.'

'We got you champagne,' Ginny said.

'So I should think. For you as well, Sister?' He smiled at Agnes as he joined Ginny on the bench.

'She's French,' Ginny said.

'Is that right? And what has she been telling you?' Andras leaned towards Agnes.

'We were discussing the advantage of having small feet when buying decent footwear,' Agnes replied.

Andras tasted his drink, gave a small nod and placed it on the table. Agnes watched Ginny watching him, and wondered what he would have done if it hadn't met with his approval.

'And have you found those artefacts yet?'

Agnes shook her head.

'But you're still searching for them?'

'Yes,' she said. 'And so are you.'

'For me, it's my work. But for you — why?' The question was abrupt.

Agnes looked at her glass, which the waiter had filled again. 'Absolution, perhaps,' she said.

'For whom?' His eyes were fixed on her. *That funny scowly thing*, she thought, looking at his face.

Ginny was drinking from her now-full glass.

'The Judas kiss,' Agnes said. 'It reverberates throughout Christianity.'

His gaze was still. 'Indeed,' he said. 'A rich tradition. And very rare on a chalice.'

'Andras could have continued as a priest,' Ginny said, with a small laugh. 'He was very good. Although, I suppose, if he was a priest I'd have had to be a secret,' she went on. 'Mind you, not sure I'd notice the difference.' Another laugh, another mouthful of champagne.

'That will do,' Andras said. Still scowling, he turned back to Agnes.

'Your friend Father Julius,' he said. 'Are you sure he hasn't heard any more from the St Fleur family?'

Agnes shook her head.

'The sand timer, at least. He must have that?' Andras's eyes were fixed on her. 'That family. It's criminal, that's what it is. Those artefacts should be in a vault. They should be kept safe. The chalice most of all. The idea that it's lost, God knows where, just because Gerard St Fleur decided to be a communist or whatever he was . . .'

'I thought he was your friend,' Agnes said.

His gaze was direct. 'Things change with the years,' he replied.

'Oh, this again.' Ginny stood up. 'I'm going to the ladies'.'

He moved briefly to let her pass. In her absence, he leaned back on his chair. 'I enjoyed our walk on Saturday,' he said. 'You're not like any of the nuns I've ever met.'

Agnes picked up her glass, watched the tiny bubbles rising.

'You know,' he was saying, 'ninety-nine percent of all monastics I've ever met were trying to put something back in their lives that was missing.'

'Ah,' she said. 'Right.'

'Your father, let me guess . . . A distant, closed in, private man. And your mother — you felt that whatever you did was never enough for her, is that it?'

Yes, she wanted to say, but instead she said nothing.

'You were an only child, perhaps. So, acquiring a community, a family . . . the attempt to find the love you missed as a child,' he surmised.

'Actually, I tumbled into it.' *Running away from a man like you*, she wanted to say, but didn't.

'Even worse, then,' he said. 'You will always be fighting your Order. I expect even now you're about to have a battle with them about some plan they've got for you . . .'

Ask his star sign, she could hear Athena saying, something about whether someone is nice or nasty . . .

The problem with that . . .

She took another breath. 'We're not here to talk about me.'

'Aren't we? The alternative is to talk about me, I assume.'

'I went to stay at Keld House.'

'Ah.' The gaze intensified. He was breathing hard. 'In that case, you'll know . . . there was a box, wasn't there? She'll have shown you — a sealed oak casket, the size of a large shoe box, with a big brass lock?' His breathing was uneven as he waited for her answer.

'No,' she answered, truthfully.

'The garage?' he asked. 'Did Iris show you that?'

'Yes, she did.' Agnes watched him. He seemed awry, twitchy, his lips working.

'All Gerard's work,' he said. 'The pieta? Still there?'

'Yes,' she said.

He seemed to recover himself. 'A huge talent. I've offered to help, but Iris won't see me.' He tried a smile.

'Help in what way?'

167

'Gerard had a value once. I'm sure I could resurrect him.'

Agnes smiled. 'Like his Christ figures?'

His gaze was level.

'Ezra's missing,' Agnes said. 'Something or someone has lured him away.'

'Ezra?'

'Francie Sorrell's grandson. Jay Sorrell's son.'

'What is that to me?'

She took a deep breath. 'Judas betrayed his friend for thirty pieces of silver,' she began. She wanted to say more, to say, *something happened six and a half years ago, and now it's back, whatever it is, and this chalice is at the heart of it* — but Andras had grasped her hand and was leaning in towards her.

'Just how much do you know?' He spoke softly, and she wasn't quite sure she'd heard him, above the approaching click of Ginny's heels on the parquet floor, her twinkly laugh, her voice.

'Glad to see you two getting on so well,' she said.

What was it Athena had said — Virgo, was it? Or was it another one, she couldn't remember . . .

Ginny was flushed and smiling as she thumped herself down next to Andras.

'I was about to ask his star sign,' Agnes announced.

'Go on, guess.' Ginny laughed.

'Virgo,'

'Oh my God. I can't believe it. Do they teach you that at nun school? Eighth of September, and he's so bloody typical too . . .'

It was just as Athena had said. Andras scowled all the more, and Ginny laughed. 'All this collecting. And he gets angry about untidiness, terrible rows if I leave a cup unwashed, aren't there, dear?' She looked up at him.

Andras rested a hand on her shoulder like a dead weight. With his other hand he drained his glass. 'I think we're going.' He got to his feet. 'I'll settle the bill.'

Ginny rubbed her shoulder where his hand had been, following him with her eyes as he crossed the floor to the bar.

She turned back to Agnes, her voice low. 'I have to tell you this. I think Gerard knew damn well where the chalice was. Probably tucked away with his sisters. But I think there was a belief he'd promised it to someone.' She spoke fast. 'All this fighting between Andras and Darius, they were the two who really wanted it, and with that promise, they were set against each other. And then Gerard died, and there was no sign of the chalice, and Andras was terrified that Darius would steal a march, is that what you say? And then for some reason, Darius disappeared. Left us in peace. Went off to Yorkshire or somewhere, he had a sister there, maybe. A niece. But Andras wouldn't let it lie, was sure he'd be back. And he kept looking for the damn chalice. Still is.' She glanced towards the bar. 'The thing is, Gerard was in pain. He said to me once, not long before he died, "Some people have to hate. If they stopped hating, they'd feel the pain." He said it was a quote from some American poet, maybe . . .' She leaned towards Agnes. 'He was in pain, Gerard. And none of us could see it.'

'And Andras?'

She looked towards the bar, where Andras was in cheerful conversation with the manager. 'I've told no one this. The other night, that man found dead, in the church. Andras was out that night. He won't tell me where he was. He came back smelling of smoke. And his jacket — there was dust. Like, sawdust. Like he'd been doing carpentry or something. It was out of character. I asked where he'd been that night, but he raged, he shouted, told me to shut up . . .' She stared at the table.

'What did you do?'

'Me? I took his suit to the cleaners. What else was I to do? Ah, Andras, all done?' She struggled to her feet, smiling brightly.

'Guido's back working here,' Andras said, as he bent to retrieve Ginny's coat and helped her on with it. 'He said he thought he'd stay in Sicily forever, but what with the mother-in-law . . .' He laughed, draping the soft dark wool around Ginny's shoulders.

A summer chill touched the night, as they spilled out from the brass swing of the door.

'Well,' Andras said, offering his hand. 'Another delightful conversation.' He turned to go, stepped away.

Ginny took Agnes by the hand. 'Next time you can guess my sign. Though it's obvious, of course.' Suddenly she reached up and kissed Agnes on both cheeks. 'Good luck,' she murmured. Then she was pulled away, and Agnes watched them walk, arm in gripped arm, towards the cab rank and its queue of yellow lights.

* * *

Agnes got off the bus, much later, on Southwark Bridge Road. She walked to her flat, glad of the quiet, glad of the silence as she put her key in the door.

Then there was the boiling of the kettle, finding a herbal teabag — peppermint, she decided — kicking off shoes.

It was only later, sitting on the edge of her bed, that she saw the text from Winifred.

I've been told to leave tomorrow. Two days early. Will you be joining me soon?

She texted back. *Yes. Yes I will.*

But first, she thought, *I know what I have to do.*

CHAPTER NINETEEN

Eddie looked up from his desk in the hostel office as Agnes inched her way through the door, half obscured by a large tower of files.

'What the fuck is that?' He pointed at the folder in her hand.

'Handover,' she said, dumping it down on his desk.

It was a chilly Wednesday morning. Outside the trees tossed their blossoms about in the wind, which carried in the loud territorial chirping of the birds.

'Handover?' He eyed the files. 'What they doing now, those nuns of yours?'

'Sending me away,' she answered.

'For ever?' His eyes widened.

She shook her head. 'No. I'll be back.'

'Thank Christ for that,' he said. 'I mean, not literally or anything . . . Going anywhere nice?' He smiled up at her.

'Not really,' she said. 'Weather same as here, accommodation more basic, clients more needy.'

'Ah.' He nodded. 'Right. Same old same old.' He turned back to his computer and carried on typing.

Agnes went and sat in the kitchen. She dialled Orla's number, left a message. Then she pulled the laptop towards her and began to type a list of handover notes.

* * *

At lunch time, her phone rang.

'How was your stay at Keld? I hope my sister looked after you.'

'Hello, Orla. It was lovely, thank you.'

'Is the house in any kind of upkeep?'

'It's charming,' Agnes said.

'Oh, nonsense, I expect you froze to death. At least you ate well, I imagine.'

'Yes,' Agnes said. 'Very well.'

'Is Duchess still out in the field?'

'She is indeed.'

'Ah, good. She'll live forever, that horse.'

'Yes.' Agnes hesitated. 'Iris said—'

'Unlike me, you mean,' Orla said.

'I hope she wasn't speaking—'

'Out of turn? No,' Orla said. 'I need people to know and I find I can't tell them myself.'

'Julius—'

'Julius knows.'

'Right.'

'Sometimes I think I've made my peace with it, and then I wake up in the morning absolutely fuming, shaking my fist at the sky . . .' Another breath, then she said, 'You saw the garage? The art?'

'Yes,' Agnes said.

'It explains everything about my poor brother.'

'Orla . . .' Agnes took a breath. 'Ezra has vanished, Jay Sorrell's son.'

'Vanished?'

'He opened a crate of his dad's belongings, threw loads of stuff out of it, and then went. Like he was on a mission.

He's only fifteen, his mother's beside herself. In her own way,' she added.

'But the police know, presumably?'

'They're aware, yes.'

'Well, then.'

'The crate in his room, it's full of letters and photographs that seem to have come from his dad and grandmother. Among them are photos of Gerard, with Andras and Darius.'

'I wish I could help.' Orla's voice was fretful now, the words brittle. 'But I'm running out of time. Francie was a friend, and she knew Gerard, of course. But why photos of him and that lot should have ended up with Jay is anyone's guess. Maybe he was just being helpful when she vanished. We all had to clear her flat . . .'

'But the photo, with those two . . .'

'Agnes, I don't know.' Her voice was emphatic. 'I can't help. Gerard had all kinds of friendships over the years. I didn't like either of those men, and in the end, I don't think he did either.'

'And they were both obsessed with the chalice.'

'Oh, that blasted chalice. I wish we'd never owned it. God knows where it is, and honestly I don't care anymore. Agnes, I have to go now. I'll see what I can do about Ezra, but I can't promise anything.'

The line clicked off.

I'll see what I can do.

It was an odd thing to say. Particularly for someone running out of time.

* * *

More lists, more files. Towards the end of the afternoon, Agnes pushed her laptop away from her, leaned back in the creaky desk chair, took a sip of cold tea.

Her phone rang.

'DS Coombes,' she said. 'How lovely.'

173

'I have news,' he said. 'Though you probably got there before me.'

'Ezra?' she said.

'No such luck. But we arrested the Preedy man. At last.'

'You did?'

'Aidan. As you know, the main suspect in the Sorrell murder. Claiming innocence as ever, but a least we've got him now. And,' he added, 'I reckon you knew where he was all along.'

'Rob—' she began.

'Aiding and abetting an offender,' he said. 'You can be arrested for that.' Agnes watched her screensaver panning its image across her laptop.

'. . . just as well we're mates,' Rob added, with a laugh. 'He'll be charged with the murder of Jay Sorrell.'

'Rob,' she said. 'Aidan might be right. About his innocence.'

'Agnes, much as I value your opinion—'

Her gaze followed the laptop image, a weirdly vertiginous panning shot across some kind of forest.

'Something happened,' she said. 'Six and a year half years ago, something happened. Reece was killed, Jay was charged with his killing, then released. It wrecked Francie's family life, she fled, no one hears from her. And now whatever it is, is back.'

'Those families never forget,' Rob said. 'That's what's back.'

The robotic drone shot was showing a seascape. *Odd for a religious Order*, she thought, vaguely. *Our laptop ought to have inspirational art. An icon of Our Lady, the Annunciation.*

Rob had gone quiet.

'Thirty pieces of silver,' Agnes murmured.

'Sorry?'

'The price of betrayal,' she said. 'It was a huge amount of money in the time of Christ. Difficult to refuse, I imagine.'

'Sister, I don't follow you.'

'DS No Name. Ezra said he knew about stuff that happened, when his grandmother was still part of his life. And now Ezra is talking about becoming very rich. And asking where to find that retired officer.'

'You've lost me—'

'Wharton. DI Wharton. He was back for a funeral, you said. Is he still around?'

'No idea. He was staying at his sister's, clearing her flat after the funeral.'

'Where's her flat?'

'It's the old almshouses. He might still be there. Number fourteen, I think. Agnes, what's this about?'

'It's about Ezra,' she said. 'We have to find him.'

'Agnes, last night, we had a case of arson up by the Peabody flats. We had two lads stabbed in a fight by the shopping centre, one in hospital saying nothing, the other legged it and is probably bleeding to death somewhere rather than talk to us. We had a shooting at the old recycling centre, a motorcycle fatality up by the river, a ramming of the phone shop on the High Street . . .'

'You mean, you can't find a teenage boy who's walking into danger.'

There was a small silence.

'DI Wharton,' Rob said. 'He's retired. I'm sure he'd speak to you. Like everyone else round here. Just don't go playing detective. If that lad is heading for danger, I don't want you following him. Promise.'

'Promise,' she said.

* * *

The sunlight flickered through the trees as Agnes crossed the tidy lawn. A blue plaque on the red brick wall commemorated the founder of the charity. The front doors were in rows, neatly numbered.

'Fourteen A.' She knocked at the door.

She could hear reluctant footsteps. The door opened slowly.

'I wasn't expecting anyone.' He was taller than she'd expected, white-haired, grey-eyed, with a wary bushy-eye-browed look.

'Detective Inspector Wharton? I'm Sister Agnes,' she said. 'Rob Coombes suggested I talk to you.'

'Rob?' The frown became a smile. 'What's he up to now? Still at it?'

'Still at it.'

'We almost met,' he said. 'My sister's funeral. Father Julius pointed you out to me, but then you were waylaid by some man in a fancy coat.'

She laughed. 'Julius and I go back a long way.'

'That's exactly what he said. Well . . .' He stepped back, showed her into the hallway. 'You'd better come in.'

He led her into the living room, which was draped with dust sheets and stacked with packing boxes. 'Here . . .' He pulled up two chairs, shook out their cushions. 'All a bit temporary here, the charity needs her flat back now.'

Agnes sat down, and he lowered himself into the chair opposite, placed his hands on his knees.

'It's about this killing of Jay Sorrell. In the old church.'

'Ah. I — I am retired, you know?' He reached up a long arm in a tweedy sleeve and scratched his head.

'Aidan Preedy is about to be charged, but he didn't do it.'

He smiled. 'Those Preedys have been declaring their innocence for generations.'

'And Ezra, Jay Sorrell's boy, he's disappeared. He's on some kind of mission, involving money, I think.'

'Ah, Francie's grandson. I remember him when he was knee-high to a grasshopper.'

'He speaks well of you.'

'Me? Can't think why, I've been away for a while now. And once this is all packed away, I'll have no reason to come back. Shropshire, that's where we retired to, my wife's family's from there.' He smiled a warm and elderly smile. 'I'll miss Ivy, though. There was just the two of us. She was rather solitary. But not alone, if you see what I mean. My wife and I would invite her for Christmas and things, although she hardly ever came. But the people round here loved her.'

'Did she know the St Fleur family?'

'Oh, them. The posh ones.' He brushed dust from the edge of the chair. 'She knew everyone round here.'

'Did she . . . was she ever . . .'

'In love?' He smiled across at her, as the sunlight caught the dust like glitter. 'Not that I know of. Although there was . . . there were a few years . . .' He looked up. 'She got interested in art. Old religious paintings, haunting the National Gallery, the Raphaels, Titian. Which was funny because she never went to church, she wouldn't hold with all that nonsense, if you'll forgive my bluntness.'

Agnes smiled.

'Funny, now I come to think of it. She could get quite obsessed about things at times. She collected postcards and all. I found this.' He got to his feet, went back to the cupboard and drew out an old shoe box. 'Postcards,' he said. 'Some are from abroad, from old friends of hers. Some are from me and the missus on holiday, Sardinia, I'd completely forgotten about it, lovely place, it was years ago . . . But a few of them are those paintings she pored over, but blank, like you'd buy in the gift shop. No writing on them.'

He handed Agnes the box and she flicked through the cards. There were various version of the Virgin and Child, scenes from the Passion of Our Lord.

'All blank?' She placed the box on her knees.

He nodded. 'I'll never know what she was thinking. But people are allowed their privacy, aren't they? In death as well as in life.'

'Certainly.' She hesitated. 'Detective Inspector, there was a young man, a long time ago, called Arthur. A boy, really. He went missing. He was close to Gerard St Fleur.'

He leaned back stiffly against the upholstery. He screwed up his eyes, thinking. 'Arthur,' he said. 'Arthur Cowell. I remember him. Blimey, he was trouble, he was, but, yes,

I remember the case. Gerard St Fleur was offering him a home, Ivy was involved, because she knew Mr St Fleur. She vouched for him, even went to the juvenile court. But then someone reported against Mr St Fleur, one of his friends, a priest, and Arthur was back with social services. No sign of his birth mother by then, but they found a stepfather and he was sent back there. He'd had nothing to do with him for years but he was known for his violence . . . and after that Arthur went missing. He was never found.' He tidied the cuff of his jacket. 'It does you in, a case like that. A lot of people were upset. Mr St Fleur took it very bad. But there was no one to cry for the boy. No mother, nothing. The stepfather was done some time later for GBH, a pub brawl it was, but the boy had gone by then.'

'Do you remember when Reece Bennett was stabbed to death? And Jay Sorrell was charged but then released for lack of evidence?'

'I remember that. Six, seven years ago, was it? I was technically retired, but I was still doing backroom stuff, training. I remember the fuss round here when that young man was released. But there was no evidence. His mum, Francie, was right, she fought and fought and she had truth on her side. The Bennett boy had gone armed and whoever attacked him had used his own weapon. All the evidence showed that Jason had come along after the attack. Only minutes after, but still. The odd thing was . . .' He ran his long fingers along his head. 'The way Mrs Sorrell argued, I always thought she knew more than she was letting on. Like, if you know your boy didn't kill the Bennett boy, with such certainty, why not say who you think did kill him? She didn't . . .' He hesitated. 'She seemed composed, you know. I remember thinking at the time, not like a mother defending her boy, more like someone trying to settle a legal case.' He smiled. 'I tried a few things, asked her what she was hiding, nothing, she'd say, I'm just fighting for my son. And she was a clever woman, a warm, sympathetic person. We always got on well. She always called me DI Wharton Retired because she reckoned

I'd stayed in the Job for so long. Which I did.' He smiled. 'Anyway, Jason was released and the poor Bennett family were left to grieve, in the belief that they had been denied justice. And it didn't do the Sorrell lot any good either, it was soon after that that Francie took herself off and vanished. An island somewhere, I heard. Hebrides, was it? All very odd. My sister missed her terribly, they were both at the heart of things here.'

He stretched out his long legs.

'In those days I'd keep up my visits to Mrs Bennett. Actually, I popped in just the other day. Poor woman.' He smiled. 'I had the feeling she knew more about where Aidan Preedy is, but she was keeping schtum as ever.'

Agnes handed back the box of cards. He bent, stiffly, placed it on the floor, by the sideboard which was half-draped in a dusty sheet. He straightened up, with an out-breath. 'I've got my work cut out here,' he said. 'All this still to clear.' A wave of his hand, taking in the draped furniture, the ornaments half-stacked in crates. 'The alms-house charity is helping, of course. Funny what remains of a person after they're gone. Just . . . all this.'

Agnes surveyed the room. Paintings had been taken down and now leaned against the walls. On the floor there was a cardboard box containing two china dogs, a couple of large vases, a carriage clock now stopped. She smiled. 'We had one just like that, in France, when I was a child . . .'

There was a pair of brass candlesticks. Next to them, an oak casket — square and sturdy, the wood finely polished to show the grain.

A sealed oak casket, about the size of a shoe box, Andras had said, with a large brass lock.

'What's that?' Agnes asked, pointing.

'That? Oh, the box. It was in that cabinet, there. I found it after the funeral. No idea what it is, ashes casket or something? About the right size. I've tried to open it, but it's very firmly locked. Can't find a key anywhere either.'

Agnes bent down, stroked the dusty surface.

'Tarnished,' Agnes said.

'What?'

'Nothing.' A thought, just out of reach.

'I don't know who it belongs to,' he said. 'My sister must have kept it for someone.'

Thirty pieces of silver.

She wondered what it was about this box that made it worth killing for.

'I wonder . . . might I borrow it?'

He laughed. 'If you can open it you can keep the bloody thing. No use to me.'

'I'll keep it safe, I promise. You'll have it back,' she said.

He laughed, and she got to her feet, picked up the casket, aware of its weight in her arms. 'If Ivy was keeping it for someone,' she said, holding it in front of her . . . 'you wouldn't know who?'

He stood up, led her out to the hallway. 'My sister — she might have been solitary but she was always at the centre of things. Just the sort of thing she'd do as a favour for someone. Maybe even stolen goods for all I know.' He smiled, opened the door for her, glanced out into the street, into the uncertain weather. 'You will take care, won't you, dear?' He touched the box. 'I may be retired but I'm still a detective. And it may be you know more about this than you're letting on.'

She looked up at him, at his kind, lined face. He reminded her of Julius. Julius in the before times, before all this, the burning of the church, the rage and the lying and the hiding of a past, a past so full of hurt or shame or damage that it still weighed heavily, like the wooden box that she held in her arms.

Len Wharton was looking at her. 'Perhaps it's too much for you,' he said. 'The weight of it.'

'I'll be okay,' she said.

'Well, at least your monastic training has given you strong arms,' he replied. 'And I suppose you know what you're doing.'

She thanked him, promised to return the box, set off down the well-tended path.

If only I did, she thought.

She made her way along the main road, the box held in front of her.

Burdening myself. Again.

She stumbled on her way. At the end of the road, she could see the spire of Julius's church.

I could go in, she thought. *I could say, Orla is dying.*

'I know,' he will say.

She stopped for breath, leaning against a wall, the casket between her feet.

I failed him, Julius had said. Gerard St Fleur.

Everyone failed him. All of them weighed down with it, a burden heavier even than this.

And not just him. That poor boy, Arthur, returned to his violent stepfather. Reece Bennett, stabbed with his own weapon. And now Jay Sorrell, lying in a coroner's morgue, still unburied.

She took the gallery photo out of her pocket, that she'd taken from Neave, from Ezra's bedroom.

Stuff from his dad and shit.

Why did Jay have a photo of Andras and Darius and Gerard, from years ago, standing in an art gallery?

And Julius.

Everyone knew Francie Sorrell, Neave had said.

And Jay's father? The story changed all the time where he was concerned . . . Always well dressed, always the latest things . . .

She stared at the photo, as if it was a clue, as if this faded image of four men could speak, could tell her . . . what?

She put the photo away, picked up the casket, walked some more.

The evening was gearing up for home time, the traffic noisy with anticipation. People walked fast, checked phones, gathered in bus queues.

Next week, I will have gone from here.

It seemed unreal to her. *France, my mother's home country. Not the France of my childhood but a sad place of refugees and exile. I could just stop.*

She found she was outside Julius's church. She sat on the wall, put the box down at her feet. *I could just carry it back to the almshouses, she thought, hand it back to Len, say, sooner or later it will find its home. Whoever Ivy was keeping it for will claim it. Why should I interfere? I could go back to my flat, start to pack, have a goodbye drink with Athena.*

I could go to Julius, and say, it's over. Whatever happened, with Gerard, and Darius and Andras and you . . . let it stay buried. Let Andras keep his obsessions, and Francie's statue stay wherever it is, and Orla have her last time on this earth in peace.

And we will say Jay died in the church, and maybe there was a fight with Aidan, and maybe someone did try to steal the St Fleur treasure.

It is just life.

So — why am I sitting on this wall, breathing in the busy fumes of the London evening, burdened with a locked wooden box that I can hardly carry?

She got to her feet, leaned down, lifted the casket again. *I know why.*

In her mind, she saw Ezra, in his blue and yellow bedroom, opening a crate of stuff from his dad.

She clicked on Ezra's number. It went to voicemail. 'I've got it,' she said. 'The thing you're being asked to find. That's worth all that money. I've got it.'

She sat on the wall in the warmth of the summer evening. Her phone rang. Ezra.

'Hi. Sister. It's me. Where are you? What you got?'

She described the box. 'Oak, brass lock, heavy—'

'Yeah. Whoa. That's it. Man, you've saved my fucking life.'

'Ezra — who wants it? What are they paying you?'

'No, Sister, it ain't about the money. Honour your father and mother, ain't that what they tell you? That's what I'm doing. Honouring my father.'

'And what about laying down your sword? What about not walking straight into danger?' She found she was shouting into her phone.

'There's a time for that, Sister. And this ain't that time. You need to come, now. You know where to find me.'

'No,' she said, gripped with fear — for him, for her, she wasn't sure. 'I'm outside St Simeon's, you know, Father Julius's church, you can find me there—'

He interrupted. 'I can't, Sister.' She heard the tremor in his voice. 'I'm in too deep. You've saved my life. Come now.' She knew, before he told her, where she would find him.

He ended the call.

* * *

It was a long ten-minute walk to the burned-out priory church. A chill was settling on the streets as the sun went down.

Agnes brushed past the now straggling police tape which lay across the doorway. The plywood boards were still nailed across.

The scent of cigarette smoke hung in the air.

She wandered round to the graveyard. The old oak tree loomed silently as if waiting to see what would happen next.

The side porch was free of any barrier. She put down the box, rattled the locked door.

She felt cold, hungry, stupid. And afraid.

There was a shifting overhead, a rustle of wildlife — a bird, a mouse, perhaps.

A leaf fluttered to her feet.

There's no one here, she thought. Was it just another lie from Ezra? Another way to hide?

Then, a sound, a muffled shout. From inside the church? Or outside, as a shifting, shrugging group of youths passed loudly by in the street beyond the railings.

She gathered all her strength and shoved her shoulder against the half-rotten door.

The door opened.

She was inside the church. She scanned the dank, dim shadows. From somewhere, a sound, a struggling rasp. Like breathing, or the flap of fledgling wings in the eaves.

The smell of tobacco was stronger now, and she could see, far away, the glow of the tip of a cigarette.

Then, suddenly, a beam of light, a torch, raking her up and down, a voice behind the beam. 'Ah. The boy was telling the truth after all. So, the story ends with a nun. How very appropriate.'

There was a clattering, a flick of a switch, and a light came on. It was a faded emergency lamp on the side wall, and it shed a sickly glow.

CHAPTER TWENTY

He was small, stooped under the low ceiling. His face was yellow-ish in the dim light, his clothes shabby, his hair grey and in uneven tufts. He surveyed her with an odd, thin smile.

'Sister Agnes, the boy called you. Is that your name?' His voice was an elderly, reedy whine. He stared fixedly at the casket, which she was still managing to hold in her arms. The cigarette in his fingers dropped and he nudged it out with his heel, absently.

'That is my name,' she said. Her voice was flat in the dim, damp air. She found she was standing where the font used to be, a raised, cracked stone pedestal.

'You have . . . you have it?' He pointed at the box.

She faced him. She saw the narrow features of the black-and-white photo — the peering eyes, the same hunched meanness, only older. He was wearing a faded shirt, gaping where buttons were missing, and ill-fitting dark trousers.

You are Father Darius, she thought. *You are the person who has crept through this whole story leaving a trail of pain, damage, rage and death.*

'Where's Ezra?' She spoke louder now.

'The boy is here,' he answered. 'But give me that casket.'

'And what do you think it contains?'

'I will be the judge of its contents. When I hold it in my hands.' His voice was clipped and old-fashioned. His face in the thin light was papery.

'Ezra told me to meet him here,' she said, glancing around the vaulted space, the uneasy, flickering shadows.

Again, the queasy smile. 'Sister Agnes,' he said. He shot an appraising gaze at her, taking in her jeans, battered boots and old linen jacket. 'A nun?'

'Yes, a nun.' She felt somehow taller than him, though perhaps it was the font pedestal that gave her height. 'Ezra Sorrell wants this casket. So I said I'd meet him here.'

He gave a brief, cracked laugh. 'Ezra Sorrell wants it, does he? When I have spent all these last few years working to claim what's mine.'

Behind him she could see the long nave, at the end of which was an ancient door of thick seasoned oak, black iron bolts rammed across it. A set of wooden chairs lay about the place, as if someone had pushed past them in a hurry long ago.

She put the box down on the floor and faced him. 'You drew him here. You told him the story and you offered him money, more money than he'd ever dreamed of. You thought he knew where this was. And he almost worked it out, but I got there first.'

'Good,' he said. 'And now you can give it to me.' His small eyes were fixed on the box at her feet.

'And the thirty pieces of silver?' she said, keeping her voice level.

His gaze flashed upwards. 'Don't talk to me of betrayal,' he said. 'I'm the one who was betrayed.'

High above them, a cracked window stood ajar, its long hooked pole leaning uselessly against the wall. The sounds of late evening traffic wafted in from outside.

Agnes took a long breath. She sat down, settling on the old stone pedestal, and gathered the box onto her lap. 'A story, then,' she said. 'Shall we start at the beginning?'

He fiddled in his pocket for another cigarette, lit it with shaking hands. The match dropped at his feet.

Agnes spoke again. 'Father Darius — what do you think is in this box?'

'I know what's in that box.'

'The Judas chalice,' she said. Her mind filled with doubts; what if the box was empty? And where was Ezra, when he'd promised he'd be here?

'The Judas chalice,' he echoed. 'Believed lost. But it's mine.' He drew a long, trembling drag of his cigarette.

'That's funny,' she said. 'Because Dr Andras Swift also claimed that the Judas chalice was lost years ago and that it was his. He's been looking for it ever since.'

A flicker in his narrow gaze. 'That man is a fake.' His lips were moist. 'A liar then and a liar now.'

Agnes faced him. 'You were here, that night, that Jay Sorrell died.'

His expression didn't change.

'You raided the safe. What a shame it was empty.'

A twitch of feeling in his eyes.

'You must have been very disappointed. Angry, even.'

'They took it away.' He shook his head. 'They took it all before I could get to them.'

'And you raided Julius's office too.'

'Not me,' he said. 'Oh no. I was outmanoeuvred.'

'But now, this.' She tapped the casket with a finger.

He eyed it silently.

There were the sounds of the dusk outside, passing cars, a distant siren, a bedtime cawing from the crows above.

Darius shifted his weight from foot to foot. After a while he sat down, taking one of the scattered wooden chairs. He looked at her.

'So a nun. I knew some of the Sisters when I was here before. The old Priory Convent.'

'Benedictines,' she said. 'Most of them moved out to Oxfordshire, didn't they?'

He nodded. 'Not many of them left by then. Falling vocations. A faithless world.'

'And you,' she asked. 'Are you still a priest?'

187

He hesitated briefly, his attention on the casket. 'Retired.'

'Ah.'

'Comes to us all,' he said, with his same small smile.

She took a breath. 'The thing is, Father Darius, in order to find this casket, I followed a trail. A long and tangled story, which twists unpleasantly around the lives, and deaths, of several people. And finally I found this box. And I carried it here, because Ezra asked me to. I brought it in the hope that it would be the end of the story.'

He was staring at the box. 'So, are you going to give it to me?' His voice was loud now.

'They say the chalice grants absolution,' she said.

He nodded, as if in agreement. 'An old medieval idea. But there's truth in it.'

'The Judas kiss. The final betrayal between two friends. I wonder why the medieval engraver chose that image.'

'It made it very rare,' he said. 'Very valuable.'

'Which one? The one that was given to you, after Gerard died? Or this one?'

There was a rustling above them. Flakes of plaster floated from the roof.

'I don't know what you mean,' he said.

She placed the box on the cold stone step. 'Six and a half years ago,' she began, with a storytelling tone, 'you made a huge and painful discovery. You tried to sell the chalice that you'd been given, and you were told it was a fake. The pain of that betrayal made you angry. You went to see Iris St Fleur, tried to explain, but she didn't listen.'

He was nodding with pretend encouragement. 'Do go on, Sister.'

'You came back to this area, in search of the truth. You confronted Andras, and got nowhere. You tried to talk to Father Julius too, but he wouldn't see you. Why was that, Darius?'

'Ah, so it's Julius who's put you up to this? I knew it.'

'No,' she said. 'Julius has turned away from me because of this.'

He eyed her. 'Really?'

She nodded, but he stayed silent.

She sighed. 'Let's try again. Six and a half years ago, you came back to claim the real chalice, to take revenge on the fakers. You got nowhere, but you had a trump card, a secret that you thought only you knew. And it involved Jason Sorrell. You thought that he was the route to the real chalice, the one you believed you were owed. And so you tried to see him. You tracked him down at Connie Bennett's house. But instead of being alone with Jay, you were ambushed by Connie's son Reece who got there first, who challenged you about Arthur Cowell and what you knew about his disappearance. He was fond of Arthur, he'd been like a big brother to Reece. You tried to leave, but instead of shaking Reece off, he followed you to the old church grounds. The silly boy carried a knife. Maybe there was a struggle, but one way or the other you managed to seize it. You lashed out and struck him, fatally as it turned out. You fled, just before Jay arrived. Did you watch as he tried to save his friend?'

He said nothing, just smiled blandly.

'Jay was initially charged with manslaughter, but then released. But that was why I began to wonder, why the silence? Francie and Jay must have known more than they were telling.'

'This is nothing more than a story.' His smile seemed stuck to his face. 'Any more fairy tales, Sister?'

'Then just a few weeks ago,' she went on, 'Orla St Fleur went to see Jay. The same Orla St. Fleur who had denied you the chalice all those years ago. Jay must have phoned you after she'd been to see him. His wife, Neave, overheard him call it a reckoning.'

His thin lips tightened.

'So you came back. You made some kind of deal with him. You were now convinced that Jay knew where the real chalice was. And, as you believed you were the trustee of a secret that concerned him, you agreed to meet him here, certain perhaps that he would bring the casket with him.'

He was motionless, waiting, his head on one side.

Again, an image of Ezra, throwing things out of a crate, searching, for something.

A load of old rubbish, knowing Jay.

My sister was looking after it for someone..

She faced him. 'Jay Sorrell knew that the chalice held the key to his story too. He was friends with Ivy Wharton, the sister of DI Wharton, and he'd entrusted the casket to her. You knew why the chalice had come to him and you were going to tell him. But he arrived empty-handed. And the same rage that erupted when Reece challenged you erupted once again.'

'Fanciful,' he muttered, rocking to and fro.

'And now—' she was trying to keep her voice level, staring at the blank, sneering smile, 'now I need you to tell me where Ezra is. Ezra's father, Jay, came here on the night he died. And you were here too.'

He shook his head.

'Orla had contacted Jay. It was urgent she talk to him and you saw your chance. Promising him, what? The missing piece of the jigsaw? The one truth she didn't share with him. The truth of his paternity.'

He tutted, shaking his head.

'You promised Jay the key to the truth about the St Fleur family, and their connections to his own mother, Francie. That's the only explanation as to why there was a box with all those old photos, including one of you with Andras and with Gerard. And yet,' she went on, stretching out her legs, 'Jay must have had his own reason to confront you. I've been trying to work out what that reason was. It must have had something to do with the shifting fortunes of the St Fleur family. And Jay, knowing that you're tied to those fortunes in some way, contacted you. And when he did, you seized the chance. You lured him here, with empty promises. But there was a price — one he couldn't pay.'

In her mind she saw Julius, the pain in his eyes as he asked her to leave.

Who was Gerard St. Fleur? she had asked him. That's when he'd told her to go.

Agnes touched the photograph in her pocket. She heard Iris's words, 'a brief love affair, just before he died . . .'

Gerard. And Francie.

She felt the paper between her fingers, heard the truth click gently into place.

'Gerard was Jay's father,' she said. 'And Jay agreed to meet you because you promised you would tell him the truth. But he never left.'

Darius's expression had changed, grown heavy-lidded and grey as stone.

'Father Julius knew,' Agnes went on. 'Gerard entrusted him with the truth. Swore him to secrecy. Made him promise . . . It was a promise too heavy to bear.' Her voice caught. 'But he kept it all the same.'

He was moving his head in a twitch of denial.

'Jay had worked it out. Orla told him the truth about his inheritance, but she left out half the story and he turned to you to tell him the rest. You were already at the church, already angry at finding the safe empty. And so you suggested you meet here, in the belief that you would get the greatest treasure of all. This — this casket. But he came empty-handed — and because of that, he never left.'

He straightened up. 'Have you finished? Because that box is mine and I'd quite like you to hand it over now.'

'What will you do with it?' She met his dull gaze. 'You can't try to sell it again,' she said. 'The last chalice you tried to sell was fake. No one would risk doing business with you, you're tainted.'

'I'd find someone.'

'You were outwitted.'

'Bastards.' The word was a shout.

'Andras used his contacts to create a perfect fake. And Gerard had hidden the real one away.'

'Gerard promised me . . .'

'He didn't trust you.'

191

'None of this is true.' He flicked his tongue against his lips.

'What will you do, Darius?'

He was shaking his head from side to side. 'Bastards,' he murmured. 'Lying fucking bastards, making stuff up again . . .'

Another shake of his head.

'Ezra had worked it all out,' she said. 'He contacted you. And once again, you saw your chance. You lured him here, as you'd lured his father. But he, too, came empty-handed. He knew what he was looking for, but, like you, he didn't know where to find it. And he came here sensing danger, like his father did. Were you angry, then? Angry enough to murder, just as you had before?'

She watched him, his gaze fixed on the box. She found herself praying that Ezra was still alive. She steadied her voice. 'You must realise the game's up. It's over. You'll be charged with Reece's death, with Jay's death, with kidnap. But if you tell me where Ezra is it might help.'

'Why should I tell you anything? They are all fucking liars. I have done nothing wrong.'

'When you meet your God,' she said, 'what will he say to you?'

A slight flinch of his face. 'I'm not here to exchange pleasantries with you.' He stared at the box by her feet. 'Now give that to me. It's mine. You have no right to take it. Gerard told me it was treasure beyond value. And he told me it was mine.'

'And if I don't?'

He looked up at her with an odd, awkward smile. 'The question is, Sister — who is going to believe you?' He shifted on his chair. 'I can't imagine your Order is going to be very pleased with you, behaving like this. Surely they expect better of you. Blundering in here, making all kinds of false accusations against me. So, I suggest we pretend that none of these accusations have happened, and that you hand over the chalice and go on your way. And I promise in turn that I shall keep quiet about your behaviour, and not, for example, report you to your Order.'

The threatening tone made her want to laugh. 'Oh,' she challenged, 'go ahead. Nothing will surprise my superiors about me.'

His expression hardened. 'You need to leave. Go now and leave the casket behind you.'

She felt her fists clench. She imagined running at him, her blow colliding with that tight, even smile. She took a breath. 'You know the guilt you're carrying. The only reason Jay came to this church was because of you and you are the reason he never left it.'

'No one will believe you,' he repeated. His voice echoed in the chill of the space around them.

'When did it go wrong for you, Darius?'

'Me?' He smiled.

'When did you become this — this—'

'This what?'

She thought of Winifred, stockpiling sedatives. She wondered what weapon might come to hand now.

Suddenly he tumbled to his feet, stepped towards the box where it sat on the floor between them. 'You don't understand, Sister.' He stared down at her. 'What did you hope to gain, bringing a locked casket here? It's of no use to either of us, is it? You can't open it. No one has been able to open it, not for years. Those women, those old women—'

'Gerard's sisters.'

'They've had their share. This is mine.'

His arms were lifted as he advanced towards her, and she wondered if he was going to hit her, his arm stuck oddly out in front of his body as if to put a stop to something. Then, he dropped his arm, stood over the box as if guarding it. 'It's mine.' His voice was thick. He crouched down by the box, rested one hand on it. 'Gerard promised this to me. This is mine.' He raised his face to her, spots of red rage on his cheeks. 'And here you are, talking rubbish about some boy, this Albert or Arthur or whoever he is, as if I know anything about him, and bringing me this box as if to do a deal with me?' He laughed his empty laugh.

Agnes eyed the hooked window pole by the wall, imagining herself bringing it down hard on his head.

He stood up, still smiling, and now seemed to be doing a dance, stepping from foot to foot as he rummaged in his trouser pocket. She realised then that he was holding a key, a big, old-fashioned, brass key.

'Ha ha,' he said, holding it up. 'As you said, I have the key. Jay was right. Gerard gave me the spare key for safe-keeping. I always knew the time would come when I would need it.'

He knelt by the box. His breath was in short bursts, his lips flecked white.

Agnes stood back and watched.

The key turned, stiffly. The lock clicked open. He lifted the lid.

He reached inside. There was a cloth — 'Ah, they've kept it well,' he murmured. He pulled on the cloth and began to draw it out.

It was thick linen, painted in bright colours. It unfolded as he tugged it, a huge roll of fabric now, images appearing, savage lines of black, splashes of scarlet, great lengths of it now emerging from its resting place.

A cross. Human hands, feet. Blood.

'What . . . ?' He pulled some more. Scenes from the life of Christ, she realised. The last inches of the long painting spilled over the edge of the box and rested on the old stone floor. She could see at the edge, two men, their arms entwined.

He peered into the box. 'Empty?' He picked it up, shook it, put it down, turned to the linen, ruffled its edges. 'Empty?' he said again.

The cloth painting was strewn against the pedestal where the font had been. It showed a cross, huge and bare, a wide black beam dripping with red. The background was sky blue, with splashes of white. Dark lines of paint traced the two figures at the foot of the cross, the dead man, the weeping

194

mother, the detail of their pale faces luminous against the jagged chaos.

Agnes looked at it. 'Gerard's painting,' she whispered. '*The Keld Shroud.*'

'But—'

'That's what he meant by the treasure locked away.'

He crumpled, as if the air had been sucked from him. He sat heavily on the step amidst the furls of fabric.

Agnes sat down next to him. 'Where is Ezra?' she said.

He shook his head. 'Cheated,' he murmured. He faced her. 'The chalice . . . to put a stop . . . Everything.'

'Is Ezra alive?' she said.

'I trusted him. Gerard. I counted him as a friend. He cheated me.'

'You killed his son.'

He was silent, still shaking his head, staring at the flag-stones at his feet. Then, suddenly, he jumped to his feet.

'You,' he yelled, jabbing his finger at her. 'I don't know how you came by this box, but I tell you, I've been cheated. Bringing me these daubs of Gerard's instead of the thing itself. That boy, lying to me, I offered him half the value, he told me he knew where it was, and now, what — *that*—' The last word was a shout, as he pointed at the shroud. 'I've a good mind to get the law on you . . .' He was darting glances around him, stepping from foot to foot, shouting, 'I've been cheated . . .' He glanced at the cloister, at the old door with its iron bolts, then at the main door, as he swivelled fast and headed at a run towards it.

'You won't get away— ' Agnes was on her feet, ready to follow him, but Darius was at the door, tugging at the lock and cursing.

A loud crash from the back of the church stopped him, followed by an echoing creak as the old oak door opened. A single male figure stood, silhouetted by the streetlight beyond the window. He was holding a gun, and he spoke.

'You'd better stop right there,' he said. 'I heard every fucking word, so-called Father fucking Darius.'

Darius froze. 'Ezra.'

Ezra stepped into the light. The pistol was small, black, fixed in his steady hand. 'Come away from the door, you little man.'

Darius took two slow steps towards him.

With a jerk of his head, Ezra indicated a chair. 'Sit down.'

Darius didn't move.

'I said, *sit down.*'

Darius sat. His gaze was fixed on the gun. 'Dear boy,' he began, 'there's really no need—'

'Shut the fuck up.'

Ezra turned to Agnes. 'Sister, I owe you. You brought what I asked for. How were we to know?' He indicated with his free hand the rough pile of linen, the splashes of colour spread out on the church stone. 'This,' he said. 'Because of this, my father died. The St. Fleur treasure. All that fucking bloodshed.' The gun was still steady in his hand, still pointed at Darius. 'Like I said, Sister, the old stories. This priest here, with the darkness in his soul, he knows something my dad didn't know. And he thinks that what he knows has a price. He's waiting for silver and all he gets is this.' He touched the edge of the shroud with his foot. 'The artist's pain. The St. Fleur treasure painted in red and black. My inheritance.' He gave an empty laugh. 'I worked it out. This.' A glance towards the shroud. My father's father.' He gave a small smile. 'I found them photos. I began to think. At school, they think I'm shit at everything. Except art. Takes them by surprise every fucking time.' His voice cracked. The fingers gripped tighter round the gun, but his arm was shaking now.

Darius's eyes, fixed on the pistol, narrowed. He shifted his weight, began to stand.

'Don't move,' Ezra said.

'Why? What are you going to do?' Darius had regained his tightened, English voice. 'Are you really going to shoot me?' He got to his feet.

Agnes stood, watching as they faced each other, the boy and the man.

'I really can't imagine it's a terribly good idea,' Darius said.

'You don't deserve to live.' Ezra's voice was shaking with his aim. 'You killed my dad.'

'And if I'm dead, you have no proof. You'll just be another statistic, another kid in a prison cell. What use is your so-called inheritance then, eh?'

'Shut the fuck up.' Ezra was shouting, his pistol hand shifting.

'Just a boy from the wrong side of the tracks.' Darius began to move towards the door.

Agnes eyed the long window pole again.

'Don't move or I'll shoot,' Ezra called out, but his voice sounded thin in the echoing space, and then there was another sound, the loud lifting of a door latch.

The main door moved, creaked. They looked up. There was a shaft of light as the church door swung open.

A woman stood there, small and straight-backed and illumined, her black-grey curls haloed by the moonlight.

Darius gasped out loud, as if he'd seen a ghost.

Francie Sorrell, Agnes thought, just as Darius breathed her name.

'Yes,' the woman said. 'It's me.' Her voice rang clear against the old stones. 'I've come to get my boy.'

CHAPTER TWENTY-ONE

Francie stepped into the church. She was wearing a neatly buttoned coat and low-heeled shoes. She glanced down at the painting, where it lay spread out on the floor. 'I remember it,' she said. 'I remember him working on that. His Turin Shroud, he called it. *The Shroud of Keld.*' She smiled. 'You must be Sister Agnes. I'm pleased to meet you.'

She advanced further into the nave. 'Haven't been here for a while,' she said, looking around. 'Changed a lot since my days. A thriving church it was, all them years ago. And now a ruin, look at it.'

Ezra was staring, the pistol still held out in front of him, now with both hands grasping it. His eyes were fixed on Francie, as she walked towards him until she stood right in front of him. She touched the gun with a finger. 'You can put that down now, Esau,' she said, and her voice was soft and firm and loving. 'I'm here now. Everything's okay.'

He seemed to crumple, his towering height folding into her, as she put her arms around him.

Father Darius stood, motionless, gaping.

Francie was making soothing sounds, her arms round Ezra as she led him to a chair. His hands were empty, now, the gun swiftly pocketed and nowhere to be seen.

'My poor boy,' she was saying.

Darius found his voice. 'Mrs Sorrell.'

Francie addressed Agnes. 'I ain't talking to that man over there, because he don't deserve the time of day, let alone me to speak to him direct, not after all that he has done to lead himself right to the fiery flames. Cos that's where he's headed. From where he is now to Hell itself, it's a damned straight line.'

Darius straightened himself, took a step, still with his gaze fixed on Ezra. Ezra was leaning into his grandmother, his eyes closed. Darius took another step towards the door.

Agnes tried to speak, tried to shout, stop —

'Don't you worry, Sister.' Francie's voice rang out. 'That piece of filth ain't going nowhere.'

Darius was now at the front door, but then there was brightness outside and noise, shouts and running feet and the door flung wide in a blaze of white and flashing blue.

'Police,' said a voice.

Francie held out a hand. 'DI Wharton Retired, am I glad to see you.'

CHAPTER TWENTY-TWO

It had played out like a film, Agnes told Athena afterwards, although as Athena said, it wasn't a film, it was real bloody life and 'It's just as well he didn't kill you, frankly, a murderous psychopath like that, and there's you sitting there all night having a chat with him, I know what you're like, you thought if only you could engage him in conversation you'd find out what had made him as he is, but the truth is, people like that don't deserve to be understood, there is such a thing as evil you know . . .'

Now they sat on cold benches in the police station corridor, Francie, Ezra and Agnes. A chill dawn filtered muted daylight through the windows above them.

Ezra had called his mum, listened, nodded, said, 'Yeah, safe, yeah, love you, yeah, love you . . .'

Now he held his grandmother's hand as if afraid to let it go.

'Orla told me what was going on,' Francie said. 'I saw then that it was time to come back.'

'Where were you?' Ezra's eyes scanned her face.

'I had to get away,' she said. 'After Reece was killed, after Jay was charged, and we got him released — but the chat, the way people looked at me, all the awfulness. I knew that Reece had challenged that wicked man. I knew Reece's death was something to do with that.' She hesitated. 'I knew what my Jay was capable of too. But . . . I knew in my heart he hadn't killed his friend. And I told anyone who'd listen. But then . . .' She looked at her hands, held as tight fists in her lap.

'That wicked man, they just left him right alone. And me, I wasn't sure. I knew him as a father of the Church. For a God-fearing woman like me, that means something. I know now, I could have done more. I could have pursued him down that path of justice. But where I was, in the community, in the Church . . . I just wanted it all to go away.

'It was a kind of breakdown, I guess. I was supposed to be a pillar of the community, and I felt hollow, empty. Dead. I knew that Jay was innocent. I told myself I didn't know the truth. And in a way, I guess I didn't. Not then. I didn't sleep, didn't eat. It was Orla who saw, Orla who could see that I was departing from them all, departing from life. It was her idea. To disappear. She promised me that I could come back when I felt the time was right.'

'So you disappeared.' Ezra kept his eyes were fixed on her. 'Like none of us needed you? Like I didn't need you?' There was a sharp edge to his voice.

She turned to him. 'You were the only one I was loath to leave. I hesitated so many times. But I would have gone the way of Gerard had I stayed. Orla was the only one who knew where I was. She let me know what was happening, my ear to the ground. But then my poor son was found dead . . . That's when I knew my days as a statue were numbered.'

Ezra turned to Agnes. 'I told you,' he said. 'Told you a statue could come back to life.'

'I wish my faith was as strong as yours,' Agnes answered.

Francie laughed. 'You know, I could do with a cup of tea. In the old days, coppers always kept you fed and watered.'

The door opened, and Len Wharton stood there. He was holding a tray on which stood three mugs. 'Ah yes,' he said. 'I remember those days. Milk? Sugar?'

He distributed the tea. 'Father Darius Samaras will be remanded in custody. Accused of the murder of Reece Bennett and Jay Sorrell, and the attempted kidnap of this one.' He patted Ezra on the head. 'And I thought I'd retired.'

Francie glanced at the oak casket which was sitting at their feet, then turned to Agnes. 'The chalice. For all you knew, that's what this box was.'

'They were after it, those men,' Agnes said. 'That's all I knew.'

Francie looked at Ezra. 'And what no one had worked out, till now — is that the only inheritor of all of it, of all the St. Fleur estate — is you.'

Two sisters, Agnes thought. *Orla and Iris. And poor Gerard, who died, leaving Jay. And now . . .*

'Me.' Ezra looked up at Francie. 'A St Fleur.' He smiled. 'I kind of worked it out, but now you say it like that . . . And all the time I thought I had to fight. Thought that box would give me the power to fight the man who killed my dad. Thought I could pick up my sword and walk towards the battle.'

Francie touched his hand. 'Esau, dear. It's a lesson. When to be still, and when to go to war. You ask Agnes here, it's a lesson she's yet to learn.'

Agnes laughed, and Francie smiled. 'And one more thing, Esau dear.' She bent to her handbag and brought out the pistol. 'I'm giving this to DI Wharton Retired. I'm hoping he won't ask no questions, but if he does — you tell the lad who lent it to you that he ain't getting it back, no way.' She touched the casket with her foot. 'Everyone thought this box was the chalice. But the funny is, I know where that chalice is.'

* * *

In the car, the two passengers sat in silence, yawning. 'I'm sorry about the lack of space,' Agnes had said, as they'd headed west away from central London, the finely tuned engine humming softly. 'It's a lovely car but not designed for families.'

'I suppose nuns don't need family vehicles,' Francie said.

'Ah. Not nuns. I've, um, borrowed it,' Agnes said.

Francie was in the passenger seat, Ezra was squashed into the back seat, dozing quietly.

'Careful—' Francie touched her arm as the engine roared beneath their feet. 'It's a fifty limit here. Or don't the cameras work for nuns?'

'Let's hope not.'

'You go left at the roundabout,' Francie said. 'Speed humps after that, even a nun is going to have to go slow.'

* * *

The house in Harrow was one in a long, tree-lined avenue. They pulled into the neat drive. Ezra unfurled himself from the back seat.

Orla let them in, taking Francie's hand as she led them into the hallway.

'Sister Agnes,' she said.

'Not quite Keld.' Agnes smiled at her.

'London suburbs.' Orla put her other hand in Agnes's. 'Such a relief when Iris insisted on staying in Suffolk, Harrow suits me just fine.'

The kitchen was large and light. It had cream-painted wood panelling, and two small arched stained-glass windows — 'I knocked through,' Orla said. 'That was the old dining room over there.'

She made tea. They sat in silence, hugging their mugs. Occasionally Agnes would catch Ezra staring at Francie, as if waiting to wake from a dream.

'I had to hide,' Francie said. 'I couldn't think what else to do. I was desperate. I couldn't live with myself. When Gerard died . . . the thing is, it's not as if I was a secret. But it was a strange, odd, passion. We were brought together through the suffering of others, which might sound noble but actually it's a crap way to start a love affair. And a short-lived one at that. And then I found I was pregnant. And for Gerard . . .' She shook her head. 'He said, give me time. I'll step up, trust me. But give me time.' And he took refuge, in his studio, in his art, in searing the blood of saints on to canvas. So, I gave him time, I raised my boy, I waited. And then he darned well goes and hangs himself, and so I'm destined to be hid, my boy destined not to have a father.'

She glanced at Orla. 'Orla saved me, not for first time, certainly not the last. And then when I really couldn't see a way out, Orla found me a place to hide.'

Orla took her spoon out of her mug. 'It came to me that she could go to Barra. The old Hebridean cottage, from my grandmother's family. No one there would know who she was.'

'I loved it,' Francie said. 'I might settle there,' she said. 'No one there who looks like me, but then no one there who looks like anyone else. I was happy, apart from . . .' She glanced at Ezra. 'I wanted you to know. But I couldn't think how to let you know without bringing danger to you and to my boy . . . and in the end . . .' her eyes welled with tears, 'in the end, I couldn't save him.'

Ezra reached out a hand towards her. 'You got me now,' he said.

Orla got to her feet. 'Shall we go?'

They went out of the back door into the garden. At the end of the garden was a large shed. Orla drew a key from her pocket and inserted it into the padlock, then opened the wooden door.

As her eyes adjusted, Agnes saw an open space, neat shelving lined with clean empty flower pots, several torches of varying size and a tool box. A large brush hung on the wall. Sealed packing cases sat along one side of the floor. On the other, a long, wrapped human-shaped form lay on its side.

'The statue,' Agnes said. 'How the hell did you get it here?'

'The removals men were very good,' Orla said. 'I brought them along the lane at the back.'

She bent to the foot of the statue, the pedestal. She pointed the beam of a torch at it.

Nestling within the pedestal was a glint of silver.

'We had it fixed in here,' she said. 'The hollow base.'

'That's why you stole the statue,' Agnes said. 'Julius wouldn't believe me.'

'Ah, Julius. How is he? Still cross with you? It won't last. I know the man well,' Orla said. 'Almost as well as you do.'

Francie had retrieved the chalice, and now held it up. 'All that wickedness, for this. The Judas kiss. Like Gerard's painting.'

'If Darius wasn't so stupid he might have seen the symbolism,' Orla said. Ezra was standing next to her, and she turned to him and suddenly wrapped him in her arms. 'My brother's grandson,' she said, and her eyes filled with tears. 'You are . . . you are family.'

Francie gazed at them. 'The land is returned,' she said.

He looked at her. 'What, like all this is mine?' He shook his head. 'Just don't go breathing a word to my mum.' He took the chalice and examined it, turned to Agnes 'Do you think it saves you from Hell?'

'There's a very long answer to that,' Agnes said.

'And what's the short answer?'

'That will take some time too,' she said, and Ezra laughed, and Francie smiled, and Orla put her arm round her. 'Come on,' she said. 'It must be time for lunch.'

CHAPTER TWENTY-THREE

'To be honest, if I were them—' Julius looked across at Agnes 'I'd keep Gerard's wonderful artwork and give that awful chalice to a museum.'

Agnes laughed. There was a lightness about the day, the late June sunshine through the leaded windows, the twittering of nesting birds outside. She wondered how this had come about, sitting here drinking tea with Julius as if nothing had happened, as if the scalded fault line in their friendship had somehow healed on its own.

'Or, in fact,' he continued, 'give Gerard's shroud to one of the top art galleries in the country and make them promise to put it on display. It's a wonderful thing.' He smiled. 'Gerard would have loved the theatre of its reappearance too.'

'I suppose theatre is the word,' Agnes said. 'If theatre means a man half-crazed with rage, a boy half-dead from dehydration and a ragtag collection of coppers coming to the rescue.'

'I can see the musical right now.'

She smiled at him. 'Silly old Julius.'

'And Ezra, being the heir.' He shook his head. 'He'll need a trustee. A lad like that owning half of Suffolk . . .'

'Ezra was going on about his mum and her dream of a huge kitchen with a central island and underfloor heating.'

'Well, it's true, it's years since I was there but Keld certainly needs updating and she sounds like just the person.' He glanced across at the sand timer on his mantelpiece. 'I'll have to give this back to Orla now. And the book. It was written by an anonymous monk, probably Benedictine, fourteenth century. It needs to be in a rare books collection, not lying around here. It's called *On the Nature of Forgiveness*. Timely, given how badly I've behaved where you're concerned.'

She shook her head.

He was silent. Then he said, 'You were right. And I was wrong.'

'You couldn't know—'

'Those past entanglements, promising to keep secrets . . . it was bad for me. Bad for us all. There was darkness at the heart of things, and when it erupted into the light I chose to run away. I'm sorry, Agnes.'

She found there were tears in her eyes. She reached across and took his hand.

'I bet Athena had strong words of disapproval where I was concerned,' he said. 'And I deserve them all.'

'She concluded you'd been kidnapped by aliens and replaced with a body-double.'

He smiled, clapped his hands together, laughed. 'The only rational explanation, as ever,' he said. 'It certainly felt like it.' He took her hand again. 'All those years ago . . .' Julius gazed down at her fingers on his own. 'Gerard and Francie Sorrell — it was a small moment in their lives. The relationship was wrong for both of them, but Jay was the result. They made a pact, forged in silence and secrecy. At the time I was the only one to say, "What about the baby?" I knew there would come a time when he needed to know the truth. And so, I became the guardian of that truth, sworn to secrecy. Eventually Francie told Orla as well. We were the only two people in the world who knew who Jay's father was.' He sighed, took his hand away from hers. 'And then the truth began to seep out from around the edges of other people's wants, other people's reckonings and it all became dangerous. That awful man, lurking round the edges of our friendship, and the other one, Anselm or whatever he calls himself now. And all I did was turn away.'

'Your hands were tied,' Agnes said.

He shook his head. 'The awful one, the one they've arrested . . . it was always his own interests, money, status, power. He must have got wind of the truth, of Gerard and Francie. Biding his time until he could use it for his own ends. Even as far as taking a life. He always was deranged.' He nudged his spectacles further up his nose. 'I should have been more brave,' he said.

They listened to the cooing of the wood pigeons on the roof.

'I wish I'd seen it,' he smiled. 'Francie Sorrell come back to life. I wish I'd seen that man's face.'

'It was . . .'

'Redemptive? Or is that asking too much?'

'No,' she said. 'Not redemptive. When the police led him out, he just shouted at everyone, said he was the wronged man. Still shouting when they loaded him into the van, in handcuffs.'

'I bet you wanted to hit him,' Julius said.

'It's a miracle I didn't,' she said.

'At the time . . .' He fiddled his mug mat into a circle. 'When Gerard died — I did hit him. Very hard.'

'You did?'

He gave a small nod. 'It was the way he stood there, being the wronged person. Being aggrieved. I couldn't bear it. I punched him in the face and walked away.'

Agnes smiled at him. 'You should have told me.'

'I couldn't. That's what was so awful. Silenced.'

'Sister Winifred tried to kill an abusive priest once,' Agnes said.

'Did she succeed?'

She shook her head. 'Her Order moved her on before she could.'

'Ah.' He sighed. 'Shame.'

She smiled.

Julius leaned back on his chair, fiddled with a pencil on his desk. 'But — how did you know? Taking that box, you had no idea what was in it, turning up at the church, and there's that awful man, and that poor brave boy.'

'I knew it had a meaning for everyone. I just hoped I was right.'

'An act of faith,' Julius said.

'Playing detective, Rob Coombes would call it.'

'It was a symbol of betrayal,' Julius said. 'That's at the heart of all of this. Gerard died, the way he did, and we were all flung apart. I should have done more, I should have kept an eye on Jay, but I didn't feel it was my place. Orla became a recluse. Francie was a shadow of herself. And then, as you know, disappeared completely.'

'And then all these years later, Jay died.'

'By then I couldn't see a way of telling the truth. But I was wrong. Deeply wrong.'

'Julius — you did nothing wrong.'

'I should have told Jay what I knew of his father.'

'But you'd promised Gerard you wouldn't.'

A pause, a sip of coffee.

'It was Andras who betrayed Darius,' she said.

'They're as bad as each other,' Julius said.

'He organised a fake. To get rid of him.'

'That must have taken some skill,' he said. 'I wondered why Darius went so quiet.'

'It was only when he tried to sell it, a few years later,' she said, 'that he found out.'

Julius shook his head. 'I always thought that man was capable of killing. And to call himself a priest . . . even in those days he was a fraud. That's why I hit him.'

They sipped their tea in silence.

'So,' Agnes said. 'Francie disappeared and the statue was made, with the chalice at its base. And all that time, Ivy Wharton had that casket with *The Keld Shroud*.'

'It makes sense,' he said. 'Gerard was very fond of her. They'd go to art galleries together. Before he died, he'd asked her to look after a few things. At some point she passed the crate of papers to Jay, but in the chaos of his life he'd ignored it. I guess she didn't know what to do with the casket, so she just kept it. And then her death brought Andras back, sniffing around. He knew Gerard had been close enough to Ivy to leave her some of his possessions. He must have wondered if she had it all that time. He knew at some point the trail of the fake would lead back to him, and so finding the real one took on new urgency.'

'What about these other things?'

'Orla thought everything was in the church safe,' he said. 'When she came back for Ivy's funeral, she asked me to look after them.'

'And then Ezra got interested in the crate of stuff.'

'But no one, not even Orla, knew where the shroud was.'

Outside, the busy cooing and cheeping was drowned out by a burst of loud drilling.

'Broadband,' Julius said. 'Or was it water? They put a note through the door last week.'

He picked up his mug, turned it a quarter turn. 'Gerard was very brave. And also very vulnerable. I loved him, Agnes. We all did.'

'Iris said he was like that. People adored him.'

'He was extraordinary. Good-looking, charming. There was a kind of grace about him, he moved like a cat. His death was unbearable.'

'And all that time I was stuck in the school up in Yorkshire, feeling sorry for myself.'

She remembered now, how Julius had seemed different after that. But she'd had her own crisis, as usual.

He shook his head.

'That's why I was so resistant to your questions . . . After Gerard's death, I felt I was to blame. Orla tried to stay in touch, and I sent her away. It was only when you started asking about it that I realised the rage was still there.

Untouched.' He turned his mug another quarter turn. 'You know, if that man were here, now, standing in front of me — I'd thump him again.'

Agnes smiled.

He picked up the chalice, studied the detailed figures. 'Judas the betrayer. But was he acting out God's plan? Did he have to be the betrayer, because someone had to be? And then he still died horribly. But was that his destiny? Or is there is a place for disobedience. Discernment,' he said. 'The greatest paradox of faith. All the abuse of our church comes from people claiming that they're doing God's work. It's a constant stain.'

They sat in silence.

'What will Francie do now?' he said.

'She wants to move back to the island. There's a community school there, which she thinks will be good for Ezra in his school holidays. There's a rewilding project, flowers, animals, I don't know, beavers, maybe? Badgers . . . ?'

Julius laughed. 'For a French countrywoman, you're the most urban person I know.'

He reached across to the timer, and turned it over. Once more they watched the filtering sand.

'I hope you'll be all right in France,' he said.

'Athena says I'll do nothing but complain. The accommodation, the food, that endless Calais drizzle . . .'

'. . . the lack of proper bathrooms, no clean towels . . .'

'Do you two text each other?'

He smiled. 'We both know you very well, that's all.'

They watched the sand settle in the lower glass.

'You'll be back, that's the main thing.'

'Yes,' she agreed. 'I'll be back.'

'You can grumble to me then.'

She laughed. 'As a wise man I know once said, taking vows doesn't make us saints.'

'Faith makes fools of us all. Believing we can make a difference, against all the evidence.' He looked up. 'When do you set out?'

'Monday. The day after tomorrow.'

He nodded. 'Come and see me before you go.'

'I will. Of course.' She stood up to leave. As he went to open the door, he stopped. 'We may be fools,' he said. 'But the alternative is worse.'

She smiled up at him. 'I'll stick with being a fool then.'

'You can still complain about the bathrooms,' he said.

He put his arms around her and held her. He began to say something, but she put a finger against his lips. They stood like that for some moments, and then she left.

Out in the street, she blinked at the dazzling sunlight. She thought about friendship, and the trickle of time, and the endless Calais drizzle.

CHAPTER TWENTY-FOUR

Her flat was cosy in the early evening sunlight. A large suit-case lay open on the floor, and strewn across it was a tumble of jumpers, jeans, hairbrushes, a sponge bag, travel slippers. *Slippers? In that mud? You'd be better off with Wellingtons, sweetie, you're hardly going for a fashion show . . .*

Sunday evening. What a weekend it had been.

Yesterday, a meeting with Ginny, afternoon tea in Marylebone. 'Meringues,' she'd said. 'Like in the old days with my grandmother.' Ginny was talkative, delighted to see her again, 'We must keep in touch, Andras is a changed man, you know, such a heavy burden he was keeping with all that silliness with that piece of tin, so glad it's all come to light and he knows where the real one is now, you do have it to show him, don't you? He's on his way now, I told him where we'd be, he's a temperamental old git — is that how you say it? But I love him.'

'Well, I don't actually have it on me,' Agnes said. 'Given that it's a rare and priceless medieval artefact that even the museum that Orla's been in touch with was nervous about keeping safe.'

'Museum? Oh. He was rather hoping to hold it in his hands before it went anywhere.'

'I have got this.' Agnes bent to her bag, took out an old shoe box and opened it.

'But—' Ginny stared at the silvery glaze, the elegant curve of the cup's stand. 'But — that's it?'

'That's the silly piece of tin. The police seized various items at Darius's home, and they didn't know what to do with this, so they gave it back to the family. But Orla said you could have it,' Agnes said, as Andras approached their table.

'Look, darling. Your wonderful fake,' Ginny pealed at Andras as his eyes fell on the box.

'Fake?' He looked darkly at Agnes.

'Agnes here made sure it came home.'

He sat down heavily beside Ginny. 'But — but the real one?'

'Oh, darling, a museum will have it. Of course. It's invaluable, that's what our Sister here is saying.'

'Well, it would be considered priceless if those two stupid women hadn't shoved it into the foot of a cheap bronze, if your story on the phone yesterday is to be believed. Completely mad, no expertise. If only they'd trusted me . . .'

Agnes had looked up at him. 'Andras — did you ever give them any reason to trust you?'

His gaze was fixed on the fake chalice, as it lay on the white linen tablecloth before them, with the background clink of tea cups and the soft notes from the piano.

'No clever-dick comments for once,' Ginny said.

* * *

Now, at her flat, she folded the mustard yellow jumper, laid it in her case. Ghastly thing, she agreed, but warm.

I'm not going for a fashion show.

'Camping? You?' Aysha had raised a manicured eyebrow earlier that day. 'That Sister Wilfrid must be some chick.'

There was lunch. Pasta, of course. Homemade falafel. Noodles. There were goodbyes, hugs from Aysha, and Dina and Eddie, promises not to stay away long, 'although Sister

Dominique is going to be so much better at this job than me, you won't want me back.'

Aysha had sent her a glance over the tofu stir-fry. 'Yeah,' she'd said. 'Maybe.'

* * *

Now she placed things in her case. Waterproofs. Thermos cup. Torch.

Camping. Me?

Winifred. Some chick.

Another fool. Like me. And Julius.

Better than the alternative.

The doorbell interrupted her. Agnes got up slowly, her knees aching.

Bridget was on the doorstep.

'I brought you this,' she said. She was holding a small bouquet of white roses. 'Cut them earlier today.'

Agnes looked down at their fresh beauty against the beige weave of her coat.

'Thank you,' she said.

Bridget followed her into the flat.

'Nice place,' she said. 'Francie told me where you live, hope you don't mind . . .'

'I don't mind at all.'

Bridget sat down, smoothing the wide sofa seat with both hands. 'Do all nuns get this, or just difficult ones?'

'Just me, I think.' Agnes filled a small white vase with water, placed the roses on the table beside them.

Bridget glanced at the suitcase. 'You're really going then? Who'll live here?'

'The Order will rent it out. They've found a deacon who needs a home.'

'Huh. Typical.' She patted one of the cushions. 'They'd better keep it for you when you're back. I can't see you putting up with living with a load of old nuns.'

'That's what my friend Athena says.'

215

'Good. You need someone on your side.' Bridget looked at the curtains, the bookcase, then back to Agnes. 'No one else ever listened to me. That's what them flowers are for.'

'You knew,' Agnes said. 'You knew that Jay's death in that church wasn't what it seemed. And you came to me. I should be thanking you.'

Bridget looked up at her. She gave a small nod. 'And they're all right now. Francie with her island, and Ezra can have school holidays there too. Orla will miss her, like before, but at least she don't have to pretend anymore. I knew she'd come back one day, didn't see how a person could hide away for ever. And Iris has invited me to stay for a bit. I think I will, later. But Orla ain't got long and it's all very well her being on her own in that great big house out west, but it ain't going to look after itself, is it? And so I said I'd look after her. I said, "Don't you go arguing about it, not now," and so we've agreed. Got to keep busy, haven't I?'

Agnes nodded.

'And—' Bridget went on, 'Connie says to thank you too. That bastard is behind bars and her Reece can rest in peace at last.'

'We knew Jay didn't do it,' Agnes said.

'Yes,' Bridget said. 'We did. Mind you, Aidan's so comfy in my spare room he don't want to leave, and Daniella ain't happy about it, she wants him living with her. I told them they've got to sort it out between themselves, and at least he ain't living at Her Majesty's Pleasure, which was how it looked a week ago, didn't it?'

Bridget gazed down at the roses in their vase. 'And the funny thing is, it all started with Ivy Wharton. Who'd have thought? She'd never have imagined it, that by dying she'd cause such a fuss.'

For the first time Bridget smiled, and Agnes smiled too.

CHAPTER TWENTY-FIVE

'All packed?'

They were in the turquoise bar again, 'For old time's sake,' Athena had said on the phone, even though, as Agnes pointed out, they'd only been there once, it's hardly a tradition. 'Well, it will be now, and we can see what the Sunday evening crowd is like.'

Now they sat on a vinyl bench in the bright glittering bar and raised their glasses.

'Setting sail, out on the open seas, seeing the white cliffs recede into the mist behind you . . .'

'The train takes about two hours,' Agnes said. 'It's no distance.'

'Ah. Train. Yeah. No distance at all.'

They sipped their drinks. 'White cliffs and blue sea, kind of more romantic, though,' Athena said.

'I'm not intending to fall in love.'

'Ah. Yes. There is that.' Athena studied her glass. 'Sauvignon Blanc,' she said. 'Austere, I thought. No more fizzy pink stuff, at least not until you're back, which will be what a fortnight, maybe? A month? I can't see you lasting longer than that, you'll run out of clothes for a start and there aren't any decent shops out there . . .'

Agnes sipped her wine. 'I packed that jumper.'

'Oh God. Yes. Very sensible.' Athena picked ice out of her water glass and splashed it into her wine. 'Oh God, sweetie, I got so distracted I nearly forgot. Here, a present—' She leaned to her feet, lifted up a large paper carrier bag, in which was something wrapped in silver tissue paper.

Agnes put the bag on her knees, lifted out the paper.

'A black leather jacket,' Athena said. 'See? I knew it was you. And so practical for unloading small children from windswept dinghies. Or whatever it is you'll be doing there.'

Agnes held it up. 'This doesn't look very charity shop,' she said.

'No, well, I thought, why waste all that time when I can go straight to a real shop and choose your size?'

'It's lovely,' Agnes said. 'Really lovely. Thank you.'

A shadow of uncertainty crossed Athena's face. 'It won't — I mean, that nun you've got to work with — she won't mind, will she? It not being very, traditional . . .'

Agnes smiled. 'She'll want one too.'

'Ah. Good. Well, she'll have to ask her best friend.' Athena sipped her wine. 'Oh, and Simon in the gallery was very keen on those photos you sent of the shroud and stuff. He thought he might show some of this chap's work in the gallery. And so, I said I'd ask if you could put him in touch with the two posh birds about borrowing it or something?'

Agnes smiled. 'A resolution. Definitely. They'll be delighted.'

'Though the weird thing is,' Athena said, 'you know that shroud, and all that religious stuff in the garage, well, Simon was looking at the pictures you sent through, and it's such a weird coincidence, he remembered seeing that bloke's work in London, years ago, what was his name?'

'Gerard St Fleur.'

'Yes. That's the one. He remembered him having an exhibition in London about twenty years ago when he was still a student, and now he can have the actual shroud that he saw then in his actual gallery. Weird, isn't it?'

'You can tweet to Doctor Mitch about it for his podcast,' Agnes said.

'Yeah. Suppose so.' She took a mouthful of wine. 'Thing is, I've sort of gone off all that stuff. It's like you suddenly finding yourself going off to join the Girl Guides, I've realised that really life is kind of random, you know, like we all just blunder through and stuff happens and, in the end, so what if it doesn't make sense? We just do the best we can. And you know, I checked my horoscope for this week and it said it was a very good time to have a big rethink, what with Saturn being in this rare conjunction with Jupiter. I think that must be what this is. Oh, sweetie, look at you, tears in your eyes, what have I said?'

Agnes smiled, shook her head. 'Julius said that faith makes fools of us all. Believing in something against all the evidence . . .'

'No. Not you. Not him. Although, if that's being a fool, then count me in.'

They sipped their wine.

'Trains can be romantic too,' Athena said. 'There's that film, isn't there? The old black-and-white one, with that gorgeous man and that lovely music. And at the end, the husband says, "Thank you for coming back to me."' She blinked, dabbed carefully at one heavily mascaraed eye.

Agnes touched her hand. 'I'll miss you,' she said softly.

'Just make sure you charge that phone. If they have electricity over there. Oh, and my car?'

'Parked outside.' Agnes pushed the keys across the table. 'It was fun while it lasted.'

'Story of our lives,' Athena said, and Agnes laughed.

Athena raised her glass. 'To setting sail.'

CHAPTER TWENTY-SIX

Agnes joined a snaking Monday morning queue. The Eurostar check-in screen said *Destination: Paris, stopping at Calais*, and Agnes wondered what it would be like to stay on the train, emerging at the Gare du Nord into a real city like this one, with smart busy people, chic women with huge wheeled cases and neatly dressed children, boulevards and decent coffee and people being loud and important on their phones.

Instead of . . .

Winifred would be there. 'I'll meet your train,' she'd said on the phone last night. 'I'll borrow a car, that way you won't be alone. I've asked for one of the bedrooms for you in the main HQ building. You'll be dealing with warehouse stuff to start with, deliveries of food and clothes. At least you'll have your own room . . .'

Agnes found herself at the front of the queue, behind a woman with perfect auburn hair and very high heels, who wafted through the security barrier as if it was an insult even to be asked. Then it was her turn. Her ticket was checked, the barriers opened and she was on the other side.

She thought about blue seas, the white cliffs of England fading into the distant mist.

Faith makes fools of us all.
The story of our lives, she thought.
Here's to setting sail.

THE END

ACKNOWLEDGEMENTS

I would like to thank Adrienne Gould, and Rebecca Carter. Grateful and appreciative thanks to the whole team at Joffe. Lastly, thanks, as ever, to Tim Boon.

THE JOFFE BOOKS STORY

We began in 2014 when Jasper agreed to publish his mum's much-rejected romance novel and it became a bestseller.

Since then we've grown into the largest independent publisher in the UK. We're extremely proud to publish some of the very best writers in the world, including Joy Ellis, Faith Martin, Caro Ramsay, Helen Forrester, Simon Brett and Robert Goddard. Everyone at Joffe Books loves reading and we never forget that it all begins with the magic of an author telling a story.

We are proud to publish talented first-time authors, as well as established writers whose books we love introducing to a new generation of readers.

We won Trade Publisher of the Year at the Independent Publishing Awards in 2023. We have been shortlisted for Independent Publisher of the Year at the British Book Awards for the last four years, and were shortlisted for the Diversity and Inclusivity Award at the 2022 Independent Publishing Awards. In 2023 we were shortlisted for Publisher of the Year at the RNA Industry Awards.

We built this company with your help, and we love to hear from you, so please email us about absolutely anything bookish at feedback@joffebooks.com

If you want to receive free books every Friday and hear about all our new releases, join our mailing list: www.joffebooks.com/contact

And when you tell your friends about us, just remember: it's pronounced Joffe as in coffee or toffee!